This new book was pr
by Bob Able, the autho

Please give it back to a charity
so that it can be sold again to make more money
for worthwhile causes.

Sarah's Kitchen

"A delightful modern story that will make you smile"

Bob Able

'We cannot know what is just around the corner and our lives can change in an instant. But don't be afraid, what is waiting for us around the next bend might just be wonderful! Embrace tomorrow!'

ANON

Sarah's Kitchen

by Bob Able

Cast of Characters:

The Frobishers:

Jane Frobisher, Penelope's twin sister.
Penelope Frobisher
Jeremy Frobisher, brother of the above.
Uncle Frederick Frobisher, elderly uncle of the above.

The Smallponds:

Andrew Smallpond, famous TV gardener.
Dame Amelia Runacres-Smythe, the professional name of Andrew Smallpond's wife who is an accomplished horticulturist and writer.

Albany Developments staff:

Sarah, our heroine.
Pete, a builder.
Derek, principle of the company.
Amanda, Derek's wife and principle of the Amanda's restaurant chain, Mario's and the Mad Hatters Tearoom.
Suzanne, Amanda's sister and Dave's wife.
Dave, a builder and Derek's brother-in-law.
Carlos, the head chef.
Steve, chef.
Mario, part owner of Mario's restaurant.
Jenny, employee in the Mad Hatters Tearoom.
Henry, Albany Development's accountant.

Others, in no particular order:

Emma, Sarah's daughter.
Matthew, Sarah's older brother.
Sandy, Matthew's wife and teddy bear maestro.
Chesney Marriott, famous TV chef and personality.

BOBABLE

Justin, an advertising and marketing specialist.
Trudy, Justin's wife and former chorus girl on the West End stage.
Jack Bolton, inspired lighting and effects technician.
Sparky, an electrician.
Lauren, a Local Authority Building Inspector and femme fatale.
Dr. Gerard Foyle, University Vice Principle.
Prof. J. G. Wimbish, University Professor.
Damian the Viking, a landscape gardener.
Small Clipboard, the head of production.
Darren Teasdale, a car salesman
Ivor, a decorator.
Miss Carter-Bone, Emma's form teacher.

Chapter 1

Originally she had set out to become a rocket scientist, of course, but that soon gave way to a plan to become a vet, then a nurse, and then, taking her brother's lead, she declared an interest in a life as a lady train driver.

Inevitably that didn't last, and now, several years after she had left school behind her, and most recently following many months as one of the growing army of unemployed single mums on the estate, Sarah was struggling to find a way to improve her lot.

She had always been a proficient and quite inventive cook, and became clever with pastry and cakes. But, as she never found a job which enabled her to use those skills, baking remained a hobby. Finances dictated that more recently she had to follow her mother's methods to produce food for the family. Those one pot casseroles and quick pasta meals were fine when she and Ricky both had jobs, and even served well enough after Emma was born. But fancy cakes were a thing of the past.

Now, though, with Ricky gone to live with his barmaid, the pneumatic Stella; Emma at primary school and growing fast; and the job, that they promised they would keep open for her, vanished; her finances were increasingly a worry. So of necessity food became fuel, rather than fun.

When they got the house everybody on the estate had jobs, and most had two cars. Things looked rosy and the future was exciting. But then it all changed.

The Government said it was not just a problem for Great Britain, the recession which followed the financial crash was worldwide. It certainly seemed to leave almost nobody untouched on the estate. Ricky was one of the dozens who lost their jobs when the factory closed down, even though he was on a management training programme.

He got a better redundancy payment than some of their neighbours because of that, but he started spending it in the pub, and after a while he seemed to stop looking for work altogether.

That led to the rows, of course. And that led to the emergence of Stella, the landlord's niece. And that explained what Ricky was doing all day after Stella's shift finished at the pub.

Now it was just her and Emma. They still lived on the estate, but now they rented one of the flats over the little parade of shops.

At least it was cheaper than the mortgage she and Ricky had on the house, but when it was sold, there was only just enough money for the deposit on the rented flat left, after all the bills were paid. Although it was embarrassing, she was forced to 'sign-on' for Universal Credit.

There were six shops of varying sizes on the ground floor of the building, although only three were currently occupied.

The launderette was still open, and so was the wine merchant. But the hairdressers, the little supermarket and the newsagent had all long since closed down and been boarded up.

The last shop at the end of the parade had variously been a wine bar, an estate agents, a junk shop and a charity shop in the recent past, but now, after a long period sitting empty, it was being done up.

The builders said a slightly leery 'good morning' as Sarah passed by each day after walking Emma to school and she wondered what they were doing. Obviously she would not have had the courage to ask, however, were it not for the accident.

On that fateful day, as she rounded the corner on the way back from the school, and the shop came into view, a truck was parked unloading some building materials outside. One of the builders, who it later emerged was called Dave, was standing in the back of the truck throwing long metal scaffold poles over the side onto an untidy heap on the pavement. As she approached one of the poles landed on its end and sprang back, catching Dave on the side of his head and causing him to fall backwards from the truck, into the road.

Sarah rushed to help. She remembered some of the first aid course she did at work not long after Emma was born, and was able to stem the bleeding. Then she helped Pete, the other builder, to make Dave more comfortable until the ambulance arrived.

He was conscious but a bit dazed and while they sat with him on the road, Sarah asked what they were doing to the shop.

'It's going to be a cafe and a cake shop, I think,' said Pete. 'Although I can't see it doing any good round here unless they are planning to make it a greasy spoon, selling breakfasts or something.'

'Nah,' said Dave, coming to the surface. 'Amanda thinks she is going to make it a bakery type of thing, serving afternoon tea and what-not. Daft cow.'

'Amanda?' said Sarah, interested.

'Yeah. They are all like that up on Barclay Woods. Got some idea that this area is gonna be done up and … what was that word she used, Pete?'

'Gentrified, Dave. Ah, here comes the ambulance.'

As the ambulance departed, Pete was finishing a call on his mobile phone.

'Derek is coming up to give me a hand to get this stuff off the pavement, although I shan't be able to do much more today on my own.'

'Derek?'

'Amanda's husband. He's Albany Developments. They've been buying up houses that have been repossessed round here and doing them up.'

'Well, that's interesting,' said Sarah. 'I knew there were quite a lot of empty ones and there had been problems with them being vandalised. It will be good if they are being done up.'

'I think he is going to tart some of them up to rent out. He has got some deal on with the Council and a housing association, I think.'

'We bought one of the houses here when it was new. It was nice round here then,' said Sarah.

'Was it? Well, perhaps it will be again one day. Derek is planning to knock some of the houses down, build new ones for sale, and do up some of the others to rent. Have you seen that leaflet he was having delivered?'

'No. What leaflet?'

'Oh, you live in the flats, don't you, so you probably

wouldn't have got one. The leaflet is asking if people who own houses here want to sell, and saying the area is going to be a regeneration project or something.'

'What? Knocking all the houses down?'

'Not all of them, I don't think. Only the ones built out of plywood; the timber frame ones with the funny roofs. There is a lot of them empty.'

'The council built them and then sold them off to some housing company. They always had problems with those odd looking steep roofs and damp getting in, especially after the original windows got replaced. I knew a couple of people who lived in them with mould growing up the walls who were desperate to get re-housed.'

'Well, those ones are nearly are all empty now and Derek's idea is to demolish them. But some of the other ones, the private ones, are rented out now and getting in a right old state, so Derek wants to knock some down and do others up for sale.'

'There have been problems with some of the people renting round there, I know. There are a couple of burnt-out cars up on the green, and the swing park is fenced off because it has been vandalised.'

'Dave told me the rumour is that there is some shady Indian or Pakistani bloke renting some of those houses out to asylum seekers and folk that even the council don't want to house. There was a drug dealer arrested ...'

'Yes, that was on the local news. There are stories like that all the time. I wish I could get my Emma away from here. I don't want her growing up amongst all that.'

'I know what you mean, love. But I guess unless your fella gets a better job somewhere else ...'

'Unfortunately he got what he considered a better opportunity somewhere else some time ago, and it's just Emma and me now.'

'I'm sorry ... I'm Pete, by the way.'

'Sarah,' said Sarah. 'Is this Derek coming now, in that big Mercedes?'

-oo0Ooo-

Sarah had had a cleaning job for a short while, up on Barclay Woods, working for a company that cleaned several of the posh houses up there.

She hoped to get Ricky a temporary job being advertised for a gardener in one of the big houses on that estate, but he wouldn't hear of it. He was a qualified engineer, he said, and was almost management trained. He considered a gardening job was beneath his dignity.

Sarah failed to get Ricky to accept that the type of engineering work he could do was history, and he would simply *have* to retrain to get another job.

His answer to that was to create a job for himself propping up the bar in Stella's pub.

Sarah liked the large houses on Barclay Woods and enjoyed cleaning them with the jolly crew of girls she worked with. It was a pity that the company folded, and that the efforts a couple of the girls made to take over the cleaning round didn't work out.

The difference between the lives the Barclay Woods residents enjoyed and those endured by the residents of her estate could not be more marked, and Sarah often wondered how they did it.

-oo0Ooo-

'How's Dave?' called Sarah as she passed Pete working on the scaffolding outside the shop a few days later.

'Hi, Sarah. Concussion. Been given ten days off, lucky bleeder!'

Hearing the talking outside, Derek emerged from the interior of the shop.

'Ah ha! Are you Sarah?' he asked, 'Can I thank you for helping Dave when he had his little accident. It was very kind.'

Sarah blushed and could not immediately think of anything to say. She thought what she did was only what anyone would do in the circumstances.

'He's got to stay at home and take it easy for a

while, but after the hospital stitched him up he was laughing and joking with the nurses in no time. Typical Dave, that is. Suzanne, Amanda's sister calls him the life and soul, looking for a party.'

Sarah smiled at the little joke.

'I'm Derek, by the way. Dave is my brother-in-law,' and he held his hand out for Sarah to shake.

'How do you do,' said Sarah coyly.

'Pete tells me you live in the flats up there,' Derek was saying. 'You are probably wondering what this shop is going to be and what we are doing with it …'

'Well, I …'

'It is Amanda's pet project. And what Amanda wants, she gets, if you know what I mean. Amanda, my wife, has a vision to turn this into an artisan bakery and tea shop. She has all sorts of plans drawn up and swatches and what-have-you prepared for the wallpaper and the fabrics covering the chairs and so on; all themed with her latest favourite. Hares. It is going to be called the Mad Hatter's Tea Rooms, she informs me, although until I can get the regeneration of this grotty old estate up and running, she is the mad one if you ask me!'

'It was once very nice round here,' said Sarah.

'Oh. Sorry, no offence meant, but you have to admit it is long overdue for a spruce up. When I've finished with it, it will be very pleasant again, I hope. And a desirable place to live.'

'Is he laying out the grand vision for Albany Developments world dominance again?' smiled Pete, climbing down from the scaffolding. 'And I thought he was just here to make the tea.'

-ooOoo-

For a change Emma ate up all her tea without a complaint. The cottage pie Sarah had made met with her approval, and she even finished up the peas.

'What are they doing to that shop downstairs, mummy?' she asked between mouthfuls, and Sarah explained Amanda and Derek's plans. 'We went to a tea shop like that once didn't we, mummy. I think it would be nice.'

Emma was referring to a trip they had taken a year ago to see Sarah's brother, Emma's uncle Matthew, who lived in leafy Surrey, near Dorking. The trip was still green in her memory and Emma adored her uncle and his industrious wife, Sandy, who ran her own little business from home making teddy bears. Emma's most prized possession was one of those bears, which when not involved in imaginary picnics and other games was always within reach, and accompanied her to bed every night.

Matthew was doing well, and since college had a job in the Local Council where he seemed to work in the office on something mysterious to do with trees. When Sarah and Ricky had split up he had helped with selling the house and dealing with the solicitors, and then finding Sarah and Emma the flat where they now lived.

With no children of their own, Matthew and Sandy spoilt Emma and could always be relied upon for the more expensive sort of Christmas and birthday presents. Emma did not know it, of course, but there had been conversations about getting her a bicycle for her next birthday in six weeks time. Sarah was very grateful to them and certainly could not contemplate buying such extravagant presents herself.

But there was a problem. If Emma had a bike, where could she ride it safely? There was no way that Sarah could let her ride it around the estate, that was simply out of the question. And riding it to school meant a main road which was much too busy for children cycling. Sarah did not want to disappoint Emma or frustrate her need to spread her wings on a bike, and she remembered the joy she felt when she was given her first bicycle. But that was down in the quiet lanes near Dorking, where she grew up, not in the run-down sprawl where they lived now.

Not for the first time Sarah regretted following Ricky to the inner suburbs and his work in the factory. The whole thing seemed like a golden dream back then, but over time it had turned into a depressing grinding disappointment, and now it looked as though there was no way out.

Chapter 2

When she was two, Sarah's father bought a victorian 'villa' in the village of Westcott, on the outskirts of Dorking from where he could take the longish walk, or more usually cycle, to the railway station, and on to his work in the City of London.

She attended the local school, following two years behind her brother, and they rode their bikes alongside Pipp's Brook and through Squire's Wood; where, in a pool near the source of the brook, they swam as children.

There were picnics in the fields and trips for walks on Ranmore Common, and on summer weekends as she grew, her parents would occasionally take her to the Prince of Wales pub for lunch, a few doors along from the ramshackle cycle shop that provided her first and much treasured bicycle.

As she grew, she joined the 'Young Farmers Association', and that is how she met Ricky.
The Young Farmers organised trips to farms,

obviously, but also to places connected with the business of farming, including, one hot summer day, to the County Show, in Guildford.

As a group they visited the various manufacturers of agricultural implements and machinery displaying their wares at the show. There Sarah met Ricky, an apprentice sent down with the company representatives to keep the Rectangular Balers and Conveyors they manufactured, and were displaying with a tractor to pull them, clean and shiny to impress the visitors and potential buyers.

When she first saw him, Ricky was working in the baking sun standing high up on the deck by the steering wheel of the tractor, polishing invisible specs of dust from the paintwork, with his shirt off. Having just turned sixteen and still quite impressionable, Sarah was instantly smitten.

Although slim and yet to develop what you might call a muscly torso, nineteen year old Ricky already had a broad chest and cut quite a striking figure in tight fitting and highly fashionable 'camouflage trousers' and rigger boots. Sarah was very impressed and became all the more-so when, now with his shirt on, he joined the young farmers in the beer tent and bought her a half pint of cider.

As the leader of their group was gathering the young farmers up by the minibus which was collecting them, Ricky and Sarah shared their first brief kiss and Sarah could not resist resting her hand on his impressive chest under his unbuttoned shirt. As they fixed up their first date, Sarah was already under Ricky's spell.

Given Sarah's age, her parents were naturally concerned that she should not spend too much time with Ricky and imposed strict curfews and deadlines to limit the time they spent together. But five weeks later, after they gave permission for a trip in Ricky's elderly car to the nearby cinema for a matinee performance; in a quiet country lane and in broad daylight, Sarah became a woman. They never made it to the cinema.

-ooOoo-

When Pete and Derek mentioned that Dave was due back to work on Monday, as she passed by and enquired after his health, Sarah did something quite out of character, extravagant and potentially foolish. But she loved doing it and was pleased with the result.

Sarah baked a selection of fancy cakes to present to the builders, to celebrate Dave's return.

There were little individual upside down apricot and orange cakes, slices of almond, blueberry and vanilla cake, two different sorts of madeleines, and slices of indulgent creamy 'millefeuille' with layer after razor thin layer of puff pastry and creamy custard topped with a rich fondant icing, decorated with a web design in chocolate. Sarah couldn't really afford the ingredients for these extravagant cakes, but something drove her to revisit her old hobby, and she throughly enjoyed making them.

She knew that Derek, Pete and Dave stopped for coffee at ten o'clock, and she turned up with the tray of fancies under a tea-towel just at the right time.

'Where did you buy these?' asked Derek; and when Sarah admitted she had made them, he made Dave put his slice of cake, un-bitten, back on the tray and took a photograph on his mobile phone of the entire assemblage.

'You really made these?' asked Dave incredulously, as Pete, taking a bite of almond, blueberry and vanilla cake, let out a little sound of delight as the various flavours danced on his tongue.

'It's just a hobby,' blushed Sarah as the two builder's men heaped praise on her after each mouthful they took.

Derek however was quiet, and while he tasted, and clearly enjoyed the cakes, he passed no comment until they had nearly all gone.

'Sarah,' he said, 'it was extremely kind and generous of you to make those, especially for an undeserving work-shy pair like these two. How much do I owe you for the cakes?'

'Oh no!' said Sarah, taken aback. 'It is nothing like that. I did it for my own pleasure as much as anything else. I certainly wasn't looking to sell you anything.'

As she spoke Derek was wrapping the last of the cakes in the tea-towel.

'Is it all right if I get the tea-towel washed and give it back to you on Wednesday?' asked Derek. 'I want Amanda to try these!'

-oo0Ooo-

Emma enjoyed the cakes too, and devoured the rest of the selection that Sarah had not taken to the builders with determination.

'Lovely, Mummy!' she said smacking her lips and wiping the last crumbs from her chin. 'When are you going to bake some more?'

Emma went to bed with a full tummy, telling 'Edward', her bear, all about the cakes and discussing with him the virtues of each one, in the order she ate them.

In the evening, as Sarah sat with the little book in which she tried to keep track of their finances and entered her expenditure for the week, she had to admit that it would be some time until she could afford another extravagant baking day like that. The rest of the month was going to be very tight. She had enjoyed doing it, but looking at the figures now, she had to face the facts and regretted her rash act.

As she stared at them, the figures in the little book began to dance before her eyes, and she found that she was crying.

-ooOoo-

Chapter 3

Derek was sitting in his Mercedes, outside the shop talking to a statuesque blond woman who occupied the passenger seat.

As Sarah approached, on her way back from taking Emma to school, she opened the door, un-wound her long slim legs and straightened her shapely form as she stepped onto the pavement.

'Ah, Sarah. There you are,' said Derek, now standing just behind her. 'Have you got a minute? I'd like to introduce you to Amanda, my wife.'

As she took the manicured hand she was offered, Sarah noticed that Amanda was dressed in a stylish figure hugging grey dress with a broad white belt accentuating her slim waist, and was clutching a small matching white handbag. Her beautifully made up face split into a broad smile, revealing perfect straight white teeth, that seemed to catch the sun and sparkle.

'How do you do?' she purred.

'Amanda wanted to meet you because she was so impressed with those cakes you made ... we both were,' said Derek.

'You are very talented, Sarah, if I may say so, and at first I could not believe that those elegant little dainties did not come from an expensive bakery. No doubt they sell like ... like hot cakes,' smiled Amanda encouragingly. 'Which bakeries do you supply and where can I buy them?'

'Bakeries? I don't know ... Oh I see what you mean. No. No bakeries, it is just a hobby,' Sarah found she was blushing. 'I hadn't actually baked anything for months, but I just thought it would be nice to mark Dave's return to work in some way, so I ...'

'But surely you do this professionally in some capacity, don't you?' said Amanda, genuinely surprised.

'Good heavens, no,' said Sarah. 'Apart from anything else I couldn't afford the ingredients to do that sort of thing very often. I only did it for Dave and the boys and to give Emma, my daughter, a bit of a treat.'

'Have you got a job, Sarah?' asked Derek.

'No chance!' sputtered Sarah. 'There's no work round here, especially since the factory closed.'

There was a moment of silence as Derek and

Amanda exchanged glances.

'Sarah,' said Derek, taking a step forward. 'I realise this is a bit sudden, but would you consider coming to work for Amanda and I?'

-ooOoo-

'Oh, the restaurants,' said Pete. 'Yes, there are four of them at the last count, I think. Derek bought them for Amanda as investments.'

'Well, it was all a huge surprise, and perhaps foolishly I said that I would need to think about it, what with Emma and school and so on,' sighed Sarah. 'I'd love to do it really, of course, but I can't see how I can, and I was flustered and I dithered, and they have probably changed their minds now, or found someone else.'

'No, they haven't. I spoke to Derek earlier,' said Dave. 'Amanda is as keen as mustard to take you on if something can be worked out that fits in.'

'Amanda doesn't actually work in the restaurants, as I understand it,' said Pete.

'Nah, she wouldn't know where to start. She just floats about looking glamorous and chatting up the customers,' smirked Dave. 'You must admit she is a bit of an eyeful, and I suppose that sort of thing is good for business.'

'But how could I do it? I can't work in the evening,

and I have to take Emma to school each day, and …' Sarah jumped when her mobile phone rang in her pocket. The only person who ever called her these days was her brother, and she was not expecting a call from him.

Then she remembered that, at their request and at the end of their embarrassing conversation, she had given Derek and Amanda her number, and now Amanda was calling.

Sarah hesitated and even considered not answering the call. She was still trying to prepare the little speech she knew she was going to have to deliver, thanking Amanda for her kind offer, but explaining the difficulties of her situation and regretfully declining …

'You gonna answer that, or just stand there looking at it?' asked Pete.

-ooo0oo-

For Derek, it all started when he managed to get a job on a City-type's house, building an extension.

Until that point he had been just another jobbing builder, putting up a wall here, modernising a kitchen there. But then he met Isaac.

Everybody owed Isaac money, and he thrived on it. Those who had failed to borrow money from banks could turn to Isaac who found ways to defray their debts in various ingenious ways, and such was the case with the City-type's extension.

The first builder on the job had disappeared, leaving the job barely started but with part of the roof of the existing single storey structure removed, and with winter approaching, an urgent need to make the house watertight. The problem was that the City-type had taken out a second mortgage to do the extension and foolishly paid most of it over to the first builder. He could not borrow any more money through a conventional route, and with property prices falling, had no equity left in his house to borrow against.

In desperation, he turned to Isaac and his rather unusual loan facilities to get him out of trouble.

When he visited the house, Isaac noticed that Derek was rebuilding the porch of a house almost opposite and contrived to fall into conversation with him about the failed extension works over the road.

It was not long afterwards that Derek, having gratefully secured the biggest job he had ever handled, was firstly making the house watertight and then organising deliveries of materials and completing the extension works, all for cash in hand, under Isaac's watchful eye.

The job went well and Isaac offered him another, then another, and so it went on for a couple of years, until Isaac took him to see some land he had bought which it emerged had planning permission for three large detached houses. One of which Isaac proposed to live in himself. Derek had by this stage gathered about him a small team of tradesmen and they built out all three houses together.

After that, and now with a taste for building new houses Derek went to see the bank.

Initially he struggled with the cash-flow forecasts, business cases and all the paperwork they required to consider funding him. But Isaac, well pleased with his new house, offered to become his mentor and helped him through the pit-fall ridden process of moving from jobbing builder to property developer.

With a rapid improvement in the property market to help him on his way as he sold the first pair of semi-detached houses he built, and with some 'seed corn' money from Isaac, he found more land, and building under the freshly minted 'Albany Developments' banner, he was up an running.

Within five years he had paid off the money Isaac lent him and was becoming established with a reputation for good quality workmanlike housebuilding that sold well and impressed the banks.

Then he met Amanda. Or rather, to be strictly accurate, he met Amanda's father who was a successful property developer with a small 'land bank', arthritic knees and looking to retire.

Because he could no longer drive himself, his daughter Amanda drove him to the block of land he had offered to sell to Derek. Their idea was to unlock the padlock on the security fence and show him round.

Derek was instantly enchanted with the tall, willowy yet stylish girl and, more in an effort to impress her than through any particular feeling for the land, agreed to buy the site on the spot.

That deal led to another and eventually to Derek taking the biggest financial risk of his life, and with support from a consortium of banks, buying out the assets of Amanda's father's company.

He married Amanda six months later and could never really believe his luck, not only in finding her, but that she had even considered dating him. He regarded her as way out of his league and he worshipped and spoilt her. As he himself freely admitted to anyone who would listen, anything Amanda wanted, she got.

The company thrived and building on its existing track record, now as part of Albany Developments, Derek started to make some serious money.

His diversification into restaurant ownership came about by chance a few years later.

Amanda loved entertaining, so long as she did not have to cook or wash-up, and did not have to have anything to do with preparing the food. Over time, they established that meeting their friends in the better sort of bistros and restaurants provided the best compromise, and Derek indulged her taste for fine dining.

He took her to theatres, shows, galleries and expensive restaurants where the patrons went to see and be seen as much as to satisfy their hunger, and they gathered a blizzard of acquaintances and a few real friends who were invited to house parties, with caterers, of course, in their spacious home in Barclay Woods.

Derek loved showing her off and watching her deal effortlessly with entertaining all sorts of people from his business contacts to the trendiest authors and playwrights, as well as her own friends and neighbours. But there were times when they wanted to be quiet and on their own.

They discovered Mario's; a quiet but quite exclusive bistro with a delightful and ever changing menu, an engaging patron and a charming and talented chef. It became their favourite place to eat, and on quieter nights they were happy to chat to the owner and his staff as they enjoyed an un-hurried dinner.

But those quieter nights were becoming more frequent as the latest economic downturn began to bite, and over the brandies, Mario admitted that his establishment was in trouble and the clientele, that until now he had been able to rely upon, was dwindling as the recession deepened.

Amanda told Derek not to start the Mercedes when they returned to the carpark that evening, and while Derek listened enthralled, she proceeded to list for him where the comfortable restaurant was missing opportunities, how the business could be expanded with limited cost and risk and how she, Amanda, could take on the role of promoting it.

They had the contacts, she pointed out, and with a few judicious improvements here and there, it could become one of those trendy, always busy, places they visited when they fancied the brighter lights.

Three months later Derek and Amanda had presented a business case to Mario and agreed to buy out his partners. Then they were engaged on a programme of business development that was so successful it left them all breathless.

Admittedly Derek and Amanda had lost their quiet bolt-hole bistro, but it blossomed into a fashionable and very busy business that turned in excellent profits consistently. Amanda was good at this, and taking on the role of elegant owner, making the customers feel special, and gently promoting the business suited her.

The profits suited Derek and it was not long before they had replicated the model by acquiring a small chain of three family restaurants which were under-utilising the advantages of their locations. With new chefs, appointed by Mario and Carlos, his capable chef and now a partner in the business, the re-branded "Amanda's" stylish little chain of bistros went from strength to strength.

Most recently, Amanda had discovered that, as part of his efforts to acquire most of the estate where Sarah lived, Derek's company now owned a small block of flats with six shops on the ground floor, some of which were empty, and one of which had previously been a wine bar, so had the correct planning category to become a restaurant.

Initially Derek gave little thought to this part of his wider regeneration scheme, but Amanda, who Derek aways involved in all his business plans, went to look at it, and finding it largely ignored on the masterplans for the scheme that Derek's architect drew up, she began to think about what to do with it.

There was no doubt that, if it came off as Derek and the architect planned it, the project overall would eventually deliver a desirable and pleasant place to live. It would be very much along the lines of the similar project on the other side of the river, in the adjacent Borough, that the Local Authority were keen to emulate.

Amanda went to look at that too, and there she found her inspiration.

Around a spacious green, by an Aldi supermarket there stood a development of newly built flats over little shops offering quite up-market independent businesses space to offer their wares. There was a boutique, a candy store, a hat and handbag shop, a posh shoe shop, hairdresser, nail bar and, of most interest to Amanda, a thriving modern restaurant on two floors which boasted good quality cuisine at sensible prices.

Amanda knew that it would take a while to establish the same sort of environment on Sarah's estate but, while she was sworn to secrecy, she also knew that delicate negotiations were underway to demolish the old agricultural machinery factory and build a Waitrose supermarket on the site. And if that came off, Waitrose trumped Aldi all day long when it came to attracting the right sort of people to a new development.

-oo0Ooo-

Chapter 4

Sarah read the letter for a third time.

The letting agent had written to inform the tenants that the building had been sold to new landlords, and while there would be no change until the existing 'short-hold tenancies' came up for renewal, the area was now part of a 'regeneration scheme' which might mean the landlord would not be renewing leases. The agent finished by stating that existing tenants would be able to find alternative accommodation through their offices, if the need arose, and assuring the reader of their best attentions at all times.

It was only two months since Sarah's six-month lease had been renewed, but that meant there was only four months left to run, and she viewed the future with trepidation.

Sarah had lived in the flat for over three years, and now it was one of only five still tenanted in the block of twelve flats. The two over the off-licence were occupied by the owner of that business and his wife; and next door was his son, who lived with their two children and his wife. A flat over the laundrette was let to some students who she never saw, and another was let to her friend Jenny and her two boisterous young sons who went to Emma's school.

Jenny had worked at the factory with Sarah, but not in the same department. While Sarah worked in the office, dealing with the paperwork for 'goods inward' and 'invoices received', Jenny worked in the canteen. But when the factory closed Jenny introduced Sarah to the short-lived cleaning company who gave them both employment looking after some of the grand houses up on Barclay Woods.

Now Jenny worked part time in the laundrette, and was just about making ends meet. The news about the sale of the flats must have come as a shock to her too, and Sarah resolved to go and see her to discuss it.

She thought she would also tell Jenny her news about Amanda and Derek's plans and the impossibility of her taking a job with them.

-oo0Ooo-

Following her inconclusive phone call with Sarah, Amanda had arranged to meet her at the shop to discuss their plans and to see if a way could be found to enable her to join the business.

Derek decided to come to the meeting at the last

moment and drove her to the little parade of shops where Dave and Pete were stripping out the last of the grotty fitments and preparing to install the new equipment. Given what Amanda hoped Sarah would be doing this was an appropriate stage in the building works to meet up, so that they could make sure that the proposal and design was what was needed.

Sarah was already at the shop when they arrived and was bustling about washing mugs prior to letting the workers make their tea.

'When were these mugs last washed, Pete,' she was saying. 'They are disgusting and I'm surprised you have not gone down with food poisoning!'

'Boys will be boys,' laughed Amanda, stepping carefully over tool bags and builder's materials in her kitten heels as she entered the building.

'Boys will be off work with salmonella or something if they don't clean up their act,' smiled Sarah, turning to greet the new arrivals.

'They had better not be!' said Derek.

'Yes, well,' said Amanda. 'Can I have the key for next door please, Dave. We will be having our meeting in there.'

To Sarah's surprise, with the key in her hand, Amanda walked through the shop and out into the scruffy courtyard where the bins were stored.

'After you,' said Derek, and indicated for her to follow with the roll of plans he was carrying.

Amanda was unlocking the back door of the adjacent shop and stepping into the dim interior and Sarah wondered what was going on.

Once Derek had found the light switches and turned them on, it was clear that they were in the back store room of what was once the local supermarket. The room was empty now, apart from a plastic garden table and six chairs, which Derek proceeded to dust off and unroll his plans on the table.

'Right, Sarah,' said Amanda. 'We would like to explain our proposals for this place and show you the plans we have had drawn up. Please take a seat and make yourself comfortable.'

Sarah did as she was told and glanced at the complicated looking drawings spread before her on the table.

'Perhaps I should start by explaining that, as part of the regeneration programme, Albany Developments now own all these shops and we have had our architect draw up plans for what we intend to do with them,' said Derek.

'Oh,' said Sarah, 'does that include the flats above here?'

'Yes, it does,' said Amanda. 'That is where you live,

isn't it?'

'Yes, but I got this letter yesterday …' and Sarah explained about the Letting Agent's worrying communication.

When she finished she noticed that her two hosts were smiling at each other and Derek was chuckling.

'You needn't worry about that, Sarah. That's just old Watty panicking that he might loose the job of managing the flats.'
Derek took his own seat at the table and continued.
'Mr Watts, of Watts and Partners, was obliged to write to you about the change of landlord, but he should not really have frightened you with rumours of the lease coming to an end.'

'We are going to need all the income from tenants we can get to make our plans a reality,' said Amanda, flashing one of her wide twinkling smiles.

'Lets have a look at these plans and hopefully things will become clearer,' added Derek.

-ooOoo-

'So tomorrow that wall comes down and we join this shop to the one you had your meeting in,' said Pete, offering Sarah a packet of chocolate digestives.

'No thank you,' replied Sarah, 'I can't stop, I just wanted to tell you about my decision.'

'And,' said Dave, 'the space that you were in

yesterday will be blocked off from the rest of it to provide more space for tables and chairs in here.'

'Then the rest of that bit, what was the supermarket,' continued Pete, 'is due to become the entrance of the offices of Albany Developments, which will be upstairs, converted from some of the flats, and a Dentist's surgery will occupy the rest of the ground floor.'

'Yup, and next to that will be the opticians shop,' said Dave.

'But that is where my flat and the laundrette is, isn't it?' asked Sarah. 'My friend works there. Is it going to close down? Am I going to lose my flat?'

'You have put your great big size twelves in it now, Dave. I'm not sure that we weren't supposed to keep that to ourselves.'

'Oops!' said Dave. 'Forget I said that. It is only plans at this stage, I don't think it is anything definite.'

'But I can't forget it,' said Sarah, 'although actually that has given me an idea.'

-ooOoo-

'So, there it is Jenny, what do you think?' smiled Amanda winningly.

'If Sarah and I can sort out which days we take each others kids backwards and forwards to school between us so that, as you say, one of us is available to do the breakfast shift, or the teatime one each day, it works perfectly. Count me in!'

'You won't be on your own either because, as I said, most of the place is going to be our "development kitchen" where Carlos will be trying out his new menus and the trainees will be coming to learn the ropes for the restaurants. Only the bit at the side where that wall is coming down and the front area will become the cafe and tearoom. The rest of it is all for Sarah to make her cakes and Carlos to train his staff.'

'And now that you have explained it all to me again, and I understand the plans, I don't mind at all moving into one of the other flats,' said Sarah. 'Emma and I are actually quite excited about it.'

Sarah smiled at Jenny who leaned over and squeezed her arm.

'Thank you for making this happen for me, Sarah. Oh, and thank you too Amanda for giving me this opportunity. I promise I will not let you down.'

'Great,' said Derek. 'Now can we discuss the sort of breakfasts you cooked in the factory canteen, Jenny, and decide what we can serve here. I confess I am getting hungry just at the thought of it.'

'Pete was absolutely right when he suggested we do breakfasts,' said Amanda. 'While the estate is being developed and the place is swarming with builders the tearoom side of things might not do that well, but all those big hunky builders will want their breakfasts so that will give us early cash flow as well as something to look at!'

'I must make a note only to employ ugly, wimpy old builders,' said Derek. 'Like Dave and Pete.'

'Oh, I think Pete is quite good looking …' said Sarah, before she could stop herself, and she blushed to her roots.

'He is rather, and single too,' added Amanda, now laughing.

'I need Pete working, not mooning about over you girls,' said Derek. 'Perhaps I ought to move him to one of the other sites.'

'Oh no, don't!' said Amanda, Sarah and Jenny in unison.

-ooOOoo-

Chapter 5

There is something uniquely satisfying about the clean lines of a brand new stainless steel catering kitchen, and as Amanda and Sarah stood surveying the finished project, neither could stop smiling.

'Amanda, it is beautiful,' said Sarah.

'Yes, it is, isn't it. And now you see it for real, rather than just on the plans, are the benches and the pass the right size, do you think?'

'It's enormous! You should see the tiny little bit of worktop I have to use in my flat, I shall wonder what to do with all that space.'

'Easy. Make more cakes!' Pete had just walked into the kitchen behind them.

'Now, about your flat, Sarah,' said Derek, joining the gathering in the sparkling kitchen.

Sarah was excited, and dreading discussing that aspect of the scheme again in equal measure. She understood now that her flat and several others were to be incorporated into what would become Albany Developments new offices, above the shops, and that they would modernise and decorate one of the other flats for her.

She had also been told that her rent would remain the same and she would be given a brand new lease, but she was still worried. Although it would be several months before she actually had to move, the prospect was concerning her.

'As I said you can have your choice of the flats over by the off-licence, next to the two that the owner there occupies. Pete here has the keys, so you can go for a look whenever you like and make your choice. But don't be too long about it because we will want to start converting yours and the others into our new offices quite soon, and Pete and Dave are going to need a bit of time to do up whichever flat you choose before you can move in.'

'Yes, you explained that, Derek, and I'm very grateful. Its just ...'

'We can choose the decorations and the carpets and curtains and things together, if you like, Sarah,' said Amanda.

'And I'll help you with the new kitchen layout before we fit it out,' said Pete. 'I'll make sure there is a bit more worktop than in your current place, in case you want to make more cakes there too!'

Everyone laughed at that, and Amanda took Sarah's arm.

'I would really like to help you with the interior decoration, Sarah, and it will be a chance to spoil Emma a bit. We could ask Emma if she would like to come with us to the shops and choose her own decorations for her bedroom. That would be fun.'

'Not,' said Dave, now standing next to Derek, 'that Amanda would dream of getting her hands dirty herself when she says decoration, you understand. Her involvement starts and stops with the shopping!'

Chucking, Derek reached into the bag he had been holding, and accompanied by the musical chinking of the glasses therein, drew out a chilled bottle of Champagne.

'And on that note, I think we should start the christening of Sarah's kitchen before Carlos and Mario arrive and start making a mess!'

-oo0Ooo-

The flats were approached up a concrete external stair leading to a deck area which extended over the shops below, forming part of their roof. The front doors were arranged in pairs next to each other with one leading to the lower flat and one leading to the upper flat, which was on two levels with an internal staircase to get to the bedrooms. Jenny and Sarah each lived in one of the lower flats, and neither had ever been in one of the upper ones.

Pete unlocked the door of one of them and revealed a staircase off a small hall, leading up. On arrival on a spacious landing they were presented with a closed door to the kitchen, which Pete said they would look at in a minute, and double, partly glazed, doors leading to an enormous lounge/diner which covered the entirety of the rest of that floor. It was very much more spacious than Sarah's existing flat, and they had not even seen it all yet.

Up an open tread wooden staircase from the lounge there was another landing and doors to two good sized bedrooms and a bathroom with a window. In Sarah's flat the bathroom did not have a window and ventilation was provided by a noisy fan.

It was all badly in need of re-decoration, and the bathroom had a shocking pink suite, which Pete hastily pointed out was going to be replaced. He also explained that the few sticks of grubby furniture which remained in some of the rooms and the dirty threadbare carpets would also be removed.

'Right, let's go down and see the kitchen now,' said Pete. 'I did warn you that it is in a bit of a state, didn't I? But it will all be replaced and freshly decorated and tiled, so try to look past what you see now.'

Pete had not exaggerated. The kitchen looked as if it had been wrecked by vandals with doors hanging off or missing altogether from the once white units which, at some point, had been badly hand painted black. There was a grimy ceiling with several polystyrene tiles about to fall off and a few more already on the filthy floor, and a dirty sink, still full of unwashed cobwebby saucepans.

'Nobody has lived in here for a while,' said Pete, stating the obvious. 'Mr Watts, the letting agent said it had been let to students once, but when they left nobody bothered with it until now.'

'It is disgusting. How on earth can people live like that?' said Sarah. 'But the flat is huge, much bigger than mine, and sunnier too, on this side of the building.'

'You wait until Dave and I have done it all up, Sarah. There are going to be new windows, and new heating and smart new paint everywhere, it will be a home anyone would be proud of. And in case you didn't know, Dave and I are a bit good at this sort of thing, though I say it myself!'

'But Derek is never going to let me have this one for the same rent as my much smaller one, is he. I won't be able to afford it.'

'Derek said you might be worried about that and that I was to reassure you that, if you want this one, the rent will be the same as you pay now,' Pete smiled. 'But he also said to ask you, if you were interested in this one, if you would mind not telling anyone else the rent you will be paying, because the other ones like this are let for more money.'

'Would he really do that for me?' Sarah asked incredulously.

'Derek and Amanda are all right, Sarah. They play it straight and don't muck people about. They have always looked after me and the other folk who work for them, and that is why people stay with them,' said Pete. 'They are good people, and Derek sticks to his promises.'

Sarah could not believe her luck.

'In that case then, yes please, Pete. I would very much like this one, if that is OK.'

-oo0Ooo-

'It is going to be the best birthday present ever!' said Emma excitedly.

It might not be a bike, thought Sarah, but a new bedroom, decorated entirely to her choice was certainly something she had not expected to be able to offer her daughter.

'And Mummy says the whole flat is huge, Edward,' she explained to her teddy bear. 'So we will have to invite Auntie Sandy over to bring some of her bears so we can have the biggest teddy bear's picnic in history!'

'Yes, we will!' said Sarah. She had not yet told her

brother and his wife about the new flat and was looking forward to doing so. With Emma's eighth birthday just two weeks away they had been asking what they could buy for her, and Sarah wondered if it would be too much to ask them to contribute to buying Emma a new bed. The second hand one she used now was showing its age and the mattress sagged in the middle. It was all they had when Sarah moved into her flat, but now with a new bedroom to put it in, it was time the old bed was replaced.

-oo0Ooo-

Chapter 6

*F*or all his bluff and bravado Pete was actually quite shy.

His lack of self confidence dictated that he had never had much success with girls as a result. Although he was certainly good looking and personable, and had had plenty of opportunities, when it came to finding romance he was always awkward and usually found himself unable to think of anything to say.
He desperately wanted to ask Sarah out, but he could not find the right moment, or the courage to begin.

Surprisingly he found it easy enough to talk about impersonal work matters, however. His time with Sarah, as they went over the plans for the kitchen in her new flat, spread out once more on the garden table, was concluding, and he began to be aware of those all too familiar butterflies in his stomach which began to dance and swoop.

He had practiced what he was going to say for days, but feared that he was more than likely to fluff his lines, or be unable to say anything at all when, now that it was here, the moment came.

'Well, that will work really well,' said Sarah. 'There is loads of worktop on your sketch too, just as you promised. You are good at this, aren't you, Pete. Have you done it before?'

'Once or twice,' said Pete, clearing his throat and reaching for the kitchen brochure again.

He had to clear his throat twice more before he could bring himself to say anything else.

'Sarah, I wondered if … if you would like …' he said.

'Yes?' said Sarah turning her big blue eyes on him.

'I mean if you would like …' Those eyes began to dissolve his already shaky courage.

Sarah watched Pete squirm. She wondered what he was trying to say.

It was no good. Supposing she said no, thought Pete. He would die of embarrassment.

'Would you like wood effect or just smooth finish on the doors …'

The words burned like acid in his throat. He had failed again. He cursed his inability to get what he wanted to say out, and he barely heard her answer.

-oooOoo-

Carlos was like a human whirlwind.

He arrived with the little 'Amanda's Bistros' van crammed full of all the utensils and store cupboard ingredients he could need, and as Mario tried to keep out of his way, once he realised he could not do anything to help, Carlos bustled about arranging the kitchen just as he wanted it.

Mario did have one job to do and that was to get the big TV monitor on the wall and DVD player to talk to each other while making sure that the teaching aids Carlos had prepared ran properly when the laptop he plugged in was connected.

'Don't forget you have to leave space for Sarah's baking stuff, Carlos,' he said. 'Sarah is going to be working in here every day, and you will only be here a couple of times a week.'

'I haven't forgotten, Mario. Don't panic. I have left these cupboards over this bench for her. It is the most practical place to keep her things. I also think that I shall ask her if she would like to use the left hand oven, and I'll use the right hand one. Then there is no danger of a clash.'

'You have got it all figured out, haven't you, Carlos. I hope you and Sarah are going to get on.'

'Get on? Of course we will get on. We are both professionals working a commercial kitchen. I don't know Sarah very well yet. I have only met her twice, but I am sure we can get along just fine and she will fit in well.'

'Don't forget she works for Amanda, Carlos, she is not one of your kitchen staff.'

'Yes, yes. Of course I remember, Mario. You worry too much. Now, get out of the way I want to re-arrange some of my pans.'

-oooOoo-

For Sarah, there had only ever been Ricky.

She had never even dated any other boys, and when he left she had certainly not considered finding anyone else. Sarah decided that she could live without men, and with Emma to look after she needed little else.

And yet in her quieter moments, after Emma had gone to bed, she did sometimes wonder. And now she found herself replaying that odd conversation with Pete in her mind, as they finalised the kitchen design.

Why did he suddenly look so uncomfortable and seem unable to get his words out? He only wanted to know the finish on the cupboard doors ... unless ... perhaps there was something else he wanted to ask.

No, it couldn't be. This was Pete we were talking about. Pete probably had swarms of women chasing after him. Surely good looking cheeky chap Pete didn't need to be coy. And why on earth would he give her, of all people, a second glance. Sarah had no delusions about her situation. Who, she told herself, would want a skinny, ordinary looking little half portion like her, with a ready-made family?

It was just being fanciful. Even if she wanted to date again, which she told her self firmly she did not; she wouldn't want to go out with someone like Pete who probably had a different girl for every day of the week.

OK she knew he was single, hadn't Amanda said so, but that didn't mean he was lonely enough to want to hang about with someone like her.

Lonely? Now why had that word popped into her head? Sarah had never considered herself to be lonely … she had Emma and … and … Sarah shook herself and got up to make a cup of coffee before she went to bed with her favourite baking cookbook.

Soon she would be baking in that wonderful kitchen and she needed to make sure she had done all the homework she could, to brush up her rusty skills. That was quite enough to be thinking about.

-ooOOoo-

A few days later they were ready to go.

Mario was due to arrive at a little after eleven o'clock in the van to collect the first complete batch Sarah had made, and after a couple of trial runs to get used to the oven, and correct the shape and size of the scones amongst other things, Amanda was happy that Mario's would be the first restaurant to offer afternoon teas in addition to its current menu.

The plan was to roll it out to the other three restaurants over time, once they had gauged how popular it was at Mario's, and refined the product as much as was practical.

On the first day, and somewhat anxiously, Sarah had arranged for Jenny to take Emma to school and started in the kitchen at a little after seven in the morning. The cafe and tearooms were not yet open to the public and Pete and Dave were still putting the final touches to the decorations in preparation for the arrival of the furniture, so with no breakfast service to worry about, Sarah could concentrate on getting her afternoon tea menu just right.

She was ready quite a while before Mario was due to arrive, and with the tea cakes and scones and delicate and decorative patisserie all boxed up and ready to go, she allowed herself a little break and offered to make Dave and Pete coffee.

Naturally there were a few cakes left over, so she had no difficulty in getting them to accept her offer.

They sat once more around the plastic garden table in the recently converted area, now decorated in shades of pale blue with sections of wallpaper featuring Amanda's favourite hares. Some of these creatures were in top hats looking at pocket watches, some at rest and some running, and with the decoration done, it was very different to the first time she had sat at this table.

'The tables and chairs are due today,' said Dave through a mouthful of cake. 'I thought they would be here by now.'

'What do you think of it?' asked Pete, indicating the entire room with a sweep of his arm.

'It is very pretty,' said Sarah honestly. 'Unless you have a phobia about hares, I suppose!'

'You wait until you see the chairs,' said Dave. 'There are more hares in the fabric of the seats, and then there is all the other bits and bobs she has ordered.'

'Yes. There are china hares, teapots with hares on, cups and saucers covered in hares and little metal hares that will appear to hang off the side of the dressers we made.'

'You made,' said Dave. 'Pete is the cabinet maker, not me. My unique expertise lies more at the sledge hammer and brickwork end of the proceedings.'

'You made these dressers, Pete?' asked Sarah. She had seen the well crafted units with stylish turned legs and decorative shelf supports being unloaded from the truck, but had no idea Pete had actually made them. 'They are lovely.'

'Amanda wanted something to be solid and practical as well as being nice to look at,' said Pete blushing and looking at his shoes.

'Took him hours that did. Derek was getting well fed up with him using all the space up in the workshop in the end,' scowled Dave. 'So was I. His first job is helping me modernise your flat and working on the new offices, not fiddling with Amanda's stuff.'

-ooOoo-

Chapter 7

Things soon took on a regular pattern for Jenny and Sarah, and with the cafe now open for breakfast, the rota they devised to take and collect the children from school was working well.

It turned out that it was easier for Sarah to collect the children in the afternoons when her teas were being consumed rather than prepared. So Jenny took over the breakfast preparation and Sarah found herself starting ever earlier each morning to get everything ready, as the volumes of patisserie required increased.

While Sarah worked what amounted to full time, Jenny was still a part time employee, although Amanda had said that if the afternoon teas at Mario's took off, they might be able to increase her hours running the cafe as Sarah needed to spend more time in the catering kitchen.

Carlos used the kitchen a couple of afternoons each week and mostly when Sarah had finished for the day, although on a couple of occasions they did need to work round each other while Carlos tried out new recipes. But that worked well too, because it usually meant Jenny and Sarah got to take home exotic meals for the children's supper, prepared by a chef who was quietly building quite a reputation in the world of fine dining.

So far, for the cafe itself, it was also going very well. After an initial flurry, as the various demolition contractors and builders working on the main part of the estate tried out the breakfasts, and on two occasions they sold out of some of the raw ingredients; that part of the business settled into a busy and sometimes hectic flow, with the take-away side doing particularly well. The afternoon tea trade was pretty well non-existent, unless you counted Derek and Amanda's visits, but that was understandable as the building work on the estate gathered pace. Perhaps, they thought, it would improve when buyers stared to come and look at the new houses, and were in need of refreshment.

The afternoon tea trade at Mario's was also slower to start but as the word quickly spread, Mario began to have to take bookings rather than just offering a 'walk-in' service. He joyfully told Amanda that he would have to organise it into two sittings if it got much busier.

It was a confident Amanda who added the first of the three bistros to the list of her establishments offering afternoon teas and created flyers to go in the local papers and advertising to announce the start of the new service.

-oo0Ooo-

By Friday afternoon Derek was becoming excited and worried in equal measure, and he needed a discussion with Amanda.

'If it gets too busy we are going to have to take on extra staff, or start making the teas in the individual restaurants, and there is only one of Sarah, and she can't be everywhere,' he said. 'And the afternoon tea business is increasing the number of people who want to come back for an evening meal too.'

'Well, wasn't that the idea, Derek?' purred Amanda. 'Surely the busier we get the more money we will be making, so the more staff we can look to employ. And there doesn't seem to be any lack of people wanting to train under Carlos. He is inundated with un-solicited CVs.'

'Amanda, I need to talk to you. Something has come up which might be a great opportunity, or might just be a step to far ...'

As was their habit on warm evenings, they sat enjoying the last of the sun on the wide deck which stretched from the french doors leading out from the study, round to the dining room. This part of their large garden had been the venue for several parties in recent times and always caught the last of the late summer sun. Derek and Amanda liked to sit here to wind down after their busy working days and talk about what they had been doing. The peaceful garden outside their large modern house always seemed to help Derek relax, but tonight it was not having its usual effect, and he was sitting on the edge of his side of the elegant wrought iron love-seat.

'Derek?'

'Amanda, I got a call from Henry at the accountants. He told me he works for the family that own the old Barclay Court Hotel, down by the tennis club. They have asked him to discretely look into the possibility of doing something different with it, and he agreed that he can talk to Albany Developments in confidence about it.'

'The hotel?'

'Yes, the Frobishers are also the family that once owned the agricultural machinery factory. It is them, and a bank, I think, that Waitrose are talking to about re-developing the factory site. Henry said they had considered selling the hotel, but wanted to explore a series of ideas, before making a final decision.'

'Okay …' said Amanda, intrigued.

'Yes. Well, at first I thought it wouldn't interest us because it is a listed building so you can't just knock it down and build houses on the land, but then

Henry explained that about ten years ago they had planning permission to build six or seven nice big houses on part of the garden, accessed of Barclay Woods Drive, so that got me interested.'

'Yes, it would.'

'And then Henry said they wouldn't just sell the plots, and they wanted to look at a more comprehensive range of options which involved the hotel itself in some way. Henry found out that at one point it became a catering school and that there are classroom facilities and some of the bedrooms were originally built for catering students studying and working there. The main classroom is basically an enormous kitchen and is currently unused. You can see a bit of the building through the trees as you go down Old Oak Drive towards the main road. Do you know where I mean? It looks a bit like a village hall.'

'Good heavens. I thought that was a squash court, or an indoor swimming pool or something,' said Amanda.

'Well, according to Henry, all the bits of the catering school are still there and years ago the hotel used the building to cater for wedding receptions held there, when they put up a big marquee in the garden, or used the hotel's ballroom. Henry said the Frobisher's who run it now are the three grandchildren of the original family, and they want to still keep running the hotel. But it is not viable as it is currently configured and is losing money.'

'It does look a bit run down. It looks like the sort of old Gothic place your car breaks down outside in a horror film.'

'Ha, yes. I can imagine that! And creepy old Pop Frobisher himself comes to open the creaking door when you knock and ask if you can use the telephone …' laughed Derek.

'Thank God for mobile phones is all I say!' chuckled Amanda.

'Well, anyway. There are about twenty bedrooms, I think Henry was saying, and the only food they offer guests is breakfast at present, although they once had a roaring evening trade up there, with people eating and dancing in the ballroom, which is now all shut up and needs a new roof.'

'When did they have dancing up there?'

'In the 1930s and 40's I think.'

'Ah, no chance of inviting the old crowd back if the roof was fixed then.'

'No, but the more I talked about it with Henry the more an idea started to form in my head. But, it is a bit ambitious, and it might take quite a lot of investment to pull it off.'

'I'm all ears …'

'No you are not, you have perfectly proportioned

ears, I've told you that before.'

'Well, shelving my anatomical proportions for a moment, what is this big idea?'

'I love your anatomical proportions, Amanda.'

'Stop it. We are talking business here, and I'm intrigued.'

'Sorry. Well, the thing is, the Frobisher's won't sell the land for the houses to be built unless we come up with a comprehensive package. Henry wondered if we might consider opening their dining facilities up as an 'Amanda's' bistro and run it while they run the rest of it as a hotel. The money we made from building the houses would subsidise the cost of setting up the restaurant part of it and employing the staff and so on ...'

'Nice try, sweetie, but until the houses are built and sold there is no money to develop the restaurant and employ the staff unless we take on more bank borrowing, and 'Amanda's' is too new as a business to contemplate that yet.'

'You are right, and obviously the Frobisher family won't want to wait while we build and sell the houses before the bistro gets going. So that is when I came up with my idea.'

'OK partner, shoot!'

'No, not a shooting gallery, darling. Don't be silly ...

I'm thinking a catering school with accommodation on site and a venue for weddings and other events in the ballroom, all fed and watered by a fine dining restaurant.'

Amanda was quiet for a while and Derek knew her well enough to give her time to absorb the concept. When she spoke she was standing up and pacing round in little circles.

'We couldn't call it 'Amanda's'. It is too close to all the other restaurants and would pinch their business. And what if we couldn't get enough weddings to make it pay. Might it be better to think of it as a sort of very up market dining club, with dancing and entertainment. Exclusive dinner dances where the students serve their food. A membership club, perhaps. An exclusive venue with fine dining and guest appearances by famous singers ... not noisy ones, of course. And exhibitions and wine tastings. Artists exhibitions and all that sort of thing, I mean, during exclusive evenings for invited connoisseurs ... with huge stylish flower arrangements and maybe an ice sculpture ... Hold on, maybe gambling ... a swish casino night for members and guests ... formal dress required. Croupiers and all that sort of thing. It would be like dining in a Bond movie.'

'All right 007, don't let's run before we can walk. It does have possibilities as a catering college, don't you think. We could base Sarah and Carlos there doing their stuff for all the venues as well as demonstrations, perhaps. If we could get it up to the point where other good restaurants were sending their staff to be trained, and maybe get some guest chefs to do master classes...'

'Derek, let's go to bed. No, let me re-phrase that. Derek, we need to sleep on this. It is a big project and will take some thinking through.'

-oo0Ooo-

Chapter 8

*H*enry's Bentley looked somehow right as it drew up the drive to the once elegant old country house that had become the Barclay Court Hotel. There was still an air of olde world charm about the setting of the building, if you disregarded the need for a spruce up and the overgrown garden.

Derek and Amanda's large Mercedes completed the effect and the three youngest Frobishers formed a sort of guard of honour as their guests walked through the tall pillared porch to the front door.

The Misses Penelope and Jane Frobisher were twins and had celebrated their fiftieth birthday some little time ago. Their brother Jeremy was a few years younger, but still wore the scowling countenance of the ladies, as a family resemblance. After the introductions were complete, they invited their guests into a dimly-lit parlour with a view down the drive, and a fireplace with crossed antique shotguns over the mantle. Evidently this was where the initial discussions were to take place.

'I thought,' said Jeremy, taking the lead, 'we could show you round it all after we have had a chat. I've got some photo albums here which give a flavour of the history of the place and what it used to be, if you would like a look.'

'Oh, that first one is a delightful picture,' said Jane. 'It is the ballroom in about 1938, I think. Look at all the dancers and the chandeliers glowing! Our grandparents always had a full house in those days.'

The much thumbed black and white photograph did indeed show what appeared to be a crowd of young people enjoying themselves. Some were dining, seated at tables set for four and being served by white coated waiters, some danced and a band could just be seen, no doubt playing the latest jazz sensation for the enjoyment of the revellers.

There were several more photographs covering the same theme, and then, as Jeremy turned the pages, some group photos, now in colour, of smiling people dressed in chef's 'whites' holding certificates, outside what appeared to be a large schoolroom.

Then there were more modern pictures of various bedrooms, dining rooms, and people, which Jeremy flicked through until he reached some images that were obviously private family photographs.

'That is dear Uncle Frederick,' offered Penelope when an image of an irritable looking old gentleman in a tweed suit appeared on the top of the pile. 'He lives in a care home now, of course. But we have him home here every few weeks. It was his idea to sell this whole place off to become a nursing home but Mummy and Daddy would hear nothing of it because it meant that we three would not have had employment or an income, which had always been the plan.'

'That's right,' said Jeremy. 'Our grandfather, who was also Uncle Frederick's father, made it quite clear that they wanted our parents to continue to run the hotel as he had, and then to leave it to us to continue the tradition when our turn came.'

'Yes,' offered Jane now, 'Uncle Frederick was the younger son you see, and life took him on a different course, away from the hotel. First the military … he was in the Guards, and then in the City where he worked in insurance, I think it was.'

'The thing is it is becoming increasingly difficult to make it pay, since the financial crash and now this recession. And we haven't the capital to develop the other parts of the business, so we asked Henry here to see if he could think of a way forward,' said Jeremy.

'We would want to still run the hotel part of it, if that was possible, though,' said Penelope looking daggers at her brother.

'If it was possible,' said Jeremy returning his sister's

glare. 'You have to accept that we need proper advice and ideas as to what to do with the place, Pen. That is why Henry bought along our guests.'

'Perhaps we should have a look round now.' said Jane, taking charge and stepping towards the door. 'Can we show you the garden first? The weather forecast said there was a chance of a shower and poor dear Penelope is very susceptible to colds and chills, so I don't want us to get caught in it.'

-oooOoo-

The garden, though still large by modern standards, had once been much bigger, and in the 1970s most of the land was sold off for development. Derek and Amanda's house was built in the 1980's but was on land that once formed part of the grounds of Barclay Court, as the house was originally called.

Now, with only one gardener, in the form of Jeremy himself to look after it, the once charming flower borders, lawns and separate walled kitchen garden were all in dire need of some attention.

Externally the slightly fussy ornate brickwork of the original victorian house was still in good condition, but the various later additions, ranging in vintage from the 1930s to the 1970s were all showing their age. All of the woodwork was looking very tired and, as they rounded a corner of the old house, they came to a large structure with boarded-up windows, joined to the main house by a flat roofed corridor.

This, they were informed, was once the catering school.

While Jeremy fought to undo a padlock which secured a door on the flat roofed corridor, Jane explained that the catering college opened in 1965 but closed twenty-five years later when the last of the specialist staff left. More recently the buildings and kitchens had been used to provide catering facilities for wedding receptions and parties held in the ballroom, and later on, in a large marquee erected in the grounds, but they had not been used for the last ten or more years.

'There has been a bit of a problem with the roof here,' added Jeremy. 'The Council said this building was what they called a 'dangerous structure' because damp had got into the roof timbers, so we boarded it up to keep people out.'

'It might not be very pretty,' explained Penelope, 'but the cost of repairs were such that we had to shut it up until we had the money to do something about it.'

'Thank you, Pen,' said Jeremy with a scowl. 'I thought we agreed that we were going to allow our guests to look around without burdening them with any more detail than was necessary about the background.'

'Oh, yes. Sorry Jerry, I forgot that you said not to say that we were short of money.'

'Pen!'

'Perhaps,' said Jane, 'we should take a look inside now. Jeremy seems to have managed to get the door open at last. Please do be careful, though. We have to remember to tell you that this is a dangerous structure and you enter at your own risk, according to our insurance company.'

-ooOoo-

What had once been the ceiling of the corridor was now mostly on the floor and there was a strong smell of damp.

The double doors leading to the bigger structure stuck in their frames as Jeremy wrenched them open and, fishing in his pocket for a flashlight, illuminated the scene.

Before them, where the beam of the torch touched it, lay another corridor with small rooms off to either side and then, through a further set of doors, this time propped open, to a vast almost clear space with a high open style roof and visible trusses festooned with cobwebs.

All along the walls there were stainless steel work benches, tall fridges, sinks and cupboards. In the centre there was a bank of ovens at eye level separated by further metal work stations, interspersed with large gas hobs and vast extractor hoods. At one end, behind a tall room divider, there was a raised stage with a wide steel peninsular and an another large separate area currently being used to store a collection of stools, tables, and metal framed wooden chairs.

This was the main teaching room of the former catering college, Jane informed them and, as she steered them round a shallow puddle in the floor, she explained that beyond lay the college offices, a separate bakery, and further smaller teaching rooms as well as the caretakers accommodation.

'And the toilets, of course,' added Penelope. 'But you can't use them anymore because the water tank burst.'

'Thank you Penelope,' said Jane, as Jeremy suppressed a groan. 'We will look through there in a moment.'

Although, with the windows boarded up and no natural daylight, it was difficult to see much of the room, Derek glanced at Amanda and was unsurprised to see her registering astonishment as they looked around the damp and dismal, but never-the-less huge space.

-oo0Ooo-

The little party had returned to the main hotel reception, after a brief inspection of the building plots. There Jeremy had explained that the small area with moss-covered foundations and a little low wall constituted what was officially termed as a 'material start'. This, he explained, stopped "those idiots" at the Local Council from being able to cancel or remove their ten year old planning consent to build houses on that part of the land.

'Fortunately,' said Jane, 'there are currently no guests in residence, so you can look at all the bedrooms.'

Back in the reception area, just as the threatened drizzle started outside, Jane took charge once more.

'There are twenty letting bedrooms, three of which are now large family rooms which were originally built as dormitories for the catering school students. They are all 'en-suite'. One is the original master suite of the house and has a lounge, as well as a dressing room and a bedroom as you will see when we get there. But first, perhaps we can have a look around the hotel building.'

'Starting,' said Jeremy, 'with the ballroom that you saw in the pictures.'

'This way, please,' said Jane.

-oo0Ooo-

The approach to the ballroom had the same elegant high ceilings as the rest of the ground floor of the hotel and they arrived now at wide heavy double doors which stretched right up to the ceiling.

Jane unlocked one of them with a massive old

fashioned wrought iron key and, as the huge door creaked loudly and slowly opened on its hinges, Derek thought he detected a tiny stifled giggle from Amanda.

What was now revealed to them however was no laughing matter.

The enormous and obviously once very grand room had suffered somewhat since the days of the joyous pictures they had been shown.

In the far corner on the right, just above the raised staging occupied by a band in the photos, a large chunk of the once ornate plasterwork had fallen and smashed into a thousand pieces on the dance floor, and above it the underside of the roof slates could be seen.

It was obvious that pigeons had once got into the space and made themselves at home. Every surface showed the unpleasant signs of their presence.

Floor to ceiling red drapes kept prying eyes from looking through the tall windows. Though faded now, they once would have matched the decorative tasseled padded covers on the balcony wall of the mezzanine structure that spread along most of one wall at first floor level.

The grubby dance floor, beyond the carpet they were now standing on could possibly be restored, Derek thought, but not the collection of chairs and tables stacked and scattered here and there that the pigeons had clearly used as perches.

The elaborate and obviously ancient metallic wallpaper would once have glittered to add sparkle to the proceedings, but the massive chandeliers featured in the photographs had gone, leaving only wiring to show where they had been.

'What happened to the chandeliers?' Derek asked.

'Oh, Uncle Frederick sold them some years ago,' said Penelope. 'They went to another hotel in London, I think.'

'Yes, well, this area does need total restoration, of course,' said Jeremy. 'And the roof over there needs a sort out.'

'There are doors to the kitchen and the bar facilities over there,' said Jane, pointing. 'I suggest that we view them from the other side rather than walk any further into this room.'

'I'm certainly not going in there,' said Penelope. 'It stinks!'

Chapter 9

'And so,' explained Derek, 'when we got to the bedrooms we were not expecting much, but they were all clean and tidy. They might have benefited from a lick of paint here and there but other than that they were fine.'

'What was the restaurant and bar like,' asked Dave.

'The kitchen was a bit messy, but they only serve breakfast in there now. The resident's dining room was what you might call serviceable. It had rather nasty cheap plastic chairs and tables, so not nearly as grand as the rest of it. But the cocktail bar is a sight to behold and the high spot of the whole place.'

'Not more pigeons?' said Pete.

'No, it was lovely. It is all done out in 1920s or 30s style … art deco is it? And every surface gleamed. There is marble everywhere and big stylish lights with sculptures of women in elegant 1920s clothes, and pictures of jazz bands and people dancing. And there are loads of mirrors. All very glamorous.'

'Pity they couldn't have kept the rest of the place up like that,' said Dave.

'Yeah. They are very obviously skint, but they won't hear of selling the whole thing and have turned away several interested parties, so Henry told me.'

'So do you think it is something you and Amanda want to get involved in, Derek?' asked Pete.

'Well, initially I thought it was too much, unless we could get the whole place and perhaps sell the listed building bit off, but when I saw that bar I changed my view. And Amanda loves it, so we are going to do some figures and see what we can do.'

'And anything Amanda wants, she gets,' smirked Dave.

'Cheeky,' smiled Derek. 'Anyway I need you to keep all this under your hats because it is not on the open market or anything, and Henry got us involved on a confidential basis. We don't want the word getting out and all and sundry snooping about there. Anyone want more tea?'

'I'll get you some,' said Sarah.

-oo0Ooo-

'So, this is exciting isn't it, Emma!' said Amanda.

'Thanks for dropping us off, Derek,' Sarah called

to his retreating back. 'This is very kind of you, Amanda. Emma has been so looking forward to it.'

'So have I,' said Amanda. 'This combines my two favourite things. Spoiling children and shopping!'

'Do you spend much time spoiling children?' laughed Sarah.

'Only the nice ones,' chuckled Amanda. 'And at Christmas Derek and I always go to the Hospice and give out presents there, but that is different.'

'You have a lovely house to bring kids up in,' said Sarah, looking around the spacious lounge they sat in now.

Amanda's shoulders fell. 'I suppose you are right, Sarah, but I'm afraid that is impossible.'

'Oh Amanda, I've said the wrong thing. I'm so sorry … I didn't think …'

'It is quite all right Sarah. We found out a couple of years ago that we can't have children. It is just something we have had to come to terms with.'

'Please forgive me, Amanda. I wish I had never said that … I'm so sorry.'

'Please don't apologise, Sarah. Let's forget it, we don't want anything to spoil our shopping trip, do we Emma.'

'I'm sorry too,' said Emma. 'But if you like you can be

my auntie. Then you can come and see me and we can do shopping and things, and I can help you with stuff whenever you like.'

'Thank you, Emma, that is very sweet. Auntie Amanda … I like that! Come on then, let's go and choose that wallpaper before they sell out.'

-oooOoo-

'She was just so generous!' said Sarah. 'After the wallpaper and the paint she started picking out bedside lights and cushions and curtains. And then she moved on to the matching bedding and wouldn't let me stop her until she had even bought Emma pictures for the walls!'

'You don't surprise me, Sarah,' said Pete. 'She loves kids and is very kind.'

'She absolutely blew Emma away, and is now her adopted Auntie.'

'People sometimes think Amanda is a stuck up glamour-puss and Derek's trophy wife. But once you get to know her she is a clever, thoughtful and delightful person. People don't see it, but Amanda is his business partner as well as his wife. Derek is a very lucky man.'

'And their house is perfect …' Sarah sighed.

'Did you go in the main lounge? That is an extension. Dave and I built that.'

'Yes, it was lovely.'

Much to his surprise Pete found he was beginning to relax in Sarah's company, so long as he kept the conversation light. Looking at her now, nicely but subtly made up and smartly dressed for her shopping trip, he thought how petite and attractive she was.

Her big blue eyes were framed in her face by her fair hair, now loose and not raked back into a practical ponytail for a change. And her slight frame was shown off to best advantage by the wide loose-legged trousers and white blouse she wore under the inevitable anorak style blue puffy jacket, that was her constant companion.

He was surprised when he heard the words 'Sarah, you look very nice, can I take you out for a drink one day?' and realised he had spoken them himself.

-oo0Ooo-

'Really, it is no problem, Sarah, and I think the idea of that "high sleeper" bunk style bed with the desk underneath it is ideal. Emma will need somewhere to do her homework soon, so we would be delighted to get it for her.'

'Thank you very much indeed Matty!'

'Do you think you will be able to put it together, though? These things from Argos are bound to come flat packed and need assembly.'

'I think I know someone who might be prepared to help me with that, at least I would like to think he would …'

'So come on sis, tell me all about this bloke. You are obviously smitten!'

-ooOOoo-

Chapter 10

*T*he thing about time is that it passes, and if you don't keep an eye on it, it passes quickly. So it was for Emma and Sarah.

For her birthday Sarah laid on a special tea in the Mad Hatters Tea Room and invited Pete, Dave, and Derek and Amanda, and with Jenny's help they served up an epic feast to Emma and her school friends which they are probably still talking about.

The move to the refurbished flat went without a hitch, and while Sarah could not stop looking at her new kitchen, and would sometimes go in there for no reason other than just to admire it, Emma adored her new bedroom and the 'high sleeper' bed that her aunt and uncle had bought her.

Pete and Sarah shared a shy drink at the Red Lion and then a kiss in the car park, and since then there had been a curry and a pizza, and next week a trip to the local steakhouse was planned. There had been more kisses too, but so far, apart from holding hands, that was as far as it went.

For Derek and Amanda things had become very busy indeed. The proposal they put to the Frobishers, whereby they continued to run the hotel but Albany Developments took over the rest, was with the solicitors to make into a reality. Under this plan Derek purchased the building plots. In addition, a new company which Henry the accountant arranged for them to set up, took on a long lease, with the option to purchase, on the ballroom and bar, the former catering school, and the caretaker's accommodation that went with it.

Albany Developments new offices were also nearing completion and Derek called Pete into a meeting there.

'I'd like to offer you the chance to be the project manager of the Barclay Court Hotel scheme, Pete,' he said. 'It will mean a bit more money in your pay packet and taking on some responsibility, that I am more than confident you are ready for. Its a big project, and I don't say it won't be tricky, particularly working round the Frobishers and keeping the hotel open throughout, but I know you can do it and I can trust you to get it right.'

At the same time Amanda called a meeting with Jenny and Sarah in the Mad Hatters Tea Room and laid out her proposal.

'So if you are up for it, Jenny, when the time comes

you can take over this place as manager, with a new assistant, and Sarah can work at the Barclay Court Hotel Catering School. She can serve all the restaurants and the new facilities from there in a separate dedicated kitchen. It will mean full time hours for you both, if that is OK, and if we can find another of the mums round here to work with you with similar needs to get kids too and from school, Jenny, it should work as well as it does now.'

Amanda paused and looked from face to face.

'Of course the project is going to take a while to reach fruition and there is a lot of work for the builders to do before we are ready to put this into action, but I'm telling you now because we want to be sure that we have a solid supportive team of great people behind us that we can rely on.'

Jenny jumped at the chance, of course, and Sarah, who had been briefed beforehand shook her hand.

'But how are you going to get there, Sarah?' Jenny asked. 'You don't have a car.'

When she first moved into the flats Sarah did have a car, but terminal rust had led to a comprehensive and damning MoT test failure, and she had to pay to have it towed away. Now though Amanda proposed that the Catering School should purchase one of those small vans with side windows and seats in the back which could be used to transport people as well as cakes and patisserie.

The biggest shock came when Amanda explained that the new Catering College could not be called 'Amanda's' so that it did not compete with her other restaurants, and that she proposed to call it "Sarah's Kitchen".

'Why not Carlos' Kitchen? After all he is the head chef,' Sarah had asked. 'Or Mario's Kitchen?'

'No, we have thought about this long and hard, Sarah. The fine dining and dancing club we are proposing to create is going to be called "Carlos at Barclay Court" and Mario is thinking about retiring so doesn't think it would be right to use his name for a new venture.'

'But …'

'And we will have "Sarah's Kitchen" sign written on the side of the van stroke people carrier thing to make it easy to recognise in case you go to pick students up from the station or something. The vehicle will be yours to drive to work and use all the time for whatever you need to do, provided you don't mind driving around in an advert!'

Sarah was already beginning to think this was all a dream, but then Pete asked her to let him take her over to the hotel to show her something.

-oooOoo-

The area at the back of the former catering college,

where it opened onto a secluded walled kitchen garden, was very overgrown.

As they stood amongst the weeds now looking back at the building, Pete drew Sarah's attention to a door and some windows in the otherwise blank elevation.

'There,' he said, 'I'll show you.'

What they were looking at was built as accommodation for a
live-in caretaker who would have been dedicated to the college in its heyday. It had not been occupied, at least as a home, for many years and Pete initially had to shoulder barge the door to get it open.

'Ouch!' he said, rubbing his arm.

'Careful,' said Sarah replacing his hand with her own and gently rubbing where it hurt.

'Sarah,' he said gathering her into his arms. 'It is all right, I don't think I am broken.'

'I'm glad,' she said looking up into his face.

When finally he released her she was hot and flushed and somewhat embarrassed.

'Someone might have seen us …' she stammered.

'Nobody can see us, don't worry, and we were only kissing. I'll protect you from the ghosts of the Frobishers past!'

'Don't! This place is creepy enough without you talking about ghosts.'

'Do you believe in ghosts then?'

'No. Well, I don't think so.' But in spite of herself she gave a little shudder.

'I'm sorry, are you cold?' said Pete gathering her into his arms again.

'No, I'm fine.'

'Oh Sarah,' said Pete, kissing the top of her head, 'you are so dainty. You are so small and perfect, I could eat you, just like one of those little pastries you make ...'

'But I'm not nearly as sweet if you bite me, so just watch yourself,' she laughed, pulling away from him.

'I'd better show you why I asked you to come here,' he said. 'Come and have a look at this.'

The caretaker's accommodation, once they got inside, was arranged over two floors like a normal house. Upstairs there were two bedrooms of reasonable size, a small third bedroom, presumably intended to be a nursery, and a bathroom. On the ground floor there was a cozy lounge with a fireplace, a separate kitchen, and a dining room with french doors leading to a little private garden that could not be seen from the front and used two of the kitchen garden walls, making a corner, as its boundary.

It was all a bit dated, of course, and having obviously been used as a store for the collection of garden implements that were now scattered about in the downstairs rooms, it had not been lived in for some time. It was untidy, but it had the makings of a pleasant little home.

'Derek says if I do this place up on my own time, when I'm not supposed to be working, I can live here rent free while I'm managing the project and getting the new houses built.'

'Wow!' said Sarah. 'Lucky you. Think of the money you will save not having to pay rent to your mum and dad!'

'So what do you think?' he asked now.

'It is sweet. Or at least it could be once you have sorted it out. How long will you have the use of it for?'

'Two years initially, but maybe longer if things work out as Amanda and Derek currently plan. It might even become a permanent thing, although I should imagine I'm going to have to pay a rent at some point.'

'It is like little secret cottage but, being on the Barclay Woods estate, it is in one of the poshest addresses round here!'

'Do you think Emma would like it?'

'Pardon me?'

'I mean do you think she would think it was a romantic little hideaway cottage. Girls like to imagine that sort of thing.'

'She might.'

'Well, when you are working up here, when all this gets going properly, maybe you could bring her round and show it to her and perhaps I could cook you both supper.'

'You cook supper?'

'I can, you know. When not scrounging off you in the cafe I can cater for myself quite well.'

'Oh yes? And what do you cook?'

'Well, my signature dish is beans on toast, of course. But I can also rustle up a mean salad when the mood takes me.'

'No wonder you are thin.'

'I prefer wiry.'

'You'll need someone to look after you when you can't come and eat at the cafe so easily.'

'Will you do it, Sarah. You don't want me to starve in here do you? And you will have the run of an entire catering school with all sorts of ovens and so on to rustle up exotic and wholesome grub.'

Sarah, laughing, gave him a little push.

'Ow! That's my bad arm!'

'Sorry, sweetie …'

-oo0Oo-

Of course Barclay Court had stood witness to considerably more of the passage of time than its current occupants, and it had not always been well received.

Pevsner's guidebook described it as 'architecturally muddled' and Winston Churchill, who called in briefly, described his visit in a letter where he explained that his party had to take 'pot luck' at lunchtime, and that the architect of the house seemed to have taken pot luck more than once when designing it. He suggested that the draughtsman may have stopped work on one day, gone off on a 'monumental toot' for three days, and on his return, having forgotten where he was up to in his drawings, continued in a different style altogether.

He would have noticed that the roof is a mixture of artificial battlements, towers and dormers finished off, in one corner, with a square clock tower, apparently stolen from a French chateau and plonked on the top as an afterthought.

The original house may not have been entirely

pleasing to the eye as a result, but that did not stop the Local Authority 'Listing' it and applying the troublesome category of 'Grade 2' to it.

This 'Listing' proved a bureaucratic nightmare for the Frobisher family, who had to seek permission to do pretty much anything to the ageing structure, and engage in a long winded and frustrating paper-chase whenever work needed to be done.

The final straw came for the last generation of the Frobishers when part of the ornate plaster roof in the ballroom collapsed, and repairs were needed to its roof. The ballroom incident happened to coincide with some ongoing negotiations they were having with the local Building Regulations Officer, about the plots where the new houses were proposed to be built.

The Building Inspector was called in to sign-off some works which their architect assured the Frobishers would secure the longevity of the planning permission, which was otherwise about to expire.

While looking at the 'material start' their builder had organised, and prior to issuing his certificate, the Building Inspector noticed that the roof of the adjacent catering college appeared to be sagging on one side. Before long the Town Hall mannequins had declared the building unsafe and issued notices to categorise it as a 'Dangerous Structure' which must not be used.

While the Frobishers were trying to argue that away, during very heavy rain, part of the ballroom roof collapsed and the fire service, called in to make it safe, notified the Building Inspector, who notified the Conservation Officer, who visited the ballroom and promptly issued a sheaf of papers containing exacting details as to how the repairs to the 'Grade 2 Listed Structure' were to be carried out and threatening fines if the work was not done to their specification.

At that point, Jeremy Frobisher, who was responsible for the buildings and maintenance side of things, seemed to give up and retreat into his shell.

He kept his pride and joy, his grandfather's wonderful period cocktail bar, cleaned and polished but with no customers, and now only a thin trickle of travelling salesmen staying in the hotel, usually just on a 'Bed and Breakfast' basis, there was no getting away from it, the rest of the hotel was becoming shabby and had been allowed to deteriorate.

Penelope, who struggled a little to understand what was going on sometimes, cheerfully devoted herself to cleaning and laundry as before, and Jane continued to run 'Reception', cook breakfast for the guests, and do the books. But Jeremy began to neglect his duties in the gardens, and with no gardener anymore to help him, things inevitably began to go downhill.

-ooOOoo-

The Frobishers lived in an enormous apartment, covering much of the top floor of the original house. It had four bedrooms, a drawing room, a dining room, an office, and a small library where Jeremy kept his precious family archives.

The guest's lift did not reach the top storey of the house, although the battered service lift clanked up as far as a half landing, a little way from the door to their apartment. But there were three staircases serving it, and one internal flight of five steps up, and three down to travel from one end of the apartment to the other, avoiding the awkward dormer roof supports, low ceilings and occasional oddly positioned beams obstructing easy circulation.

In what their most illustrious guest might have described as the chateau clock tower 'plonked on the top', there was a further narrow and very steep staircase that was little more than a ladder. These uncomfortably tight stairs served three tiny, oddly shaped, cold rooms. They were arranged one on top of the other, and anyone visiting had to crouch to avoid hitting their heads on the ceilings. They were now kept locked up behind a stout door. Since the building was first constructed, nobody had managed to find a use for these impractical rooms, and they remained completely empty and forgotten.

Now Jane wanted to retire, Jeremy needed help to run the facilities, and they had to make a plan to look after Penelope.

In conceding that they were no longer coping with it all, the three Frobishers called in their accountant and asked for his help.

He was already working with them to finalise the negotiations with the company representing Waitrose, over the sale of the site of the old agricultural machinery factory, but those discussions were only progressing slowly and were tangled up with tax. The financial saviour that that deal represented for the family was some time off yet.

The proposal from Albany Developments they had been presented with was timely, and enabled them to find a way to resolve some of their immediate problems. It allowed them some respite from the pressures facing them while they waited to plan for the future with what they referred to in their conversations as 'the Waitrose money'.

-ooo0oo-

Chapter 11

*B*uilding work on the estate where Sarah and Jenny lived was progressing at pace.

The first of the refurbished units to be offered to let were beginning to be occupied, and the those which were for sale were being snapped up by eager buyers.

The show house in the area of brand new housing was up and open and the first phase of the new houses were about to receive their roof trusses.

Amanda took Sarah and Jenny to meet the two charming ladies who had been employed to greet people and show them round the show house, and Amanda thoughtfully gave the ladies some slips of paper she had printed off to hand out to prospective buyers, which would entitle them to a free cup of coffee or tea at the Mad Hatter's Tea Shop.

The first cup would always be free for the sales ladies, she announced, who were welcome anytime and now that Jenny and Sarah had been introduced to them, they were sure to be recognised.

It was clever marketing, and the sales ladies; middle aged Mary and young Sally, said they would be sure to collect their refreshments from the cafe and send the foot-sore prospective buyers along too.

Amanda had already ordered a little notice board, which was being prepared with a holder for the development's sales brochures, to go on the wall in the cafe; so the arrangement was entirely reciprocal.

While the sales ladies showed them round the show house, to the inevitable 'Ooohs' and 'Ahhs' from very a impressed Sarah and Jenny, Amanda was on the phone to Derek.

She explained that the sales ladies only had one desk between them, as the second had not yet arrived, and asked him to hurry it up. She told him that the automatic watering system in the garden did not seem to be working and the new turf was in danger of giving up the ghost if something wasn't promptly done about it. She went on to point out a blown lightbulb in the entrance porch, and comment that she had not seen the boards of wall tile samples in the show house, and wondered why they had not yet been delivered.

Amanda was nothing if not observant and was always absolutely at the top of her game.

On the way back from the show house, in Amanda's posh four-wheel drive, they drove past Sarah's old house. She did not mention it or make any comment, but she was pleased to see that a removal lorry parked outside was unloading furniture, and a young couple were standing in the entrance porch holding hands. She silently wished them luck.

-oo0Ooo-

Now that the solicitors had done their work, Derek spent much of his week with Pete at the Barclay Court Hotel, meeting decorative plasterwork restorers, specialist damp company representatives and the Director of the company who had provided the equipment and stainless steel furniture for the catering kitchen behind the Mad Hatters Tea Room.

He also spent time with his architect in the Council offices discussing the design of the new luxury homes to be built on part of the garden of the hotel, and meeting the Building Inspector who had given the Frobishers so many problems over the previous years.

It was getting cooler and the sun was setting earlier, but for now Derek continued to sit on the wide deck with Amanda, as the sun went down and they swapped news. He was able to chuckle delightedly as he told the story of his meeting with the Building Inspector.

'We have come across him before, of course, when we extended this house, and he knows all about our business, but he is not such a bad old stick when you give him a chance to explain things.'

'The Frobishers made him out to be some sort of a Machiavellian ogre.'

'Well, if he was, then he has mellowed now. He is due to retire this year and I got the distinct impression he was fishing to see if there were any part-time openings for someone with his experience at Albany Developments.'

'Crafty old blighter!'

'But he was really helpful and encouraging about the designs we propose for the new houses. It transpires that the Frobishers had engaged a whacky young newly qualified architect to design some ghastly ultra-modern boxes for the site, all blue glass, flat roofs, and white stucco walls, and he hated them. Our house types might be a bit more traditional, but they will fit in well with the rest of the Barclay Woods estate, and he appreciated that.'

'What did he have to say about the catering college?'

'That was quite enlightening too. He agrees with me that the shoddy flat roofed link to the main house needs to go and be replaced with something a bit more in keeping, and gave me a heads-up that the conservation officer would be watching that one like a hawk. He thinks we will have to completely strip the roof off the main part of the big classroom and start again with that bit. He said the failed roof trusses in there appear to be untreated timber and they have all had it. He suggested replacing them with lightweight steel or modern engineered wood but re-using the same slates as far as possible to cut costs and keep it looking the same.'

'It sounds like you have really been getting down to the detail.'

'Yes, and so have you with your observations at the show house. What with one thing and another I haven't had a chance to go over there recently and it was useful to have that feedback. Sarah told me about your free coffee for the sales ladies and the buyers idea when I popped in there at tea time. She was most impressed.

'Were you impressed too, honey?'

'Certainly ...'

'Well, it's getting chilly, so let's go inside now and open that bottle of wine in the fridge. Then you can tell me how much you appreciate me.'

-ooOOoo-

'So, with the kids off school tomorrow, have you got any plans?' asked Jenny.

'We have to go food shopping in the morning, but at tea time we are going up to the Barclay Court Hotel to meet Pete. He wants to show Emma the catering college before they strip the roof off and mess it all up. He also wants to show her the little house he will be living in up there.'

'Things are going pretty well with Pete, aren't they.'

'Between ourselves, I haven't bothered about men for so long that it is all a bit new and I'm quite nervous.'

'Oh, it will soon come back to you, once you get him in the bedroom …'

'Stop it! That's not what I mean, Jenny,' giggled Sarah. 'And we are certainly not at that stage…'

'Yet.'

Sarah pulled a face.

'That sort of thing is impossible anyway. He lives with his mum and dad, and there is Emma …'

'Emma could always come and stay with me for a night …'

'Not yet, but thanks for the thought, Jenny.'

'Oh look', said Jenny, glancing out of the cafe window. 'Here comes Mary from the show house, and she has got a couple of rather hunky blokes in tow. Is she expecting to sell them a house or is she after something else, do you think?'

'Jenny! You are incorrigible!' giggled Sarah.

-ooo0oo-

Chapter 12

'So about thirty or forty percent of the stainless steel units and benches can be saved and refurbished, but they don't recommend trying to rescue any of the ovens and certainly not the extractors.'

Pete was on the telephone explaining the results of the inspection at the former catering college that the specialist company, who supplied the fitments for the development kitchen at the cafe, had undertaken.

'Well, that is not as bad as it might have been, I suppose,' said Derek. 'When are they going to collect them?'

'Friday, and I hope it is OK, but I agreed that he could offset the scrap value he gets for the rest of the metal stuff off the refurbishment costs of the good bits that he will return. He said it would be no problem to remove most of the units from the kitchen at the cafe and install them in the smaller kitchen at the back too. Also, on Monday the demolition crew will make a start on knocking down the corridor. The guy who came over confirmed that the tests show there is no problem with asbestos, so they can get straight on with it.'

'That is good. Asbestos could have held us up for ages, and given the age of the buildings it is lucky that there isn't any in evidence on this project. And that is fine about the scrap metal ... good thinking.'

'The other good thing, if you will sanction it, is that I've spoken to Trevor at the groundwork company. He can spare a team and a digger for two days towards the end of next week to do the site strip and get the first couple of foundations dug on the new build site, if you like.'

'The site strip yes, but the foundations not yet. We are expecting a letter from the council approving our amendments but it hasn't arrived yet. I don't anticipate any problem, but we made a good impression with the Building Inspector and I don't want to rub him up the wrong way now.'

'Can I ask Dave to pick up some pallets from his site and drop them over here?' asked Pete now. 'I can knock up some containers with them which will remove the need to hire cages to store the slates when they come off the roof, to avoid them being damaged.'

'That is an excellent idea, Pete. Dave is knee

deep in pallets and they never seem to come and collect them after materials deliveries, so he will be delighted to off-load them on you, I'm sure!'

'Hang on, I don't want hundreds of them! Just about fifteen should do it. Don't let Dave dump his problem on me!'

Derek laughed at that, and said he would call Dave and explain, as they ended their call.

'Sarah, that boy Pete is turning out to be very resourceful, and I think he might want to ask you out, you know,' he said smiling into the kitchen where she was working.

'Try to keep up, Derek,' said Amanda, sitting beside him, 'They have been dating for weeks!'

'Ah,' said Derek, 'I see. Well, he never stops taking about you, Sarah, and I don't want a broken hearted Project Manager moping about the place, so I hope you like him too.'

Sarah, blushing deeply, could only say 'More tea, Derek?'

-oooOoo-

Emma was swamped by the large size fluorescent 'HiVis vest' Pete gave her to put on, which came down to her knees.

At least the bright yellow 'hard hat' had an adjustable band so it could be made to fit, and when Sarah was also similarly attired, Pete insisted on taking mobile phone photos of the pair of them, prior to their tour of the catering college.

'You are supposed to have boots with steel toe-caps as well,' he said. 'But I doubt they make them in small enough sizes for you, Sarah, never mind about for Emma, so we will turn a blind eye to that requirement this time.'

'Can we go in now, Pete … please!' said Emma, who was getting cold.

'Come on then, my pretty little builders, let's go and have a look.'

-oo0Ooo-

Emma's "Wow!" and Sarah's "Gosh!" made Pete smile, as he watched them take in the size of the main classroom.

He had rigged up powerful work lights on yellow tripods in each of the corners of the vast room, making it much easier to see what they were looking at, despite the boards attached to the windows which blocked out the natural daylight. They were able to see the scale and potential of the building much better than when Derek and Amanda had first visited.

Almost as soon as they entered, however, Pete's phone rang. It was Dave who had arrived with a truck load of pallets and wanted help unloading them.

'You stay in here, ladies. I won't be long. It might be best if you don't touch anything and don't wander off into the other rooms, if you wouldn't mind, some of them might not be safe.'

-ooo0oo-

Chapter 13

He didn't like being left on his own, even though he realised that he was home.

They all had their jobs to do, he knew that, but he had watched the television news cycle round three times now and was bored, so he turned it off.

It was very quiet without the newsreader's babble.

He looked around the familiar room, but felt uneasy.

Crash!

What was that?

His training kicked in, and took over. He was up, grabbing one of the shotguns from over the fireplace and racing towards the noise before any further thought occurred to him.

He bustled through the double doors, noticing that the corridor was in something of a state, with debris all over the floor, and he decided that the blast must have caused it.

He flattened himself against the wall. The enemy could be anywhere. He must be close to the place the blast happened, judging by all the plaster on the floor, and who knew what lay beyond the next set of double doors, which were wide open in front of him.

Cover. He needed cover, but the area ahead of him was brightly lit and there seemed nowhere to hide. Then he heard the voice …

'Don't touch that. Come here and wait with me as you were told.'

A woman speaking. And then another …

'I think I would like to be a chef when I grow up …'

A child's voice! And he recognised it. He tightened his grip on the gun, put it to his shoulder and burst into the room.

'It's all right, Penelope, I'm coming! Stand away from that child!' he bellowed. 'Stand away, I say, I am armed!'

A scream.

He leaped forward and grabbed the back of the child's peculiar loose coat and gathered her up.

'It's all right Penelope, I've got you.'

Why had the kidnapper screamed? Must get control of the situation. Need to secure the area.

'You, down on your knees and keep your hands in the air where I can see them ... NOW!'

Sweep round the room. Nobody in sight. Hold on tight, Penelope.

She is screaming.

'Stop screaming, Penelope. It's all right, I've got you!'

'You! Keep your hands up. Keep them right up! Look down at the floor.'

Stop screaming!

-ooOoo-

'Here you! That is quite enough of that!' yelled Pete.

He had grabbed the gun, threw it behind him and pushed the man down onto the floor in one fluid action.

Sarah was sobbing.

'Oh Pete!'

'Emma is fine, Sarah. She is fine.'

'Right,' said Dave, a little out of breath. 'I've got the gun, Pete, pull him up and let's have a look at him.'

Running footsteps.

'What the hell? ... Uncle Frederick!'

'It is all right Mr Frobisher, I've got him,' said Pete

tightening is grip as Jeremy ran up.

'Mummy!' wailed Emma, enfolded now in Sarah's arms. 'Mummy.'

-ooOoo-

'So the silly old devil thought Penelope was being kidnapped and his military training took over,' said Jeremy. 'He was in the Guards.'

'Well, he scared the hell out of Sarah and Emma. He should be locked up!' said Dave.

'Unfortunately he can't help it. He has dementia, you see.'

'I don't care what is wrong with him,' spluttered Dave. 'What the hell was he doing wandering about here with a gun?'

'He would have had a job shooting anyone with that, it is a replica. We have two of them. They are for decoration purposes only, and normally mounted on the wall over the fireplace in the parlour,' explained Jane.

'Uncle Frederick comes home for a visit every few weeks and is usually no trouble,' said Penelope. 'I don't know what came over him.'

'Ah, here comes the paramedic,' said Jeremy.

The florid burly man who came in now was smiling. 'I've given him a sedative and he is sleeping now,' he said. 'He was saying he was sorry and understood now that it was not Penelope... Now how did he put it? ... He thought if it wasn't a kidnapping then it was a burglary.'

'I thought I had talked him out of that one,' said Pete, now joining them, 'I was explaining that even in these days of so much hands-on vocational education it was a bit unlikely that a lady burglar would take an eight year old girl to a break-in. He conceded that he imagined lady burglars would be a bit more on the brawny side than Sarah. Then he started to fall asleep.'

'Is the little girl all right?' asked Jane.

'Yes, she is sitting in the ambulance with her mum now,' said the paramedic. 'And when I left her she was asking how to turn the sirens on.'

'What you did was very brave, Pete,' said Dave. 'I dunno if anyone else saw it, but he wrestled the gun off him and pulled Emma away. He wasn't to know the gun was a pretend one! That old loony could have murdered them. He should be in an institution!'

'He is only a confused old gentleman,' said Pete. 'There was nothing of him when I grabbed him, he is just skin and bone. In his mind his niece was being kidnapped, so he just did what came naturally to him.'

'I wasn't being kidnapped, thank goodness,' said

Penelope. 'And Uncle Frederick seems to have thought I was still at school.'

'Bit of an odd school uniform though, an ill fitting HiVis jacket', said Jeremy, which broke the tension and everyone laughed.

-oo0Oo0-

'Yes, and Pete was so brave and saved us all, Auntie Amanda!'

Now back in the cafe, with hot sweet "builder's tea" made by Dave for everyone, Emma was on her third round of explaining the events of the afternoon, which she had embellished, just a little more, each time.

'Pete let out a roar and ran at the man who was holding me up in the air by my jacket. He grabbed the gun, wrenched it from the man's hands, and then threw him on the ground and stood over him. He was like a gladiator, Uncle Derek, you would have been proud of him. I think you should give him a pay rise for danger money!'

'That's enough now Emma,' said Sarah, chuckling. 'Pete was undoubtedly brave though, and we are very grateful.'

'Where is Pete, by the way?' Derek asked.

'He went back to work while I bought Sarah and Emma over here in the van to get a cup of tea,' said

Dave.

-ooOoo-

Chapter 14

'But we haven't been to see the little house Pete is going to live in, Mummy ...'

'I think you have had quite enough excitement for one day, young lady,' said Sarah, steering Emma out of the cafe and towards home.

'But I thought we were going back with Dave. I have some ideas for how Pete can decorate the house to make it cozy and ...'

As they approached their front door they noticed a figure leaning on the wall beside it.

'Pete!' squeaked Emma, and ran into is arms.

'Hello, you two. I just popped over to see if you were OK, but there was no reply ...'

'We were being plied with hot, sweet, builder's tea for the shock, by Dave, in the cafe,' explained Sarah.

'Yuk!' grimaced Pete.

'And what about you,' said Sarah, unlocking the door and turning on the light. 'Are you all right?'

'Oh yes, thank you …'

'No, I think I had better check you over,' said Emma. 'I have a full nurses kit in my room and I'm sure Dr. Edward would like to take a look at you.'

'Dr. Edward?' said Pete as he was being propelled up the stairs with a determined little hand in the small of his back.

'Emma's bear. I understand he can cure most ills.'

-oooOoo-

With Dr. Edward Bear on the floor beside her, Emma slept in what looked like a most uncomfortable position on the edge of the sofa.

'She would be more comfortable on her bed, I should think. Would you like me to carry her up there?'

'I bet you can't do it without waking her up. I never can, and the bed is too high for me to lift her in.'

With infinite care, Pete gathered the little girl in his arms and, as Sarah followed with Edward, they quietly went up the stairs.

On reaching her eye level bed, Pete carefully laid her down but as she settled, she wrapped her arms around his neck and murmured his name. It took Sarah a moment or two to disentangle her arms and giggling, they escaped downstairs.

'She was dreaming about you!' chuckled Sarah. 'Her hero!'

'Well, I dream about you, Sarah, although my dreams are different.'

'I bet you snore,' laughed Sarah.

'I have no idea, but I would love you to tell me if I do.'

Pete gathered her into his arms.

'Oh Pete, no. Not with Emma upstairs …'

'But Sarah, I find it so very hard to resist you.'

'I don't want to resist you either, Pete, but not here, not like this. Emma might come down at any moment and …'

'Mummy, Edward wants a glass of milk,' said a sleepy voice from halfway up the stairs, and then I need my hair brushing to get ready for bed.'

'Go,' whispered Sarah. 'If she realises you are still here I will never get her to sleep.'

'Oh. Yes. OK. Can I see you tomorrow?'

'Yes, please.'

-ooOOoo-

'This is Steve,' said Amanda. 'He is the new chef working for Carlos and based at Mario's. He will be using the development kitchen here from time to time; and Sarah, I'd like you to explain about how everything works here and what it is you do, when he comes over on Monday, please.'

When they had gone, Jenny had something to say.

'Fwooar! What about him! I wish I was your age, Sarah. I'd never let him get away.'

'Very dishy,' said Sarah. 'What was Amanda saying about him being part Italian?'

'His mum is Italian,' she said. 'Shows, doesn't it. Definitely one of your Latin lover types, and single too.'

'He seems very charming,' said Sarah.

'He could charm me any day of the week, and twice on Sundays!'

-ooo0oo-

'No bookings at all?' said Jeremy.

'Not so far. It looks like next week is going to be very quiet here,' said Jane.

'Good. I can catch up with cleaning the carpets in the hallways,' said Penelope. 'The carpet cleaner makes a funny smell and leaves a bit of dampness, and I never like doing it when there are guests about.'

Jane smiled at her sister. Penelope was eternally cheerful and lived in her own little bubble where nothing seemed to disturb her.

When she was younger she could be quite tearful, especially if, as was often the case, she was not keeping up at school, or was being bullied. But she had gradually built an invisible defensive wall around herself, which protected her from the parts of life that she did not understand or would rather not notice.

Now with clearly defined tasks to perform she could cope perfectly well, although her siblings did wonder how she would react to all the changes taking place at the hotel, and especially the building work.

What the future held for her and how she would manage was of constant concern to Jeremy and Jane, and no solution had presented itself to them yet.

-oo0Ooo-

'Hi! I'm Lauren, from the Council. Are you Pete?'

The Building Control Department had taken on Lauren to work alongside the existing officer for the area who was working towards his retirement. She had recently qualified and was keen to make a success of her new job.

She had already made a considerable impression in the Council offices and was never alone at the water cooler, having attracted a cloud of young men eager to chat her up. But she was used to that, and as a young woman in what was traditionally a man's world, she had developed a series of strategies to deal with everything form drooling colleagues to leering building site workers.

Tall and shapely with her mother's dark eyes and her father's caramel skin, she could have chosen a more glamorous profession, trading on her looks, but Lauren was a down-to-earth girl who knew that she wanted a proper career which would enable her to use her mind and her not inconsiderable intelligence.

'Yes, that's me. I was expecting you. How do you do?' said Pete.

Whilst it was true that he was expecting a visit from someone from the Council, he was not expecting the bright smiling and very attractive young woman who stood before him now, and his natural shyness tied his tongue for anything much more than the initial pleasantries, so it was Lauren who did most of the talking.

Chapter 15

Matthew and Sandy arrived slightly ahead of Sarah returning from collecting Emma from school, and were waiting in their car.

Emma, seeing them as she turned the corner of the building, let out a little whoop of joy and rushed to greet them.

Sarah's brother, Matthew, was small in stature, but there the family resemblance finished. He was brawny and had a dark complexion in sharp contrast to Sarah's slight frame and fair skin and hair. His wife was chubby and jolly and always wore loud colours, which offset her mousy brown hair and comfortable proportions.

Emma buried herself in Sandy's ample bosom as they embraced, and Matthew planted a brotherly kiss on the top of Sarah's head.
'Can you give us a hand with our luggage, Emma?' asked Sandy now. 'I've bought one or two friends to meet Edward and they are in that big bag on the back

seat.'

Emma produced another squeal of delight as she saw the bulging bag full of soft toys. 'You didn't forget about the Teddy Bear's Picnic, Auntie Sandy!' she said.

'Of course not. All the bears in my workshop were very keen to come, and they have invited one or two friendly hares for your new Auntie Amanda to put in the cafe, if she would like them.'

'I'm sure she would,' smiled Sarah. 'And maybe if we put a little notice on them you might get some orders for some more from the customers.'

'I thought you said it was all grubby builders using the cafe at the moment,' said Matthew.

'No, at least not so much, now. New people are moving onto the estate and starting to use the cafe, and the builders just get take-aways most of the time,' Sarah explained. 'And, although you could hardly call them grubby builders, Amanda and Derek also seem to use it as an extension of their offices next door and are often in there.'

'They sound like nice people, Sarah. You certainly landed on your feet when you landed a job with them,' smiled Sandy.

'I hope we will get to meet them,' added Matthew.

'Come on,' Emma was jumping up and down on the

spot. 'I want to show you my amazing bedroom!'

-ooOoo-

While Emma and Sandy had their Teddy Bears picnic, Matthew suggested that he and Sarah should go and find their hotel and drop their baggage off so that, having found it in daylight, he knew where it was. Then they could relax and enjoy themselves into the evening without having to worry about locating it.

'And then I can show you where I'm going to be working, in the catering school, perhaps ...' said Sarah.

'And introduce me to this marvellous Pete we hear so much about,' said Matthew.

They had booked a room pretty much at the last minute at the Barclay Court Hotel, when Sarah pointed out that it was still open for business, and they realised that the hotel they originally selected was some miles away. It was a few pounds cheaper than their first choice too.

As they drove down the long bumpy drive and Matthew caught his first glimpse of the imposing building, he said he was impressed.

'It is like some old country house,' he said.

'That,' pointed out Sarah, 'is because it was once a country house, and the old family still run it today.'

It was only when they got to the end of the drive and Matthew noticed the overgrown gardens and the general air of decay that his expectations were lowered.

'Needs a bit of TLC, doesn't it?' he said.

'Parts of it do, yes, but it has great potential and I'm told the actual hotel rooms are perfectly OK.'

'In the dark it must look like one of those places in a horror film, where your car breaks down and the old retainer opens the creaking cobwebby door when you approach to ask if you can use the telephone ...'

'Not original, Matthew, others have said the same. But the rooms will be just fine for the two nights you will be staying, I'm sure. Just watch out for the ghosts of Frobishers past!'

'Oh dear. I hope this doesn't freak Sandy out,'

-ooOOoo-

Once Matthew had checked in and put the baggage in his room, which he admitted to Sarah was perfectly acceptable, they made ready to leave.

'Don't drive straight out, Matty, drive down that little lane there and you will see the catering college,' explained Sarah. 'If Pete is about I can probably get you a guided tour.'

Having stopped by the building and noticed that

it was now surrounded by high wire panel fences, bolted together, Sarah hopped out of the car and approached an open access gate by the single storey flat roofed corridor that linked the buildings.

'I'll just nip across and see if I can see Pete,' she said. 'You stay here.'

She was back in a trice.

'No, he is not in there, but the gate is open so he can't have gone far. Perhaps he is round at his little cottage. You just hang on here, Matty, and I'll pop round there and see.'

-ooOOoo-

Sarah came running back to the car, and she pulled open the door and threw herself in.

'Please just drive, Matty. I need to get away from here. Now!'

'Are you crying Sarah? Has something upset you?'

'It is nothing, I just stubbed my toe, that's all. Please just drive.'

'Stubbed your toe?'

'Well, if you must know, I stubbed my toe on a dusky beauty coming out of Pete's bedroom when I got to the cottage.'

'You are joking!'

'Unfortunately not. The front door was unlocked, and when I opened it and looked up the stairs I saw her. He hasn't moved in there yet, but I happen to know he had a bed delivered last week and …'

'Are you sure about this, Sarah? You couldn't have misinterpreted what you saw?'

'No, he didn't see me, but Pete was behind her coming down the stairs and he had a wide grin on his face.'

'Oh dear …'

'Yes, and she was wearing a HiVis vest, just like the one he gave me …'

-oo0Ooo-

'Hi, Sarah. I'm just ringing up to see what time I can collect you tomorrow,' said Pete.

'You can't collect me tomorrow,' stated Sarah.

'Oh. Why has something come up?'

'I should not be surprised, you would know better than me. But as you obviously have plenty to do with your spare time, don't bother picking me up tomorrow, or at any other time, for that matter.'

'Sarah?'

'Goodbye, Pete … Goodbye,' and she cut the connection.

Chapter 16

Sarah was late for work.

She had never been late for work in her life. In fact, as a rule she usually arrived at least half an hour early.

Until she had turned it off completely her phone kept ringing throughout the night and she kept on having to dismiss the calls. There were nineteen voice messages for her when she turned it on again in the morning, and she deleted them all without listening to any of them.

'You are cutting it fine!' said Jenny as she stumbled across the threshold. 'Derek has been looking for you.'

'And now,' said a voice behind her, 'it looks as though I have found you.'

'Oh, hello Derek. I'm sorry I'm late …'

'Never mind all that. What on earth is all this with

Pete? Dave tells me you won't take his calls and you have given him the brush off. I have to tell you he is in quite a state about it.'

'He should have thought of that before ...'

'Before what?' said Jenny. 'What has he been doing to you?'

'I'm sorry,' Sarah could not keep the catch out of her voice. 'I'm late and I have masses to do. I'll talk to you later.' And with that she dashed into the development kitchen and shut the door firmly behind her.

'Best let her be,' said Jenny.

'Let her calm down a bit, you mean?' asked Derek.

'Yes. Leave her to me. I'll have a chat to her bit later, and I'll let you know what happens.'

'OK, Jenny, but if there is anything ...'

'I know. You go on, and leave this to me.'

-oo0Ooo-

'Oh yes? That is what he told Dave is it?' sniffed Sarah. 'Well, she might well be a Building Inspector, although I highly doubt it, but what was she doing in his cottage? What has that got to do with her work?'

Jenny made to fold Sarah into her arms, but she stepped back.

'If she really was a Building Inspector, she is quite entitled to look at the college buildings, of course. But there is nothing she needs to sign-off in his cottage, is there? And yet they were coming down the stairs ... from the bedroom, no less; and it was clear she had been inspecting him, and he was delighted about it!'

Now Jenny succeeded in enveloping Sarah in her embrace as the tears began to flow.

'Honestly, Jenny,' hiccoughed Sarah, 'I really thought he ... I mean we ...'

'I know, honey. I know. All men are bastards, it is just that some take longer to show their true colours than others,' Jenny stated.

'Oh Jenny, what am I going to do ...'

'Well, the first thing is to block his number on your phone, after you have sent him a text to say if he tries to come near your flat you will have the Police on him. That will hold him for now. Then ...'

'Then?'

'Then we have got to plan your revenge.'

'Revenge!'

'Absolutely! You don't think he should be allowed to get away with behaviour like that, do you? You are such a sweet trusting little thing, Sarah. When you have met as many like him as I have, you will learn that they need to be taught a lesson and shown, in no uncertain terms, what it is they are missing out on.'

'I'm not sure I ...'

'Now, I've got a pretty good idea what we can do about this ... let's sit down and have one of those delicious cakes of yours and I will outline my plan.'

-oo0Ooo-

On Saturday, in order to enable Sarah to work through her problems, Sandy and Matthew took Emma out for the day to the zoo in the hopes that time would allow the frosty atmosphere to dissipate. But Sarah was not much better when they got back.

She had obviously be crying a good deal, and she had found the first of a series of letters from Pete in the letterbox, which had not helped.

In them he begged and pleaded and stated again that it was all a misunderstanding.

It emerged that her rival for his affections had a name and while, with no sibilant, it was difficult to say Lauren with a hiss, Sarah managed it as she poured out her heart to Jenny and then later to Sandy, while Matthew, to keep out of the way, subjected himself to a medical examination at the hands of Dr. Edward Bear and Nurse Emma.

-ooOoo-

On Sunday, with Matthew and Sandy due to return home after supper, Sandy did what she could to jolly them all along.

She had bought with her a bear from a new line she was developing, which contained a battery operated digital recording device, on which it was possible to record something and play it back. Sandy envisaged mothers and fathers reading stories that the child could listen to when they were not around, but now she saw a way to engage Emma in something entertaining.

'What if Edward was to tell a story which we could then play back? Emma, if you do some of the voices, Uncle Matty can do Edward Bear, and perhaps mummy could join in too.'

'Yes, but what story shall we read?' asked Emma.

'The best stories are the ones you make up,' asserted Sandy. 'We can all make up the story together.'

'OK,' said Emma enthusiastically. 'Can we do the story of the Great Big Teddy Bear's picnic and the Auntie and Uncle who bought all the bears to see Edward.'

'Certainly!' said Sandy. 'That sounds great. Who is going to start … Mummy?'

But Sarah had heard the distinctive sound of the

letter box flap, and knew that, with no post on a Sunday, another letter from Pete had just arrived on the mat. Not wanting to collect it, and afraid that she might breakdown into tears again, she asked her brother Matthew to take the lead.

'I used to make up stories for your mummy when she was little, you know,' said Matthew. 'And she used to sit on my knee. Do you want to sit on my knee now, Emma, then I can begin.'

-oooOoo-

Chapter 17

On Monday, the weather was sultry and the TV Weather Man spoke of an Indian summer for a few days before the autumn began in earnest. Sarah knew how hot it got in the kitchen and decided that a short skirt and a teeshirt was called for. Her only concession to style was her new trainers, which she had been longing to wear, and she decided she could wait no longer to try them out.

While Jenny took the children to school, Sarah was alone in the cafe and busy setting up to create her cakes, scones and fancy patisserie in the development kitchen, with the door propped open. Today, she was also responsible for periodically serving take-away coffees and sausage or bacon sandwiches, or the like, to passing builders, until Jenny got back.

She had not been told that Steve, the new chef, was going to want to use the development kitchen today and was a little surprised when he turned up. It was the first time he had used the facilities.

'I'll try not to get in your way, of course, Sarah, and I'll use the oven on the right, as agreed,' he said. 'I've come up with an idea for a slow roasted lamb dish with a bit of a twist which I want to play with, so once it is all prepped and in the oven it will pretty much take care of itself.'

The news that Steve would be roasting convinced Sarah that her choice of clothes was the right one, as things were going to get pretty hot in the kitchen. She just hoped she could control the chocolate decorations she was using and that they would not melt into an unsightly heap.

'Fair enough, Steve,' she said. 'Are we OK if I use these benches here and you work over there?'

'Perfect. I'll get my stuff from the car.'

-oo0Ooo-

Steve was trying to carry much too much in his arms into the kitchen, and tripped as he tried to deposit the stuff on one of the benches.

Unfortunately, as he did so, his foot caught one of the large tins of sunflower oil which he had placed on the floor beside his bench.

The tin fell over, and the lid came off, spilling its contents which began to spread rapidly over the floor as Sarah yelped, exclaimed that her new trainers would be ruined, stepped out of them and grabbed them.

'Let's get you out of the way,' said Steve and without further ado he lifted her bodily up, turned and sat her on the bench nearest the door where she would be out of the way.

'Sarah, you weigh almost nothing!' he laughed 'I almost threw you through the door!' And as she laughed at his silliness and he put her down, Pete came through the cafe door.

The sight that greeted him could be readily explained, if he had remained in-situ long enough to hear it. But seeing the girl who had broken his heart being lifted, barefoot, in a short skirt, swung round and deposited in a sitting position on a bench, laughing with a Latin matinee idol, was too much. He turned on his heel and departed, unseen.

-ooo0oo-

Shortly afterwards, Jenny returned from taking her own children and Emma to school, and sighing as she watched Steve bending over a mop and bucket full of an oily sludge, she rolled up her sleeves and joined in the clear-up.

Sarah, previously barefoot, with her trainers carefully stowed out of the way was dispatched to look after the counter in the cafe, where she could at least put her shoes back on in safety.

-ooOoo-

'Well, that changes things a bit, I thought I saw Pete driving away in his van as I approached the cafe' said Jenny after Sarah had recounted what happened with Steve. 'If he saw what was going on, there might be no need to use our plan to get your own back on him.'

'How do you mean?'

'Well, if he saw you being plonked on a bench with your legs out by Romeo in there and as you say, laughing, he might have thought ...'

'Oh gosh! He might have! And perhaps he did!'

-ooOoo-

There was another letter from Pete awaiting her when she got home, but this one was very different in tone and only a few lines long.

In it he explained that he now saw all and realised that he had been made a fool of.

He went on to state that whilst he could not help the fact that he had fallen in love with Sarah, he now understood that his feelings for her were not reciprocated, and he would leave her alone, as she had requested.

He hoped, he said, that when they met she would forgive him if he kept their conversations short and relating only to business, because longer exposure to her company would be unbearable for him.

Then he thanked her for allowing him the short space of happiness he had enjoyed with her, and hoped that she would be content with her new boyfriend.

-oo0Ooo-

Chapter 18

'And there is a letter from Henry saying the Waitrose deal has gone through and now the Council will start a public consultation prior, Henry says, to determining the planning application.'

'Well, that will please the Frobishers,' said Derek. 'Anything else?'

Derek had been in the little workshop Albany Developments used since early that morning. It was located at the back of some houses on the edge of the second small development the company had undertaken some years ago. He had kept the workshop which came with the site and used it as a joinery shop and general storage area.

Amanda was in the office reading out the post to him, over the phone.

'No, other than some bills and the usual junk,' she said. 'I wasn't really with it when you got up so early this morning. Why was it you had to go over to the workshop, honey?'

'I had forgotten that I had arranged to meet the man from the steel framing roofing company here so he could measure to be sure he could get his machine in the workshop, and I'm clearing the space. There is such a lot of junk in here that you can't see what you are looking at.'

'His machine?'

'Yes. I thought I had explained. His company makes extruded steel sections which will connect together to make a sort of web to replace the rotten trusses in the college and support the roof. They actually cut them and shape them out of rolls of steel on the site, or in this case nearby, in our workshop, to exact laser measurements and tolerances, which makes them ideal for refurbishments where nothing is ever square.'

'Fascinating. Well, you can tell me all about it when you come home,' yawned Amanda.

'What did you say you were doing today?'

'I'm going over to Mario's at tea time to try out a new lamb dish Steve has come up with. Carlos thinks it is good and wants to try it out as a "special" with a view to adding it to the normal menu.'

'Very nice,' said Derek, who was not really listening. 'Oh, I've got to go, the man from the extrusion company has just arrived.'

'Have fun, honey.'

'And you.'

-ooo0oo-

The rush of dinner service at Mario's was yet to reach full flow, but now it had added glamour as Lauren, the Building Inspector, came in with her mother and father to celebrate her father's retirement.

She was dressed stylishly and inevitably attracted admiring glances as she passed through the restaurant in Mario's wake as they found their table.

She did not know it, but one of those admirers was Steve, who having finished showing off his lamb dish to Amanda and now preparing for his evening service, was taking a breather by the kitchen door and looking out into the dining room.

'A good crowd for this early,' he said as Mario returned to the kitchen, having settled Lauren's party and introduced them to the wine waiter.

'Not bad, not bad at all,' said Mario.

'Do you know that gorgeous girl who you have just seated, by any chance?'

'No, but I know her mother a bit. She is coming here with her ladies for the afternoon tea, regular.'

'Are you proposing to do your thing where you bring out the chef half way through service and take him round to meet the diners tonight, Mario?'

'I dunno. Why?'

'Well, with Carlos away and me in charge, I just wondered ...'

'If I can a take you over, introduce you that lovely girl, I bet,' smiled Mario. 'All right, Steve, but you behave you self, yes? Remember the Mario's reputation!'

'Always,' smirked Steve and went back to work.

-ooOoo-

Just as he was getting into his car to return home from the office, Derek's phone registered the arrival of an email.

It was from the Local Council and was the letter he had been waiting for confirming that the 'minor amendment', replacing the ghastly white boxes the Frobishers architect came up with, had been approved and development could now proceed with Albany Developments own house types.

Settling himself in the car, he put in a call to Pete, who he expected to be delighted with this news.

'Oh, hello Derek,' said Pete, as the call connected. 'Everything OK?'

'Cheer up, it might never happen!' said Derek, noting Pete's depressed voice.

'It already has,' said Pete, dully. 'Was there anything, Derek?'

'Eh, yes the letter has arrived from the Council, you can get on with the foundations for the new houses. We have got our approval!'

'Oh. Right,' said Pete. 'I mean good.'

-ooo0oo-

The flat tyre was a surprise and an annoyance for Lauren as they prepared to go home after a splendid meal at Mario's.

'Well, your father can't do it with his back, and I wouldn't know where to start,' scowled her mother. 'Why don't you pop back into the restaurant quick before they close and see if anyone there can help.'

'Certainly, yes, I can no be changing the wheel, I'm a sorry,' said Mario, exercising his Italian charm with a smile. 'But maybe a Steve here, our chef, he can help. He is a big strong boy, as you see!'

-ooo0oo-

Chapter 19

'This is Dr Gerard Foyle, the College Vice Chancellor,' said the plump little woman who had met them at the door and taken them through the corridors to this office. Now, with an apologetic look, she withdrew.

'Ah, how do you do? I have been looking forward to meeting you. I have heard such good reports of your enterprises, all very much of interest, I may say. Yes, very much of interest. We are always keen to meet people from the business world …'

'Nice to meet you too,' said Derek, extracting his hand from the grip the slightly startled looking Vice Chancellor was exerting on it. 'But it is actually my wife, Amanda who is the brains behind this project. She is the Managing Director of the Company formed to take it forward. She wrote the proposal we are here to discuss.'

'You are … Oh, I see, yes well, erm … how do you do, Amanda?'

'Glad to meet you, Dr Foyle,' purred Amanda. 'What did you think of the prospectus and projections I sent you?'

'The ... ah, projections ... Well, yes, I have them here somewhere.'

As the embarrassed academic rifled through the mess on his desk, while frantically pressing the button to call his secretary, Amanda came to his rescue.

'I have another spare copy here, if it would be easier for you,' she smiled. 'The executive summary appears on page two.'

'Well, now you see, what with one thing and another, I have been rather hoping young Wimbish had read all that sort of ... I mean had studied your proposals. He will be with us in a moment or two, I'm sure ...'

The door opened and a harassed looking little man in an ill fitting sports jacket worn over a yellow buttoned up cardigan came in.

'Ah, Wimbish. There you are, my dear fellow. Our guests from ... from the business world have arrived, as you see. Wimbish this is David,'

'Derek,' corrected Derek.

'And Alison,'

'Amanda,' smiled Amanda winningly.

'Yes, yes. Quite so. They have come to talk to us about … ah … well perhaps you can describe it better yourselves.' And with that he subsided in a flustered heap into the old wooden chair behind his desk.

'Thank you, Vice Chancellor.' The little man inflated his chest and scratching one of the leather patches on his elbow, he addressed his remarks to Derek and Amanda. 'I'm very glad to meet you. I have studied your proposals with great interest. As Dr Foyle probably mentioned, we have been looking for ways to increase our Hospitality and Catering offering, and your ideas do seem to offer a practical way forward. The constraints on the space we have here in College have always to be taken into consideration, and your new facilities might offer a ready made solution.'

'Thank you, Mr Wimbish, you are very kind.'

The door opened again and the dumpy woman bustled in with a tray containing a cafetière of coffee and a teapot. She was followed by a thin dreamy looking older woman wearing crocs and a full length satin evening dress, carrying a tray of cups and saucers and a bowl of sugar. Space was made on a side-table for these items, and without a word the two women withdrew.

'Ah, tea,' said Dr Foyle. 'Tea. Yes Tea. Excellent. Did you know that the tea bush, Camellia sinensis, an evergreen shrub native to East Asia, produces the most widely consumed drink in the world? Tea was sold in a coffee house in London as long ago as 1657, and Samuel Pepys tasted tea in 1660. It is said that Catherine of Braganza took the tea-drinking habit to the English court when she married Charles II in 1662 …'

He might have gone on indefinitely in this way had Wimbish not intervened.

'Right-ho. Returning to your proposals then …'

'I don't think I made any proposals, Professor Wimbish …' said Dr Foyle looking ill at ease again.

'The proposals in Amanda's document … Would you mind if I ask a few questions …'

'Certainly, certainly, dear boy,' smiled Dr Foyle. 'But I doubt if I shall be able to assist you. You might do better to address your queries to Desmond and Angela here.'

Having poured himself a cup of tea, Dr Foyle subsided into his chair again, and with a little cough, Professor Wimbish restarted the meeting and took control.

-ooo0oo-

Jenny could hear them talking as they approached the door of the empty cafe.

'And the weird thing was the tyre centre people said

they couldn't find any damage or anything wrong with the tyre. When they pumped it up it was fine.'

'Well that is odd,' said Steve as they came through the door.

'They did think that I might have broken something called the bead if I hit a kerb or a pothole or whatever, but I don't remember doing anything like that …'

'Oh, hello, Jenny,' said Steve. 'This is Lauren, she has just come to help me sort out the DVD system, out the back, and look for a recipe.'

Jenny looked askance at the Hi-Vis jacket and the lanyard with the name of the Council on the card dangling at its end. She realised that she was considerably out-ranked by Steve so could not really make any objection as they passed through into the development kitchen.

'Ah yes,' Lauren was saying. 'That is the same set up we had at College, I'm sure we will soon find the Classic French Sauces menu on there for you.'

Steve cast a slightly lascivious glance as he allowed the door separating the cafe from the professional kitchen to close on it's spring, and Jenny had to sit down on the stool behind the counter to gather her wits.

Sifting the evidence, Jenny was certain that she had been introduced as Lauren; that she wore a lanyard with a card dangling on the end giving the Local Council's name; and that, without a shadow of a doubt, she was very attractive indeed. This was her. This was THE Lauren. And she wasn't with Pete, she was with Steve!

Unable to contain her curiosity a moment longer, Jenny gently raised herself on her heels, on the foot rail of her stool, until she could see through the little wired glass window in the kitchen door, and peeped inside.

There, with a DVD in one hand, suspended in mid-air, she observed Lauren locked in what used to be called a 'passionate embrace' with Steve.

As it looked as though it might be some time before they came up for air, Jenny lowered herself onto her stool again, and with a triumphant smile on her face, took her mobile phone from her pocket and started to type a text to Sarah.

-oo0Ooo-

At least Pete had his work, and he threw himself into now with singleminded determination.

The little site office he had converted from one of the rooms behind the big classroom had a door to the gravel path that he had laid himself outside, and a window overlooking the land where the new houses would be built.

He constructed his 'cages' from pallets for the roof

slates to be stored and set them aside ready for use as soon as the sub-contractors for the roof work arrived.

He oversaw the demolition of the single story corridor and worked with the skip company to create an effective schedule of delivery and removal of the demolition materials, separating up some to be used as hardcore under the driveways of the luxurious houses to be built.

He worked with the architect to set out the foundations and oversaw the groundwork as the trenches were dug and the concrete required, calculated, delivered and poured.

He started early and finished late, and when all the day's work was done, he started again decorating the little caretakers house, building a pretty lattice work porch to attach over the front door, repairing the kitchen, and clearing the neglected garden.

But it didn't help.

The ache he felt in his heart was more than a physical pain, it filled his mind. He was grieving for what might have been, and he could not get thoughts of Sarah out of his mind, no matter what he did.

-oooOoo-

Chapter 20

'But in his last but one letter he said he loved me. Oh Sandy, I have made such a mess of things, and it seems he might have been telling the truth about this Lauren.'

'I thought you saw him coming down the stairs from his bedroom with her.'

'I did, but maybe I misunderstood the reason. Matty said I might have done, although I find it difficult to imagine how.'

'Well look, Sarah, if you still feel the same way about him, you are going to have to get to the bottom of that, and that means you have got to meet.'

'But his last letter said he …'

'I know, you read it to me.' Sandy thought for a moment. 'It might not be possible to meet him by arranging it, but you could meet by chance.'

'I don't understand?'

'Well, presumably he has to come to the offices next door to the cafe occasionally. Derek and Amanda sound really nice, from what you were saying, and perhaps you could arrange with them ...'

'They are lovely, but you also have to remember that they are my employers. I'm not sure it would be appropriate to ask them to get involved in my love life ...'

'I see what you mean. But they don't have to get involved, just tell you when Pete is coming in, so you can arrange to bump into him, perhaps.'

'I'll have to think about it. I do wish we could just wind the clock back, Sandy. Now I have had time to think about it, I honestly don't think I have ever been so happy as I was when I was with Pete.'

'Not the same as you and Ricky, then?'

'I was very young then. Too young. I think Ricky would have left before he did if Emma hadn't come along, and it is different with Pete. I haven't even slept with him, but I feel sort of connected ...'

'I recognise the symptoms, Sarah. It is known officially as love.'

'I thought I loved Ricky ...'

'But that was just lust?'

'No! What a thing to say! Although ...'

'Well anyway, I still think the only thing to do is to engineer a meeting and have it out with him, especially about this Lauren being in his bedroom. At least then, one way or another you can draw a line under this and move on with your life.'

'Thank you for listening to me, Sandy. I'm sorry if I kept you from your work, and I know you are right. But ...'

'Why don't you have a chat with Amanda. She is not just your boss you know, she is Emma's adopted auntie, and that role brings special responsibilities. She will be concerned about her happiness and yours too, you know. We all are!'

-oo0Ooo-

At that moment Amanda was sitting with Carlos, the chef, in Mario's restaurant.

Amanda was outlining the proposal for the University to use the new catering college to train would be cooks and kitchen staff, two days a week.

'The rest of the time will be taken up with private lessons and demonstrations, and I'm meeting the advertising agency this week to discuss how we go about marketing that part of it, as well as the private dining club.'

'It is all coming together, Amanda.'

'Yes, although what I would really like is to get some

well known chefs to come and give talks and so on. That would draw the customers in, I'm sure.'

'Well, I've been thinking about that and maybe I can help.'

Carlos picked up the small black leather bound book he had laid on the table when they sat down.

'When I was training,' he said, 'I met one or two people who have become quite well known over the intervening years, and I still keep in touch with a few of them. Perhaps I could ask them to pop along.'

'Really? That would be marvellous. Would I have heard of any of these people?'

'Quite possibly,' said Carlos, opening the book. 'Ah, now, he might be prepared to help ... have you heard of Jonty-Adair de Groot?'

'The South African TV chef?'

'Yes, that's him. I could ask him. Or how about Chesney Marriott, he and I go back a long way. Mind you, I'm not sure you would want Chester Vayperwurst. He offered me a job once but I thought he spent too much time playing with his chemistry set to really call it cooking. And there is Stewart Shepherd, he is on TV all the time these days, but is more well know for being bad tempered than cooking, so maybe not him then ...'

'How do you know all these people?' Amanda asked

incredulously.

'Well, I trained in several places, big hotels and so on, and I met a lot of people on the way up.'

'How did you come to end up at Mario's then?'

'Ah. Well, that's a different story. I followed somebody here some years ago, before it was called Mario's. It had quite a reputation back then.'

'You followed someone? I don't understand …'

'Love, Amanda. I was desperately in love with him, you see. Long before he became well known, and I still had to finish my training.'

'Who?' said Amanda, and then realising she was prying into his personal life, 'I'm sorry, I didn't mean to …'

'Not at all. We were talking about famous chefs after all, and you may well have heard of Barry Lane. He made a bit of a splash with a couple of eponymous restaurants in Covent Garden a while after he left here.'

'Barry Lane! The Nouvelle Cuisine guy?'

'I'm afraid so. He was a lot older than me, of course, and we fell out professionally over the use of too much creme-fraise; and wasabi, of course. I said it was just a fad, but he said it wasn't. He was right and I was wrong. There were rows, he moved out of our flat, and we went our separate ways after that.'

'But you stayed here.'

'Yes. I sort of came with the premises when Mario bought this place, and I suppose it has become a bit of a habit. Lazy of me, but there it is.'

-oooOoo-

Chapter 21

There were smiling faces as Derek greeted the Frobishers on a visit to the Barclay Court Hotel on this afternoon.

'Yes it is wonderful news,' confirmed Jane.

'Always assuming the public consultation does not mess up the chances of getting planning permission,' added Jeremy.

'Well, nothing is ever certain when it comes to Town Planning, of course,' said Derek. 'But the old factory has been an eye-sore for years and I think even the most vocal of "antis" would want to see it finally gone.'

'Are there "antis", Derek?'

'There always are, in my experience, Jane. Planning applications seem to bring out the worst in people, and there are those who object just for the hell of it, it seems to me.' Derek was anxious to offer reassurance. 'But in reality a nice new Waitrose there has to be better than how it is now, so I can't really see any objections holding it up.'

'I do hope it happens soon,' said Penelope. 'I'm promised a new vacuum cleaner when it goes through and we get the money. And there has been talk of a holiday.'

'I'm convinced it will be fine,' said Derek. 'I'm wondering if I could borrow the key and have another look at the Ballroom, please. I should have done it last time, but I would like to take some "before and after" photos of it.'

'I'm looking forward to the pictures of the opening night,' said Jeremy.

'Yes, so am I. And Amanda is working hard on it, so that it is inching closer all the time.'

'Young Peter, I mean Pete, your Project Manager, is such a nice young man,' said Jane. 'But he must be feeling the pressure a little, I think.'

'He never seems to stop working, but just recently he doesn't seem so happy,' added Jeremy.

'He always had such a ready smile,' said Jane. 'Do you think he is all right?'

Before Derek could offer any explanation, Penelope presented her view.

'If you ask me he is suffering from a broken heart. Some unfeeling woman has hurt his feelings and left him flat. It's such a shame.'

'Actually Penelope, you are not far from the truth there. Poor old Pete thinks someone has stolen his girl.'

'I knew it would be something like that! Men are such brutes. Fancy muscling in and stealing his girl.' Penelope shook her head in dismay. 'Is there nothing to be done?'

'It would be wise if you kept your nose out of other people's business, Pen. If you start interfering, or even letting on that you know there is a problem, you are quite likely to make it worse,' snapped Jeremy.

'Jeremy! Penelope is only expressing concern …' said Jane.

But Penelope had turned on her heel and headed for the stairs.

'As I said, all men are brutes!' she threw over her shoulder as she departed.

-ooo0oo-

As he was taking his photographs, Derek's phone rang.

It was the architect, informing him that the third version of the proposals and sets of sketches he had presented, each with different ideas on how to build a replacement link between the college and the hotel, had met with the approval of the Town Planners and the Conservation Officer.

'I don't believe it!' said Derek. 'You mean to say they want to go with that ultra-modern blue glass thing that you put in just to give them something to object to, and to make them hurry up and choose one of the others? Well, I'll eat my hat!'

The peculiar world of the Town Hall, Planning Officials, and even staid Conservation Officers, always has the potential to surprise even the most seasoned of professionals, let alone laymen. The Frobishers were right to worry that things may not go as smoothly as one might hope when dealing with them.

-ooo0oo-

Derek and Amanda's little empire was playing host to a representative of another wing of the activities of the Town Hall as all this was going on.

Sitting in the cafe enjoying a coffee together as they looked through the complicated instructions for uploading the DVD tutorials, were Steve and Lauren. Although, because she was now in jeans and a bomber jacket, it would have been difficult to guess that Lauren was a Building Inspector, if you didn't know.

Jenny, who was in charge of the cafe whilst Sarah collected their respective children and delivered them home, had been surreptitiously sending her a text message urging her to hurry back as quickly as she could so that she would not miss all the fun.

And now, as the door opened to admit an intrigued Sarah, the fun could begin.

'Oh hello Sarah,' said Steve. 'This is Lauren, she is showing me how to unravel the mysteries of the DVD Tutorial machine in the development kitchen. Sarah works here making the most astonishingly fine patisserie, you know, and her creations are served with afternoon tea in all the Amanda's Bistros as well as Mario's.'

'You make the afternoon tea at Mario's?' said Lauren giving Sarah a wide smile as she turned in her seat to face her. 'My mother and her friends rave about those and go there every three or four weeks!'

'How do you do,' said Sarah meekly, as nothing else presented itself in her mind to say to the stunning caramel skinned vision beaming at her.

'Now I know why Mario won't tell them where they can buy the cakes,' smiled Lauren.

'That's right,' said Steve. 'Sarah here is our secret weapon, and you can only buy the cakes in the restaurants because we don't supply anyone else.'

'Well, I can't say I blame you for keeping her talents to yourselves. According to mother, Mario's is always packed to bursting point with people ordering afternoon tea, when she and her friends go there.

You are quite a celebrated local baker, Sarah!'

Sarah could not get the picture of this smiling viper, coming down the stairs from her boyfriend's bedroom in her HiVis jacket, out of her mind, but she managed to say something polite.

'Thank you very much, I'm glad your mother enjoyed her tea.' And then, as she could feel the tears starting to prick behind her eyes she said, 'You will have to excuse me I am rather busy,' and she dashed through the door into the development kitchen.

'She is rather shy,' said Jenny, by way of explanation, as Lauren and Steve exchanged confused glances.

-oooOoo-

Chapter 22

The last of the old stainless steel kitchen equipment was being loaded onto a truck, as the roofing contractors men started to swarm all over the classroom.

The catering college's kitchen equipment removal was only just finished in time, as the roofers men began hurling scaffold poles about, and an intrepid pair climbed up on to the roof outside to examine the task of stripping off the roof coverings.

Pete had just finished fashioning a solid looking door from some of the panels previously used to keep people out of the now demolished single storey link. It was the second one he had made, the first now blocked the gap where the doors led to the demolished corridor from the hotel, and this one was to temporarily block off the offices and other facilities which lay beyond the main classroom.

The toilets just beyond Pete's wooden structure were still awaiting repair, although when that was done, his new door would give site operatives access to them in accordance with his 'health and safety and site accommodation plan', which had just been approved.

Without a printer in his site office, Pete would have to go to Albany Developments office to pick that document up, and print off copies to be displayed on the notice board he had made with some cork tiles in the little room he used as his base.

He had asked Derek if he could have a printer which could also make photocopies, and one now awaited his collection in the office, along with a free standing electric heater, for use now that the weather was getting distinctly chillier.

The problem was that, to collect the printer and the heater, he would need to go to the offices, which were next door to the cafe where Sarah worked. He was aware that he couldn't avoid Sarah for ever, but he couldn't face it just yet, and he kept putting it off.

He knew that according to the site programme, coloured up and pinned to his noticeboard, there would be a period during which Sarah would be working in the classroom next door while he finished the new houses, and whilst the final touches were being added to the ballroom. Unless Derek appointed someone else to manage the site, he could not avoid that.

He had already decided that he would ask Derek if

he could be moved to work on another project, if and when one became available, even if it meant not seeing the hotel scheme through to completion, although he had not said anything yet.

He knew that to get right away would also mean giving up his rent free house, and as he had almost finished working on it, he was very sad about that. But he could not bear to live there while Sarah was so nearby.

What made it worse was the thought that the blasted matinee idol chef who he had seen her dancing with barefoot in the kitchen was quite likely to turn up at the college too. It would be all Pete could do to stop himself knocking his block off, irrespective of the consequences.

-oo0Ooo-

Justin Trowbridge was a hyperactive little weasel of a man, who never seemed to be still, and with whom it was difficult to maintain eye contact.

He had done a fine job in the past in creating marketing materials and 'branding' for Derek's new housing developments, but now he was faced with a very different challenge.

He had just finished presenting his Advertising Agency's proposals for the "brand launch" of the dinner and dining club to be called "Carlos at Barclay Court".

The glittering 'power-point' presentation they used had music and words spinning round with pictures dashing in and out of the screen, amongst backdrops of images of fine dining and 1930s style jazz clubs. But with the best will in the world, whilst it was certainly very pretty and quite noisy, it lacked any real substance.

'Yes,' said Derek, 'but where are we going to get the people to join this club? Unless I missed it in all that fluff, I didn't see a single thing about that. That is what we asked you to look into and make proposals on, Justin.'

Justin looked crestfallen. He had not expected the glaring hole in his exuberant presentation to be spotted so quickly.

'Well, it is always difficult with a new and totally original concept to know how to position it ...'

'But that is why we asked you to help us,' said Amanda. 'Have you no ideas on that score?'

'Well, I ...'

'Look, it is dead simple,' said Derek rising to his feet. 'Draw a line through Ronnie Scott's, up to the dinner dances at the Dorchester, via places like the Brasserie Zédel on Sherwood Street, and you have an idea of what we want to achieve. People won't just come for the music, and they won't just come for the food or the dancing; they will come for a stylish combination of all of it. I've just sat here for an hour listening to you talking and looking at some sort of disco on a screen with what you called 'key words' floating about and you haven't hit on anything like that at all.'

'Derek ...' Amanda started to say, but Derek was headed for the door.

'You will have to excuse me. I've got to go and earn some money to pay for all this stuff,' said Derek.

-oo0Ooo-

Back at his desk, Derek found an email from the specialist plasterwork restoration company who had been to look at the damaged ornate ceiling in the ballroom. It was their quotation to do the works.

'Oh my good God almighty!' said Derek to himself as he read the figures.

-oo0Ooo-

The central scaffolding 'tower' the roofing contractors had erected in the middle of the classroom was something of a work of art.

It encased the substantial brickwork structure which housed the original extractor fan pipes and would eventually be linked to the external scaffolding the men were building outside, while the roof covering was removed and until the new roof was completed.

Then it would serve to mount the so called "combined HVAC/MVHR, with run-around coil exchanger" plant to be installed by a specialist company who would be fitting this complicated heat recovery system to provide the classroom with clean fresh air ventilation and extraction pipes, alongside air conditioning.

Pete did not profess to understand the workings of the system, let alone all the acronyms, but he knew it would make the classroom a very much more pleasant place to work than it must have been in the past, and represented the 'state of the art' in managing the working environment in professional kitchens.

The scaffolding's third and final function was to enable the emergency fire sprinklers, insulation materials and internal finishes to be added to the roof, which would finish off the job. But first the web-like matrix of extruded steel roof supports had to be installed.

Derek had admitted that he had never been involved in anything so technical or complicated, but fortunately the architectural practice they used had experience of this type of work. Albany Developments would be leaning heavily on them for guidance as the project proceeded.

Organising it all, and managing the programme and sequence of works was pretty much a full time job in itself, but in addition, Pete still had to keep up with all the sub-contractors and oversee activities on the new build houses.

'How are you going to manage it all, Pete?' asked Dave, only half teasing.

'I'll have to learn to sleep faster,' said Pete with a grin.

-ooOoo-

Chapter 23

You had to admire Jenny. As a matchmaker her slightly underhanded manoeuvres were inspired.

A quiet word with Amanda had led to a quiet word with Derek, which had led to a reminder for Pete to come and pick up his printer/copier and his heater, and it was agreed that he would be at the office at four o'clock.

Now that it was getting dark earlier, work of necessity finished earlier on Albany Development's sites. But, if you took any notice of the television advertisements, you would think Christmas was next week, not the end of the month after next.

Amanda and Derek had fallen into the habit of going into the cafe for a warming cuppa at around half past three, and once or twice Amanda had covered for Sarah when she had to rush to collect Emma from school after Jenny had finished work.

On these occasions there was rarely anything much

to do, but today, even Derek had to pitch in and help when, with Sarah away, a small flurry of middle aged ladies descended on the cafe.

'I promise you, this is where they are made,' said their leader, a smiling woman in a warm cashmere coat. 'And my daughter has actually met the girl who bakes the cakes.'

The ladies, having rearranged the tables and chairs so they could all sit together, placed orders with Amanda for tea and, if possible, a plate or two of the wonderful patisserie they had enjoyed so much at Mario's.

'And is,' said their leader, giving voice one more, 'the baker here? We should like to meet her.'

For a while, as Derek flapped, Amanda did her best with the complicated machinery involved in tea making. But fortunately Sarah and Emma were only moments away, and took over immediately they arrived.

'Excuse me Auntie Amanda,' said Emma. 'You are doing that all wrong. Here, let me.'

Gratefully Amanda and Derek resumed their seats and engaged once again with the ladies as they extolled the virtues of Sarah's cakes.

'And this is Sarah,' said Amanda, as she arrived with heaping plates of cakes, some of which had been intended for Emma's tea.

The ladies twittered and squeaked as the cakes were handed round, and Sarah, blushing, asked Amanda what she should charge, given that the full range of patisserie was normally reserved for the restaurants, and only a limited selection was served in the cafe.

Before she could answer the door opened again, and Steve and Lauren walked in.

'So you found it all right?' said Lauren smiling broadly at each of the ladies in turn.

'Ah Ha!' said their leader, 'So this is your boyfriend, Lauren! Aren't you going to introduce him to your mother?'

Sarah almost dropped the last plate of cakes and had to restrain herself from throwing them at Lauren. That two timing sunny, smiling, sly, slithering, snake in the grass.

While the ladies were distracted and Amanda moved into her benevolent patron routine, meeting and greeting, with Emma, enthralled, at her side; Sarah decided she needed air, and opening the front door stepped out onto the pavement. Just as Pete climbed out of his truck.

-oo0Ooo-

'So is Steve Lauren's boyfriend, not yours?'

After the initial shock of meeting Sarah, Pete could

see Steve had his arm round Lauren through the brightly lit window of the cafe.

'I beg your pardon? What do you mean, my boyfriend?' said Sarah.

'But I saw you dancing with him in the kitchen ...'

'Dancing with him? Whatever do you mean?'

'You had propped the kitchen door open and taken your shoes off, and he twirled you round lifted you up and sat you on one of the benches and you were laughing. I saw you ...'

Sarah laughed.

'Why are you laughing, it is not remotely funny. I saw you with my own eyes. You definitely weren't working because you were wearing a really short skirt and a tee shirt, not your chef's stuff.'

'No Pete, no! I've just realised what you thought you saw. We weren't dancing. Steve had lifted me clear of the sunflower oil he had spilt all over the floor so I didn't ruin my new trainers.'

'How do you explain the short skirt, I suppose that was just for his benefit then ...'

'Certainly not. Have you forgotten how hot and sultry it was that day?'

'The only thing looking hot that day was you, and after you told me you didn't want to see me, you went after him ...'

'That's not true at all! And you are a fine one to talk. What about you and that snake Lauren?'

'What? I hardly know Lauren ...'

'Oh yes? And what was she doing coming down the stairs in your cottage, from the bedroom.'

'What did you say?'

'I realise that, as a Building Inspector, she has every right to look at the college buildings, of course. But there is nothing she needs to sign off in your cottage, is there. And yet I saw her coming down the stairs from your bedroom, no less, with you behind her looking like the cat that got the cream. She had clearly been inspecting you, and you were loving it.'

'When did you see her coming down the stairs?'

'Perhaps it was not the first time then! I went over there with my brother to show him where I was going to work, and I couldn't find you so I went round to the cottage. I don't think she saw me, but I saw you all right, and of course I did not want to hang around after that.'

Pete was laughing now.

'Oh, so now you are laughing at me,' the catch in Sarah's voice betrayed how upset she was. 'Silly little Sarah, made a fool of again.'

'No. You have got it all wrong, Sarah. I realise what you saw now. Lauren had just been to look at the roof timbers in my loft …'

'And I'm one of Santa's elves …'

'No really, I mean it. She had! The timbers in the classroom are all rotten and I needed to know if the ones in my roof were made of the same stuff …'

'Oh come on, you can't really expect me to believe that!' Sarah was beyond tears now. She had moved on to anger. Pete was a liar, just like Ricky. All men were brutes.

'But it is the truth, I swear! I and the reason I was looking pleased is because she confirmed that my roof was fine …'

'Absolute nonsense. We will soon sort this out, come on'

And with that she opened the door of the cafe and stepped inside.

'Lauren,' she said. 'Could I have a word, please.'

-oo0Ooo-

Chapter 24

'Yes, of course, I would be delighted, Carlos. It would be great to see you again too.'

'Thanks, Chesney, that is very kind of you. It would be good to see you in the flesh, as it were, rather than just on telly!'

Chesney Marriott, Carlos knew, was very proud of his television work, and praising that was bound to make the popular chef preen.

'Are they still churning that stuff out, Carlos? It is all repeats now, of course. It is nearly three years since I did anything new.'

'Three years! You surprise me, Chesney. Are you working on anything new at the moment?'

'Well, yes. Funny you should mention that. Later in the new year the first of a new series about teaching celebs to produce something a bit more fresh and adventurous in the kitchen was going to air, I had hoped. We had started on a three episode pilot and got one in the can but then the hotel kitchen we were using suffered a fire, so we have had to stop while the network people look for a new venue.'

'You need a new venue to make these shows?'

'Yes, but it is not straightforward because the thing is based around the celebs becoming involved in learning how to grow veg, and fruit and so on as well as cooking it. The hotel had a lovely kitchen garden, but we can't keep nipping back there to do the outside bit and then cooking somewhere else, the celebs won't do it. To tie the celebs down we need to do it all in one place and all at the same time, in one go.'

'Chesney, old pal, I do believe it is your lucky day. I might just have exactly the venue you are looking for!'

-oo0Ooo-

'And then, apart from just maintaining the gardens you have seen, there is the walled garden area,' said Jeremy.

Given a new lease of life following the Waitrose news, the Frobishers had agreed that they could once again employ gardeners to relieve Jeremy of the responsibility of upkeep of the once delightful gardens around the Barclay Court Hotel.

'Of course it has got rather neglected recently,' said Jeremy, pushing open the gate to the weedy walled garden which was overlooked by Pete's little house, but otherwise completely secluded. 'If our business partners, the developers of the catering college, are interested they might want you to do some work on this.'

Jeremy had decided that, although it was now leased off as part of the catering college deal, offering the potential restoration of the once productive kitchen garden might act as a tempter to the gardening contractors he was interviewing, and encourage them to keep their prices keen.

-oo0Ooo-

'So I said I was very sorry to disturb her, but could she confirm that she had been in Pete's loft and that, in her professional opinion as a Building Inspector, the roof was safe.'

'That was very clever of you Sarah,' laughed Sandy. 'What a great piece of quick thinking!'

'Thank you, I was quite proud of it myself.'

'So obviously she did confirm that she had been going to look in the loft, and so on?'

'Yes, and then she asked me why I wanted to know, so I said that if I was ever to think of moving in there one day I would want to know that the roof was safe first …'

'You didn't! And what did Pete say?'

'I thought he was going to pass out! He went as white as a sheet and couldn't stop dancing about.'

'I'm not surprised! Then what happened.'

'Well, we stepped outside again and Pete was babbling about the house, and could I ever forgive him for doubting me, and so on. Oh, and he told me he loved me about four-hundred times.'

'And what did you do?'

'What, after the kissing, you mean?' laughed Sarah. 'I said I was sorry I doubted him too. Then I phoned Jenny, arranged babysitting for tonight and told Pete to pick me up at seven o'clock.'

'But it is nearly half past six now!'

'Yes, I know. And I'm all ready with the short skirt he likes and my face-paint on. Tonight we go to Mario's for dinner, Pete's treat!'

-oooOoo-

Chapter 25

Amanda had decided to take Justin Trowbridge for a meal at Brasserie Zédel on Sherwood Street, on the edge of London's theatre land.

She and Derek had eaten there on a couple of occasions and been impressed by what the venue had to offer.

Located in the heart of Piccadilly, Brasserie Zédel is a grand and bustling Parisian brasserie combined with a live music and cabaret venue. It did not precisely represent what they were trying to achieve for 'Carlos at Barclay Court,' not least because it lacked the dancing element, but it had the atmosphere of sophistication they wanted and exuded the sort of 1920s style they hoped to emulate.

Justin met Derek and Amanda there with his wife, who seemed rather overwhelmed by the grand style of the venue.

'Coo,' she said. 'This is a bit posh, innit? I'm glad we are not picking up the bill in 'ere!'

Derek and Amanda had not met Trudy before, and only learned that she was once on the stage when Justin explained that the venue for their evening was close to one of the theatres where she had appeared in a musical comedy.

''Course that show didn't last more'n a few nights. The songs was no good, you see. No memorable choruses to get the punters whistling on the way home. And the writer wasn't one of your names. Never 'elps that don't. You need catchy songs and a name on the programme to make that sort of show go.'

Justin, aways somewhat twitchy, was skipping from foot to foot as he drank in every detail of the Brasserie Zédel.

'I'm beginning to understand what you meant now,' he said, looking somewhat embarrassed. 'Look, I'm sorry Derek. I made a frightful cock up of that presentation and I fully expected you to sack me and not give me any more work. You would have been quite within your rights to do so …'

'No, Justin. That is not the way we work. You have done great things for Albany Developments in the past and our business relationship has been very successful. I realise that this new venture is very different from anything we have asked you to do before, but you did say you wanted to take it on so, if you like, coming here tonight is by way of giving us a chance to make our brief a bit clearer, and for you to redeem yourself and have another crack at it.'

'Assuming you are still interested,' added Amanda.

'Oh yes, my Justin is more than still interested. He talks about nuffink else,' said Trudy. 'He's got all these books about the night-clubs and dancing venues of the 1930s out of the library and sits up nights reading them.'

Justin was blushing now.

'Come on then, let's eat,' said Derek.

-ooOOoo-

'Jenny will want to be going home soon,' said Sarah.

'Oh. Yes, I suppose she will,' said Pete, sitting up.

'We really should have gone to Mario's, it was rude not to turn up.'

'It's all right, I phoned them to cancel.'

'When?'

'When you went to the bathroom.'

'Where are you going, Pete?'

'I was going to get dressed, you said we had to get back for Jenny.'

'Not quite yet,' said Sarah, wrapping her arms around his neck.

-ooOOoo-

'And tomorrow,' Emma was saying, 'Mummy said perhaps we can go and see Pete's house when I get home from school. I've never been, and I've been asking her if we can go for ages.'

'Well, that's nice,' said Jenny. 'Ah, here comes mummy. Now you get off to sleep again, young lady or your mummy will be cross with me for staying up playing bear's picnics with you. Good night Emma, goodnight Edward.'

'Edward says thanks for looking after us, Jenny,' yawned Emma. 'He hopes you enjoyed the tea party.'

-ooOOoo-

Chapter 26

*P*ete didn't think there had ever been such a beautiful morning.

The frost glistened on grass and weeds alike, and the scaffold poles seemed to glow in the early morning sunlight. Even the skips seemed to grin at him as he passed by.

The sky, he noticed, had patches of blue between the clouds, and the thin layer of ice on the puddle by the door crackled musically under his site-boot as he unlocked the office.

Everything was for the best, in the best of all possible worlds, he thought, and he began to whistle a little tune.

The only possible girl was his once more, and the whole world smiled as he plugged in his little heater and blew steamily on his hands to warm them up.

-oo0Ooo-

'I thought it was a huge amount of money,' Derek was saying. 'But what choice do we have?'

'But at least we know now, honey,' said Amanda. 'And the good thing is it won't take them that long to do the plasterwork, so you can tell Pete to start clearing out the ballroom.'

'Pete is very busy at the moment. This is the busiest couple of weeks in the programme, what with the new roof steel lattice being erected, and the first of the brick deliveries coming to the new build. And now it gets dark so early, outside work is limited.'

'But we did say we would try to get the ballroom done for Christmas, didn't we. And working on the ballroom is inside work, after all.'

'It is too late to get any bookings to use it for Christmas or the New Year celebrations, I only said that because I thought it would be nice to have the firm's Christmas do in there.'

'I think that would be nice too, but with nothing else arranged and all our own restaurants booked up solid, we have got to do something for the staff, and they won't all fit in the cafe.'

'I heard of one building firm who had their Christmas do in June. It always gets frantic in the lead up to Christmas before the sites shut down, and you can't expect people to turn out for a bash in their holidays.'

'Do you know, that is not such a silly idea, Derek! Maybe not June, but how about March or April, before the Grand Opening, to celebrate the completion of the kitchens ... then we will be able to use our own facilities ...'

'Right-ho,' said Derek, and picked up his phone to start his regular morning calls around the sites.

-ooo0oo-

'Well, there is not that much to see yet, Chesney. It is all grimy builders and mess and rubble. But I could probably get a set of the plans over for your network people if you like, and I'll also send you some pictures of the old walled kitchen garden.'

'That would be great, Carlos. Can you send them straight to their office ... I'll give you their address ... only I've got a guest appearance at a hotel opening in Dubai this weekend, so I won't be around until later in the week.'

'Very nice!'

'Well, it pays the bills. You know you should get into this telly work Carlos, you would be good at it.'

'Opportunity has never knocked, I'm afraid.'

'Well, if we are going to be using this venue of yours, I can put that right for you. I could insist on having you on as a guest, as a condition of accepting the venue. I can be quite a little Prima Donna when roused you know. And then, when the network people see what you can do, who knows where it might lead!'

'Would it really be that simple?'

'Absolutely, old mate. You leave it to Uncle Chesney!'

'I'd better tell my boss that you are interested. I'm sure she will be excited about it, but until our conversation just now, I have to be honest and say I thought it might all be a daydream, so I haven't said anything.'

'You won't catch Chesney Marriott allowing his people time for daydreaming, Carlos. Now get back to work!' laughed Chesney.

-ooOoo-

'I seem to be getting in your way,' said Steve. 'Sorry, Sarah.'

'No, I'm getting in your way, Steve. I should be the one saying sorry.'

'There will be stacks of room when we can use the new college kitchen won't there. I'm looking forward to extending myself in there!'

'I'll clear down this bench for you Steve. My apologies, I seem to have spread my stuff all over this kitchen this morning.'

'Not to worry, you didn't know I was coming, and

you got here first after all.'

'I'm sorry Steve, what did you say?'

'Are you all right, Sarah?'

'Oh yes. I'm very all right thank you,' sighed Sarah. 'Very all right indeed. In fact, I don't think I have ever been more all right, actually.'

-ooOoo-

Chapter 27

'Hi Derek, it's Justin.'

'Hello Justin, how are you?'

'Fine thank you. I've got a message from Trudy for you. I think it is quite exciting.'

'Go on?'

'Well, Trudy worked with Desmond Tweedy in pantomime, and they became great friends. I don't know if you have heard of him, he has been on the Royal Variety Performance a couple of times with his band. And what made her think of it was when you told me to think about Ronnie Scott's. She says he has performed there several times.'

'I confess I have not heard the name, but then I don't get out much.'

'Well, anyway he does this sort of Glenn Miller tribute thing in the clubs in the West End, and he is getting a bit fed up with it. Trudy says he is putting another show together for the New Year, based on all the old jazz songs the nightclub crooners used to sing. He might be interested in trying it out at your opening bash, if you like.'

'Well, we had not really got as far as ...'

'No charge, of course. It will be like a full dress rehearsal for them with a live audience, before they take it on the road. Just give them a bit of dinner. If you are interested Trudy has a recording of a practice session they did for this new act, she can email it to you if you like.'

'Yes, that sounds very interesting. Thank you Justin, I'll look forward to getting that.'

-ooo0oo-

The intensity of the Christmas advertising was ramping up.

The shops were creating Christmas window displays, and moving the Christmas stock from slightly apologetic positions in the background to front and centre, and in the shops, in every lift and corridor, the Christmas music played.

Emma was getting excited in the way only an eight year old can.

Of course she knew that there wasn't really a Santa Claus, she said, although when Amanda offered to take her shopping with a visit to see him in his 'grotto,' she was soon pleading with her mother for permission to go.

Sarah drew Amanda to one side.

'Thank you very much for offering to take Emma shopping, but please don't buy her anything,' she said.

'Not buy her anything? But I wanted to …'

'Spoil her. I know you did,' smiled Sarah. 'You are much too generous you know, and I'm afraid we haven't the money for expensive presents, so I don't want her getting ideas from the shops about anything costly.'

'She told Jenny she would like a dolls house …'

'She told me that too, and a bike, not that there is anywhere safe to ride a bike round here, so that is not going to happen.'

'Can't I buy her a dolls house, Sarah? When I was little I would have loved a dolls house, but my father bought my sister and I a Scalextric. He would never say so, but he really wanted sons.'

'Dolls houses cost a fortune, Amanda! I couldn't let …'

'Yes you could. Oh go on, Sarah. If you let me, I promise to babysit when you and Pete want to go out, and Emma and I can play with it together.'

'You are serious, aren't you!'

'Yes, I am. I would love to do this and to spend more time with Emma. She really is an adorable little girl.'

'I was going to try to find one in the secondhand shops ... I don't know what to say ... '

'Then just say yes. And anyway I am hoping this Christmas will be a little bit better for you and all our team, Sarah. Derek and I will not be holding a Christmas do, well not until the Spring, so we will be giving everyone Christmas bonuses instead.'

'A bonus? Really? Well, I hadn't expected that ...'

'Sarah, I don't think you realise quite how much we appreciate how hard you work and the value of the fabulous skills you have bought to our company. What you have done has really made a difference to our business, and we would never have been able to do the afternoon teas without you ... and look how popular they are proving to be!'

'Yes, it was lovely to see those ladies enjoying them and hear the nice things they were saying about them.'

'Well, you were otherwise engaged when it came to paying for them, so I didn't charge them.'

'Didn't charge them!'

'It's called marketing, Sarah. They are regulars at

Mario's and they will tell all their friends about the teas, and maybe the dinners, so they are our best advert.'

'You are quite amazing, Amanda. How did you learn all this stuff?'

'What are you two taking about?' said Emma. 'So can we go to see Santa or not, mummy?'

'Please just say yes, Sarah ... to everything.'

-ooo0oo-

Carlos called a meeting when Amanda got back to the office. It was time to tell her, and Derek, about Chesney Marriott and the television programme.

'I don't know how much they will pay yet, but if you agree, they will get Andrew Smallpond to come down to look at it. If a deal can be done, they will arrange to plant the walled garden up properly, but they will probably use bought in plants for the celebs to dig up to start with.'

'Andrew Smallpond, the TV gardener?' asked Amanda.

'That's him. He is involved in the network company financially, I think.'

'I'm not sure I like this TV trickery, bringing in grown plants,' said Derek, 'That seems just a bit dishonest.'

'Chesney said that's show business.'

'So who is going to be on this show then, Carlos?' Down-to earth Derek would take some convincing about this, it seemed.

'I'm told the first pilot show has Hannah Sweet from Southenders, Victor Bottle, from that late night arts programme on BBC2, Jasmin Inthwaite, the presenter, and Malcolm Croucher, the weatherman. Chesney also said that they would need to book out at least fifteen of the hotel rooms for two nights minimum, each time they film.'

-oo0Ooo-

Chapter 27

The time had come at last for Emma to be taken to see Pete's house, and she was nattering on about it being about time too, as she climbed into the middle seat in the van.

As they drove down the side of the hotel and the catering school came into view, Emma gasped.

'Where has the roof gone, Pete? I thought you were mending it, not knocking it down!'

'Sometimes when you break things, you can make them stronger and better when you put them back together,' said Pete looking meaningfully at Sarah.

'Like when you build with Lego,' said Emma.

'Just like that,' said Sarah. 'And Pete is making a new roof for us to work under that will last for ever.'

'Is there no roof on your house, Pete?'

'The roof there is fine, Emma. It is only the big classroom that has to be rebuilt.'

'Just as well. You wouldn't want to be sleeping outside in this weather.'

'My house has a roof and heating and a fine old fireplace to hang my Christmas stocking on, as you will see.'

'We don't have a fireplace. Mummy says I have to hang my stocking on the end of my bed.'

'I'm sure that will work just as well, Emma. Well, here we are, let's go and have a look.'

The first thing Sarah noticed as they entered the walled garden where the house sat, was the improvements Pete had made to the outside.

'I love those pretty blue shutters on the windows, Pete, I didn't see them last time,' she said.

'I only put them up yesterday, I'd been making them in the workshop on and off when I got a spare moment and before the people from the extrusion company wanted to take it over and start using their machine in there. The paint is the stuff left over from the dressers in the cafe.'

'You made those?'

'Yes, of course. Why?'

'And you made that pretty porch with the lattice sides ...'

'Yes, and you wait until you see the shed I made for

the garden out of bits of the hoardings that came off the corridor, when it was demolished.'

'It's sweet!' exclaimed Emma. 'It looks like a little dolls house.'

The previously bland and utilitarian house now looked much better. Before it was just a functional adjunct to the catering school main building with windows looking out from a blank wall. That wall was only otherwise broken by a set of doors leading to the central corridor and the offices in the college building. The original designer must have felt that the access to the walled garden was purely functional, and a mere caretaker's house was not worthy of embellishment, so he left it at that.

'It certainly looks much more homely than it did,' added Sarah. 'Now it's a cottage, not just a house.'

'Well, let's see if I have made a similar improvement inside,' said Pete, unlocking the front door.

'You've put in a new fireplace,' said Sarah as they entered the lounge.

'No I haven't. Go and have a closer look at it.'

The fireplace, Sarah remembered, was an ugly tiled thing, typical of the era in which the house was built and surrounded an unattractive gas fire.

What she was looking at now appeared to be a rustic stone surround with a deep and wide polished wooden bessemer and a wood burning stove taking pride of place on a matching stone hearth.

'I don't see ...'

'Get right up close,' said Pete.

'It's stone ... no, hang on ... it's wood! This is all painted! Wow, that is really clever. Did you do that, Pete?'

'With my own fair hands,' smiled Pete. 'Although I have to admit the wood-burner is a fake one with a fan heater from Argos.'

'Coo! I didn't know you could paint too, Pete.'

'Oh, you know. One dabbles with one's art,' laughed Pete. 'It is actually all made out of more of that scrap plywood from the hoardings on the corridor building, so it cost almost nothing. Just the paint and the fake fire. I've found all sorts of uses for that timber. It would be silly just to throw it away.'

The lounge was furnished in a mish-mash of obviously second-hand furniture. Pete saw Sarah looking at it, and explained.

The furniture here came from my mum's house or was stuff Dave had and didn't want anymore. That is actually a sofa bed and came from Dave's garage, and one of the winged armchairs was my Grannies and lived in my mum's conservatory ... if you look you will see one side is a lighter colour where the sun damaged it.'

'It is all very cozy,' said Emma. 'I like it.'

'Well, shall we have a look at the kitchen now and see what you think of that?'

The kitchen was dated, but otherwise usable. But now the typical 1970s 'orange pine' cupboards were a subtle shade of blue and there was a new sink and a smart looking electric cooker with a digital clock.

'I was running out of the left over blue paint by the time I did this, so I mixed it with some white, which lightened it up a bit and made it go further. I did buy new handles but other than that, only the cooker and the sink are new, and I got them at trade price.'

'This is lovely, Pete. You really are very clever,' said Sarah. She had seen the kitchen before but only very briefly, and on her last visit most of the furniture in the lounge was just stacked up against the wall. But, to be fair, on their last visit, they had only used the upstairs rooms!

The dining room had a white plastic garden table and chairs.

'I recognise that!' said Sarah.

'I thought you might. That was rescued from the room at the side of the cafe and has been in Dave's shed ever since.'

'Speaking of sheds ...' Emma was looking out of

the french doors which led to the overgrown little garden.

'Do you like it?' asked Pete.

What they were looking at was a little wooden building with a lead-latticed window and a split stable style door, all painted white and relieved by two more of those pretty blue shutters Pete had made for the front of the house.

'It's a Wendy House!' exclaimed Emma.

'Well, If you like. I was thinking of using it as a garden bar,' stated Pete.

Upstairs, Emma expressed her approval of the white painted bedrooms, which Pete explained he had just quickly painted for now, to spruce the house up a bit ready for his mother's inspection, due next week.

'Now, if this was my room,' Emma was saying as they looked at the empty second bedroom, 'I should want some of that blue wallpaper with hares on, like in the cafe, on that wall, and maybe a creamy colour on that wall …'

'Not the hares again!' said Sarah. 'I can't get away from them in the cafe, and I'm even starting to see them in my sleep!'

-oo0Ooo-

'Thank you for coming,' said Justin. 'This is going to blow your minds.'

Derek and Amanda had been relieved of their winter coats in the foyer of the theatre and now Justin was ushering them into the empty auditorium.

In the background a slightly ominous beat played and it took a while for their eyes to adjust to the dim lighting. Having taken their seats they noticed that it was getting progressively darker and then, with a crash of cymbals, the lights seemed to flash and, to their astonishment the entire wall of the auditorium, to the right of their seats, seemed to dissolve and a view across the River Thames towards the Houses of Parliament appeared with Big Ben silently chiming out midnight against the night sky.

Then, across what appeared to be the sky above them, silent fireworks erupted and burst into brilliant shapes and flashes of light and colour until a few seconds later the image on the wall dissolved again and they were looking at the tired red wallpaper of the theatre once more.

Down on the stage a figure sat at a desk with a laptop open in front of him. He appeared to be sitting in the library of an old country house, with a fire blazing in a tall marble fireplace beside him.

They noticed a large St.Bernard dog lying almost at his feet, which now got up, walked in front of the seated figure and turned with its back to the fire.

Amanda let out a little cry when the dog's tail caught

fire, but laughed when it appeared to streak up the wall and across the ceiling and disappeared.

At the same moment the cosy library scene dissolved and the man at the desk was alone on the completely empty stage.

'Good morning, Derek and Amanda,' the figure said, now rising from the desk. 'Thank you for allowing us to demonstrate the capabilities of our company "Scene Illumination", we hope you are enjoying the show.'

But then, with a loud pop, the man, the desk and the laptop were gone and in its place there sat a man in a wheelchair.

'My name is Jack Bolton and what you have just seen is a mixture of a few little things I put together initially for the computer gaming industry, but more recently for film and theatre. My company, called "Scene Illumination" in case you didn't get it the first time, uses computer technology and advanced lighting techniques to create building sized scenery and illusions.'

At that moment the St.Bernard dog ambled back across the stage.

'Not now, Cedric,' said Jack, and with a pop the dog changed into an enormous teacup, then a giant egg, a deckchair and finally a rocket, which zoomed off, stage right.

'Sorry about that, folks,' said Jack, as Derek and Amanda laughed.

'As I was saying, Trudy, who I believe you know, and I go back a long way and she suggested that you might find some of our little illusions useful in your ballroom project, alongside a review of the lighting you are going to use for your dancing and dinner endeavours.'

Amanda squeezed Derek's hand and he realised that he was about to be paying for something else for the increasingly pricey Dinner Club project.

'I trust this lovely ballroom I hear so much about has full wheelchair access, because I would love to come and see it in action, but as you can see some venues are impossible for me.'

At that point, one of the wheels appeared to fall off the wheelchair and roll across the stage, before it too vanished with a pop.

'But enough of this tom-foolery,' announced Jack grandly. 'What you are asking yourself is how the hell much is all this going to cost. And well you might. Such expertise and hopefully convincing illusion does not come cheap, but boy, oh boy, can it build up an atmosphere.'

Suddenly the lights dropped again and the wall on their right became an elegant dining room with diners in full evening dress busily chatting and attending to the food in front of them. This time the image did have a sound track, and Derek and Amanda saw that on the stage a little jazz band had materialised who were playing a catchy show hit from days gone by.

'Is this the sort of thing you imagined for your exclusive club?' said Jack's voice over the music. 'I hope so because young Justin has been very concerned to get his presentation right this time.'

The images all dissolved, and the music faded away and they were left with just the bare stage and Jack in his wheelchair once more. But now, to their surprise, Justin walked onto the stage.

Derek looked to his left and saw the seat Justin had been occupying was empty, except for a blue folder, which a spotlight seemed to be illuminating.

Derek had not seen him go, but now there he was smiling and speaking to them from the stage.

'Thank you Jack, I hope you agree that that was pretty impressive, and Derek, if you look on the seat next to you, you will find a folder in which you will find my new, and I hope much better proposals for positioning, promoting and marketing 'Carlos at Barclay Court.' Coffee is available in the foyer you saw on the way in and if you would like to make your way there and make yourselves comfortable, Jack and I will join you shortly.'

And with that, the houselights started to come up,

some curtains closed across the stage and the jolly jazz the band had been playing resumed at a muted volume.

-ooOoo-

Chapter 28

In the morning, when Andrew Smallpond the celebrated TV gardener arrived, the Frobishers had formed a little welcoming party with Carlos, Derek and Amanda.

After being introduced to everyone, he went to look around the walled garden with Derek and then to meet Pete in his site office to look at the catering college plans.

As the Frobishers went back into the hotel Penelope turned to her sister.

'Well,' she said, 'he is shorter than I imagined, but other than that he looks exactly as he does on the screen. A little older perhaps, and certainly greyer, but otherwise just the same.'

'You be careful nobody hears you talking like that,' said Jeremy. 'This is a big opportunity for us and we don't want to mess it up.'

'They talked about Chesney Marriott possibly

coming over for a look,' said Jane. 'I wonder if he will want to stay.'

'Now he is dishy,' said Penelope.

'Nice pun, Pen,' said Jeremy. 'TV chef; dish ... very good.'

'Pardon?' said Penelope.

'Never mind,' said Jane, giving her brother a sour look. 'Are all the coffee cups laid out ready for our guests, Penelope?'

-oo0Ooo-

'Fifteen rooms at a time!'

'That is what he said, Jeremy. And for two nights minimum.'

'We are going to be rich!' said Penelope.

'Well, we are certainly going to be busy,' said Jane. 'Although we mustn't count on any of this yet. Derek said the deal is not yet done.'

'Will we be on the television?' asked Penelope.

'I shouldn't think so,' said Jeremy. 'Although the cameramen might come and look in all the corners and under the beds to see how clean it is, so you had better make sure you have not been cutting any corners, Pen!'

'Don't be mean,' said Jane. 'There is no need to tease

Penelope all the time.'

'Don't worry, I'm used to it,' said Penelope. 'All men are brutes and they probably can't help themselves.'

-ooo0oo-

Fortunately, though cloudy, the weather was fine as the roofers prepared to construct the complicated extruded steel web that would support the roof from the slates down to the insulated panels inside.

What had arrived on site from the workshop was a truck full of strips of steel channel with holes punched at the ends and occasionally in the middle, each stamped with a reference number. The metal extrusions were accompanied by a senior operative with a laptop.

The pieces of metal were bundled up in sections and one piece at a time the spider web began to emerge.

The power riveters popped and hissed as the channels were connected together, and webs about two metres square were assembled. The lightweight sections were then lifted into place and riveted together until, in what seemed like no time, the matrix reached the much bigger steel lintels they had positioned. These beams ran above the internal dividing walls and were connected to the exterior walls at either end and to the tall brick structure in the middle of the building. There operatives on the scaffolding connected it up and bolted it to the predrilled holes in the lintels.

Remarkably it all lined up perfectly and by the middle of the afternoon, as the light was fading, one entire side of the classroom building had an interlocking grey steel web of roof supports in place.

'Amazing,' said Derek as he watched the last connections being made before the roofers finished for the night.

'It is quite something, isn't it,' said Pete. 'When they showed us those videos of how the system worked it seemed a bit like science fiction, but watching it now for real is awesome.'

'And it is all done with such precision,' marvelled Derek. 'The chief engineer told me that so far they had not made one mistake or had to reject any of the individual sections.'

'Stunning,' said Dave.

'Hello, Dave,' said Derek 'You here too?'

'Yes, sorry Derek. This is such a spectacle I didn't want to miss it, so I stopped by on my way to the office to collect some papers.'

'Fair enough Dave, it is not going to be everyday we see something like this happening.'

'I shall have to start charging entry fees to come and watch!' laughed Pete.

-ooOoo-

'This is good, Derek, come and have a look,' Amanda was watching the rehearsal of Desmond Tweedy and his band's new show on her iPad. 'Real foot tapping stuff, and I hadn't realised that they do little dance routines too while they play and sing.'

'I've seen it,' said Derek. 'I have to admit they are very good. It is a great show. It would be even better if they were not slouching about in jeans and teeshirts.'

'They will dress in tuxedos when they do it for real, I expect.'

'I hope you are right. Still, you have to say it is not half bad for the price. Good old Justin and Trudy!'

'And I have to say his proposal, in this blue folder is really comprehensive.'

'Yes, Jack Bolton was saying Justin sweated blood over that, and he certainly hit the spot and got it right in the end. Incidentally, did you hear Jack explain that those illusions in the theatre were done by having two very fine mesh screens in front of where he was sitting on the stage, that we could see through, but which they back-projected the images onto. Very clever that was.'

'After your mean comments the first time round, Justin was like a little frightened rabbit, Derek. I hope you are not turning into a bully. Many property men do, when they get to your age and get frustrated when things don't go their own way, you know.'

'What do you mean get to my age? I'll have you know I'm only just my age and I have no intention of becoming a bully.'

'Well, I'm going to bully you instead then,' smiled Amanda. 'Now put those papers down and come to bed, we have got a big day tomorrow!'

'Yes boss,' said Derek.

-ooOoo-

Chapter 29

The following day, the rest of the metal spider web of roof supports, on the other side of the catering school roof, was up before lunchtime. Then the workers turned their attention to fixing large pre-formed panels to it externally which would be used as backing for the slates.

Just as the light began to fade, the first slates were being positioned and Pete was intrigued to see several large pots of natural yoghurt being unloaded from the roofer's truck.

Inevitably a couple of dozen slates had broken when the roof covering was removed. Where they had to be replaced with new ones, when they had them in position, the roofers were painting them with the yoghurt using an old wallpapering brush. When Pete enquired, he was told that the natural bacteria in the yoghurt would soon produce a patina which would make the new tiles match the old ones.

'Well,' said Pete, seeing the sense of this, 'That's a

new one on me, but every day is a school day!'

Pete explained what was going on when Amanda turned up at tea-time with Sarah and Emma.

'Yuk!' said Emma. 'I hate yoghurt. Won't it smell horrible when it goes off, like the stuff mummy forgot in the fridge once?'

'Thank you for that, Emma,' said Sarah as Pete and Amanda laughed.

'Well you won't smell it inside, Emma, even if it does,' Pete reassured her.

'Come on then, Pete,' said Amanda. 'Let's see what you have done to the old caretaker's house that has got Emma and Sarah so excited.'

'Another guided tour required? I really will have to start charging entry fees!'

-ooOoo-

'So, if it is all right with you, Carlos, I will drop in on Saturday morning and have a look at it all.'

'Fine by me, Chesney. I'll check if Pete, the Project Manager, is going to be around to let you in. He lives on the site now so it should be fine.'

'I shan't be able to stay long, I'm afraid. I'll be on my way into London to do a live appearance on "John Sparrow's Saturday Afternoons," in his kitchen, but I should be with you at about half past nine.'

'You do live, don't you Chesney! Always so busy.'

'Yes, I have to suffer for my art … all that eating fine food can wear a body down you know …'

'It must be nice to have people to do all the prep for you. When was the last time you peeled a potato?'

'Listen to it! I happen to know that there are no less than four trainees; four, mark you! All running about after you in Mario's … So much for your hard-done-by act! I ask you the same question … when was the last time *you* peeled a spud!'

-ooOOoo-

'And the specialist plaster people can start on Tuesday, as soon as the scaffold tower we have hired arrives.'

'No problem, Derek,' said Jeremy. If they come to the main hotel reception entrance they can get in at any time after seven in the morning.'

'Right, thank you. Can they then open one of the big French doors at the back and come and go that way to avoid coming through the carpeted areas?'

'Certainly, and you will make sure the cleaning contractors come and go that way on Monday, won't you,' added Jane. 'All that pigeon mess is going to be quite unpleasant and we don't want it coming through reception.'

'Not a problem,' said Derek. 'And we are clear where they are going to put their skip, aren't we.'

'Yes, that is all sorted out.'

'It is going to be lovely to see the ballroom restored,' said Penelope. 'We had dancing lessons in there, when we were little. Not Jeremy, of course. He has two left feet and couldn't dance a step to save his life.'

-oo0Ooo-

'I saw Mary from the show house this morning, Jenny. She was saying they can't build the houses fast enough to keep up with demand, down on the new build bit of the site.'

'Well that's good, Dave. How is your bit doing?'

'All ours are pre-let so we can work to a more set programme, which helps. We have handed over almost half of the houses now and the housing association people seem pleased with them. Mind you we have had some right old horrors to deal with. Several of the houses were completely wrecked when the tenants moved out and two were fire damaged.'

'They said on the local News that there had been another fire up there recently.'

'There has been more than one, and thats not counting the burnt out cars on the green that we had to deal with. But the worst thing was all the stuff the druggies left behind. Needles and those little gas canisters everywhere, there was. We had to be really careful how we cleared that all up.'

'Disgusting, and where children play too.'

'Played. You didn't see any children round there when we arrived, thank goodness. Still, it is all getting tidied up now, and while we have got a way to go yet, the first few people have moved into the refurbished houses now.'

'When are they going to re-do the kiddies play park, do you think. And what about the skate board area? My boys are just about old enough for that now.'

'I'm afraid that is going to be a while yet. We have to remove the whole surface of that area and replace it to make sure there are no traces of needles and so on first.'

'It was when that got vandalised and the Council shut it all up that the trouble started over there, if you ask me. Nothing for the kids to do. And as time went on the crime rates shot up.'

'Yeah, and it all started to go down hill when the factory shut down.'

'I heard that is going to be a Waitrose,' said Jenny cheering up.

'I hope you are right,' said Dave. 'That is just the sort

of lift this area needs.'

'That, and the new optician and the dentist coming in here, might even mean Amanda will start to sell some of her fancy afternoon teas in the cafe.'

'You never know. Thank you Jenny, that bacon sandwich was lovely.'

'I dunno how you could bear it with all that brown sauce on it!'

-oooOoo-

Chapter 30

Amanda enjoyed meeting Chesney Marriott with Carlos and took him to meet the Frobishers, after Carlos had shown him round the garden and the college.

Jane was all cool efficiency when she showed him a 'typical' bedroom in the hotel, and Penelope had to be reminded not to stare when she was seen gazing, slack jawed, from the doorway of one of the other rooms, clutching her vacuum cleaner.

'I'm sorry I can't stay any longer, Amanda,' Chesney said. 'I would have liked to have a chat with you about when, and how often, we could use the kitchen. Andrew ... Andrew Smallpond, I mean, was very impressed with it all, and having seen it, I agree with his comment that it was a pity we didn't discover this first before we made the initial pilot show.'

'That is very kind of you, Mr Marriott ...'

'Chesney, please. You made me jump, nobody calls me Mr Marriott! I thought my wicked old father had come back from the dead and was standing behind me with his horsewhip.'

Amanda laughed at the little witticism and showed Chesney to his car.

'I suppose there is no harm in telling you that the Network have said they are going to make you an offer, once I confirm I'm happy. And I am happy, very happy indeed.' smiled Chesney. 'But can I give you a little word of advice ... don't take their first offer. The company is run by three accountants who are as mean as can be, and struggle to see the more spacious view sometimes. We call them the Three Blind Mice. Andrew and I will push them from our end, but you take my word for it, their first offer will not be their last!'

-oo0Ooo-

Pete called in to the cafe on his way to collect papers from the office and was talking to Emma while Sarah prepared him a coffee 'to go' before closing the cafe.

'Yes, and I told Santa that, because mummy said I couldn't have a bike, I would like a dolls house.'

'I see,' said Pete, 'and what did Santa say to that?'

'He said some stuff about being good and waiting

and seeing. I heard him say the same thing to the little boy who was in to see him before me. If you ask me it was all a set-up. I don't think it was really Santa. I think it was an actor, dressed up. And he smelt funny too.'

'How did it go with clearing out all that mess in the ballroom, Pete,' asked Sarah.

'I am so glad Derek decided to hire in proper industrial cleaning contractors to do that,' frowned Pete. 'That is quite the most disgusting thing I have ever been involved with, and I'm so glad I didn't have to do it all myself.'

'It was only pigeon poo, wasn't it?'

'No it wasn't! I lost count at fifteen dead pigeons, and there were other dead birds too. Once they got in there they obviously couldn't get out again. No wonder it stank!'

'How utterly disgusting,' exclaimed Emma. 'I hope you will have a shower before you take mummy out tonight!'

'Big words,' said Pete.

'New english teacher,' said Sarah.

'Yes. Miss Carter-Bone is very concerned to make sure we use our vocabulary. She is much nicer than Mr Clough and makes it much more interesting.'

'I'm glad you like her,' said Pete.

'I've got a bit of homework to do, but Auntie Amanda is coming to our flat tonight, so I'll have to do it tomorrow,' Emma stated. 'Auntie Amanda and I are going to start to read The Adventures of Robin Hood. Miss Carter-Bone recommended it so I got it out of the school library.'

'Wow, I read that when I was at school, but I think I was older than you,' said Pete.

'Well you were a boy, so it would have taken you longer to be able to understand it anyway, but I'll have Auntie Amanda to help me with any words I don't understand.'

'I hope you enjoy it,' chuckled Pete.

'Emma, put your coat on, it is time to go home now,' said Sarah.

'I trust you will have a pleasant evening, Pete, but don't forget to have that shower before you pick mummy up, will you.'

-ooOoo-

'So would it be all right if Trudy and I bring Jack Bolton over for a look at the ballroom. He has got some ideas for lighting it and wants to look to see if his ideas are practical.'

'No problem, Justin,' said Derek. 'The contract cleaners have finished, although the plaster restorers will be working in there on the ceiling, but if you don't mind that, just tell me when you want to come.'

'Would Thursday morning be OK? It has to be a morning because Jack starts work at the theatre at about teatime each day.'

'Certainly. How does half past ten sound? I'll meet you there.'

-oo0Ooo-

Chapter 31

Sarah was nervous.

Tonight she was going to meet Pete's parents for the first time.

The plan was that they would go to Pete's parents house and then, leaving the van there and using their car, they would travel to Mario's for what for Sarah and Pete, was a second attempt to dine there.

Pete did not seem in the least perturbed by the prospect of this meeting, but for Sarah it had taken on a huge significance. How, she wondered, would they react to her. Would they like her, or were they already prejudiced against Pete hooking up with a pint sized ordinary looking girl with a ready-made family?

Emma came first in all of her thoughts, of course, and she could not for one moment resent her existence, but there was no getting around the fact that a woman with a child was not every parents favourite scenario when it came to imagining the ideal choices of partners for their sons.

Pete had prepared the ground carefully, he had assured her. They knew about Emma and had been told how well she and Pete got on. But, now the moment of meeting had arrived, Sarah imagined how easy it would be for parents to pay lip service, and pretend approval of the situation, while hoping it would resolve itself before they had to meet the woman in question.

Now that they were on their way to the meeting Sarah was becoming quite uncomfortable.

'Stop the van, Pete,' she cried, and throwing open the door she choked and was very nearly sick.

Pete was superbly sympathetic and allowed her to sit with the door open until the spasm had passed. He talked to her calmly, and attempted to reassure her that everything was going to be fine.

Having completely embarrassed herself, Sarah wanted to run and hide. In her shame, if she had her way she would have asked Pete to turn around and take her home, or got out and walked home to save him the bother.

Pete was lovely, he was wonderful, he was kind, considerate and charming, not to mention strong and handsome. How could she, a little squirt with baggage, be good enough for him. She wondered what he ever saw in her. Why was he bothering with her when he could do so much better, and to expect him to inflict her on his parents was too much.

And now she was crying, and that would muck up the make-up that Amanda had so kindly helped her with, when she arrived to baby-sit Emma.

She was being so unfair to everyone. She should never have allowed it to go this far, but now that it had, how on earth was she going to put it right?

-ooOoo-

Emma was having a great time.

Amanda had entered into the spirit of the inevitable teddy bears picnic and was happy to help with reading 'The Adventures of Robin Hood.'

When Emma's bedtime arrived, she dutifully brushed her hair, and told her a story she remembered from her childhood, as she nodded off to sleep.

Of course, just as she became absorbed in the complicated details of contracts with musicians and entertainers on her laptop, the inevitable little voice from the top of the stairs roused her, and she went to get Edward bear a glass of milk.

-ooOoo-

When she had recovered sufficiently, Pete had driven on, and stopped at a pub where he pretended to drink a Coke while Sarah went to the bathroom to repair her makeup.

She took a while, and they were already late for their table booking when they arrived at his parent's house. As a result, the relaxed hour they planned to spend getting to know each other was compressed into an uncomfortable couple of minutes while they changed cars and set off for Mario's.

Sarah was actually quite relieved about this turn of events as it shortened the awkward moments around the introduction to a minimum. But she was surprised that she was quickly comfortable in Pete's mother's company and the cuddly little woman opened the conversation in the most tactful way.

'How do you do, Sarah. Now, Pete tells me that you have been worried about meeting us, but apart from assuring you that we don't bite, can I just say that we really have been looking forward to meeting you. I don't think Pete has shut up about you for more than five minutes since he met you, and it is lovely to see him so happy. We want to thank you for that, and say we are truly delighted to meet you.'

After that, things became considerably easier for Sarah, and as they squashed into Pete's dad's little car, Pete started to explain what they could expect to find at Mario's, and all about Sarah's popular afternoon teas.

-oooOoo-

Chapter 32

'Did you have an accident?' asked Penelope, looking at Jack Bolton's electric wheelchair as he arrived in Reception with Derek and Justin.

'Penelope!' exclaimed Jane. 'I'm most awfully sorry, Mr ... er. My sister has a few little difficulties, and unfortunately no filter sometimes.'

'That's quite all right,' smiled Jack. 'Do you like bikes, Penelope?'

'Bicycles?'

'Motorbikes. I leaned mine on a wall once, that is why I'm in a wheelchair.'

'I don't understand,' said Penelope.

'I was doing a hundred and twenty miles an hour at the time, practicing for the Isle of Man TT race, you see.'

'I ... I ... Oh, I see. I'm very sorry about your accident ...'

'Unfortunately that was the end of my bike too,' said Jack, smiling.

'Er, it's through here,' said Derek, indicating the route to the ballroom. 'Amanda should have been here by now. No doubt she will be with us shortly.'

-ooOoo-

'Amanda is working towards March as the opening date,' said Justin.

'The plasterwork won't be finished until the end of January because, as you know, with it being Christmas Eve the day after tomorrow, construction work is about to shut down,' said Pete. 'And it won't get going again until the third of January next year.'

'So that gives us January and February to get the ballroom done and ready,' said Derek. 'Amanda hasn't set a fixed date in March yet, but we need to leave a bit of a contingency incase there are delays, so mid-March is looking favourite.'

'Fortunately,' said Jack, 'whilst the world of theatre is at its busiest over Christmas and the New Year, all our design and installation work is generally done by now, so other than a watching brief, incase anything goes wrong, this is actually a quiet time for us.'

'So you can get onto the job pretty soon then?' asked Justin.

'Certainly. We also don't allow ourselves the luxury of a break between Christmas and New Year, unlike you builders, so we can be working, on the technical design at least, very shortly,' smiled Jack.

'I wonder where Amanda is. She should have been here by now, and she will be able to discuss her plans much better than I can,' said Derek going to the window and glancing out at the car park.
'Can you get some heating for in here, Pete. It's freezing.'

'Well,' said Justin, 'Amanda and I have discussed the ideas we had with Jack in principle, which is why he is with us now. She will be here in a minute so she can add some detail, no doubt, but you see those chains and wires hanging from the roof, Jack? That is where the chandeliers were, which we would like to replicate.'

'Right,' said Jack. 'The plan is to mount the projectors and spotlights, as well as effect lighting in the bit of the chandeliers nearest the ceiling. I sent a sketch …'

'Yes, I saw that,' said Derek. 'Above all the frilly glass there is a bit shaped like a cone, going to a point at the top, which is where you will hide all that, isn't it?'

'That's right. As far as practical we will follow the shape and style of the original fittings, using the photos you sent over of what it was once like,' Jack was warming to his theme. 'There were six grand chandeliers apparently, and that should allow plenty of space to conceal all our kit and provide the effect we want.'

'Might it might be necessary to reinforce the ceiling up there where they are mounted to take the weight?' asked Pete.

'I shouldn't think so. Our electronics are actually remarkably light and the new lights will probably be much less heavy than the old lead crystal glass ones, depending on which design you choose from the options on the sketches we sent.'

'Ah, well on that point,' said Derek, 'we do need Amanda's input. She is not usually late for anything. If you will excuse me, I'm going to give her a ring to see what the hold up is.'

But Derek's call just went to the answering service.

He tried again with the same result twenty minutes later, when they had moved back into the Reception area to warm up a bit with a coffee.

'I must apologise again, Jack,' said Derek. 'I really can't think where she has got to.'

'Maybe she has been held up in traffic or something,' said Justin. 'It was very icy on the roads this morning and we got stuck behind a gritting truck on the way here.'

'Yes, that must be it,' said Derek, having got the

answering service for a third time.

-ooOOoo-

After Derek; Suzanne, Amanda's sister, and Dave were the first to arrive at the hospital.

As soon as Derek called, she had driven to Dave's site, picked him up, and rushed to the hospital.

Pete was not far behind and they were taking seats in the area leading to the Accident and Emergency department when Derek appeared at the other end of the corridor, walking unsteadily towards them. He was visibly upset.

'She … she has been sedated, and they have moved her to Intensive Care …'

Suzanne and Pete rushed to catch him as he tottered to the row of blue plastic seats and sat down heavily.

'The ambulance guy was still with her when I got here. He said that a lorry, an empty low-loader, jackknifed on the ice and her car went into the side of it. Two others crashed into it too. They are all in Intensive Care together.'

'How bad is she?' Dave put into words the question all of them wanted to ask.

-ooOOoo-

Chapter 33

Sarah was sitting beside Amanda's bed holding her hand when Justin arrived.

'Happy Christmas, Amanda,' he said, and deposited the substantial basket of fruit he had bought on the table beside the bed.

Amanda was gradually coming out of the sedation, and spoke a little quietly and slowly, but at least she was feeing no pain.

'Justin, how kind of you to come. I wasn't expecting to see you on Christmas Day of all days,' she said. 'And what a lovely basket of fruit, thank you.'

'It has turned out to be not quite the Christmas Day we were all anticipating, unfortunately. How are you feeling, Amanda?'

'Well, I'm a bit groggy and I still can't move my arms and legs, although I do find it comforting when someone holds my hand. That is odd because I can't actually feel anything, but it seems to relieve the constant tingling sensation a bit.'

'The initial x-rays show compression of the spine in her neck,' said Derek returning to the bedside with a cup of brown sludge which was apparently coffee. 'There is no break to the spine itself as far as they can see at the moment, and that means there is a good chance that she will recover full movement when everything calms down a bit after the initial trauma.'

'I'm not sure how much you have been told, Justin,' said Sarah, 'but Amanda also broke her arm, her ankle, and has several cracked ribs.'

'So much for air-bags,' smiled Amanda. 'Apparently, that lot, and some bruising was probably caused when they went off.'

'That is a pretty spectacular black eye, don't you think Justin? It is a good job you were driving a big strong four wheel drive, love, or the car could have been crushed in the impact and it might have been much worse. Mind you, I'm just so glad …' Derek choked back a tear and covered it with a cough.

'Ah, here comes Emma and Pete,' said Amanda. 'Did you find the cafe, sweetie?'

'Hello, Auntie Amanda,' Emma skipped to the bedside, and as she had been told, remembered to stop a pace away. 'It was boring. Can I hold your hand now? Mummy has had a long enough go.'

-ooo0oo-

Because it was Christmas Day the staff turned a blind eye to the number of visitors each patient could have, which was just as well, given the crowd gathering around Amanda's bed.

The plan, all being well, was to move Amanda across to the adjacent private hospital in a couple of days, when there was a full compliment of staff available. But nothing could happen until after the Christmas break.

For now however, she occupied an individual cubical in the Intensive Care Unit, connected up with tubes and wires to beeping machinery, and with a thin pipe feeding oxygen through her nose.

The little rooms on either side had initially been occupied by other victims of the crash, but the cubical to her right was now empty. Derek was told that the count had increased to two fatalities as a result of the crash, and he and Amanda counted their blessings.

-ooo0oo-

'Is she going to be paralysed and in a wheelchair like that man who came the other day?' asked Penelope.

'We don't know yet, and let's hope not. But you mustn't say anything like that in front of Derek or anyone else, Penelope.'

'Of course not. That would not be the right thing to say,' Penelope replied. 'Don't worry, I shan't be an embarrassment.'

'Thank you, Penelope,' said Jane. 'Now where do you think your brother has got to? Dinner is on the table.'

-ooOoo-

'Oooo! She squeezed my hand!' said Emma excitedly.'

'Did she?' said Sarah, 'Are you sure?'

Derek did not wait, he was running down the corridor looking for a nurse or a doctor to tell the news to.

Amanda was actually asleep when it happened, but Emma was adamant that it had, and that caused an eruption of medical staff who pushed her aside and started testing.

About ten minutes later, and now awoken by all the commotion, Amanda did it again.

-ooOoo-

Chapter 34

Although it was now the penultimate day of December, Pete's parents had invited Sarah and Emma over for a 'proper Christmas Dinner,' and now with the time at little after four in the afternoon, Pete was delivering them back to their flat.

'Come in for coffee, Pete,' said Sarah. 'Emma wants to show you her dolls house.'

'I'm glad you said that,' said Pete. 'But don't be too surprised if I doze off after that whacking great meal!'

The dolls house, a present from Amanda, had been delivered by Derek on Boxing Day, with an apology that Emma could not have had it on Christmas Day itself.

'I'm sleepy too,' said Emma. 'But I bet you will wake up once you see my dolls house and start playing with it. It's even got some furniture, though not much yet.'

A little later Emma was indeed asleep on the sofa, and Pete joined Sarah in the kitchen.

'That is a terrific dolls house, isn't it,' he said.

'Yes. It was incredibly generous of Amanda, although I did ask her just to get a little one,' Sarah put her arms around Pete. 'Oh I do hope she is going to be all right, Pete.'

'I know. We all do. But Amanda is strong and if anyone can beat this, she will.'

'Supposing she can't walk again, or not feel anything …'

'Now, it hasn't come to that, Sarah. You heard them say there are loads of tests to do yet, once the trauma has subsided. All we can do is be strong for her. And I'm going to make sure I continue to work really hard to deliver her dream at the ballroom and the catering college, so it is all there for her when she comes home.'

'Oh Pete, when I think how kind she has been to me and Emma, and Jenny, and … and everyone. She really is an amazing person. Poor Derek, he looked so lost and tired at the hospital …'

'Derek is being well looked after by Suzanne and Dave, and Carlos and Steve are taking it in turns to take meals round to him, so he has plenty of help.'

'I offered to do his washing, but Suzanne was already

on that, so I'm going to make him a big cake tomorrow and we can take it round there for him.'

'Normally, if you were making cakes, I would have asked if I could have one ... but after that meal ... phew!'

'I know what you mean. Your mum certainly does not believe in small portions, does she.'

'Sarah,' said Pete, clearing his throat, 'I've been meaning ...' He cleared his throat again. 'I was wanting to ask ...' A third little cough.

Sarah recognised the symptoms. Pete had something serious on his mind.

'Tell me, Pete. I'm not going to laugh or do anything horrible. It's all right ...'

'Oh Sarah. I'm so scared of chasing you away, if you think I am coming on too strong. Please don't run away, Sarah.'

'I'm not going anywhere, Pete. Now, tell me, whats on your mind.'

Pete drew a shuddering breath. Win or lose all, the time had come.

'Sarah,' he said. 'Would you and Emma like to move in with me at the cottage?'

-oo0Ooo-

'Thank you for showing it to me, Derek,' said Carlos.

'What are you going to do about it?'

Carlos handed the letter back and sat down on the arm of the sofa while Derek finished his lunch.

'Chesney Marriott told Amanda not to take their first offer, and to push for a bit more, although I have to say this seems very generous indeed. I had not realised that there was quite so much money in this telly business.'

'What about the timescale to get the catering college finished? Can it be done in time?'

'I need to talk to Pete about that. I don't want it affecting the building of the new houses behind the hotel, we have got two of those reserved already, but if we can get some more labour on the catering college side of things, I suppose we could speed it up.'

'What about the delivery of all the equipment, could that be a problem?'

'Well no. I have been holding that back a bit actually. The new equipment has all arrived at the supplier's warehouse and the refurbished stuff is nearly ready, apparently.'

'So do you think it is possible?'

'If I can get some more painters and decorators, find a plumbing firm to fit out the toilets and changing rooms, and speed up the installation of the sprinkler system, then yes, I think it could be done, so long as nothing goes wrong.'

'It would be wonderful to have it all up and running and the TV people bringing in all sorts of celebrities when Amanda comes home, wouldn't it.'

'Yes, Carlos. It would,' said Derek, wiping his eyes and blowing his nose.

'Would you like me to have an "off the record" conversation with Chesney about this offer to see if he thinks they might increase it a bit?'

'Would you mind, Carlos. What with one thing and another, I'm not really sure I'm up to ...'

'No problem, Derek. You leave all that to me. Now, have you finished that? I've got a rather special dessert for you that Steve made following an idea Sarah had ...'

-oooOoo-

'Well, if you take my sketches with you next time you go to see her, if you ask Amanda which of the chandelier designs she prefers, we can crack on with getting them built,' said Jack.

'I can do that certainly,' said Justin. 'I think if we can take a bit of the load off Derek while things are as they are that will help everyone, and it is not as though Amanda is in a coma or anything. She can still communicate.'

'Do give her my best regards,' said Jack. 'Believe me I really do know what she is going through at the moment. I only met her that once, at the theatre, but she did seem really switched on and I loved the concept of the fine dining and dancing club.'

'She is rather special, Jack, yes,' said Justin. 'I will be sure to pass on what you said.'

-oooOoo-

Another letter had arrived which Derek needed to read to Amanda.

This time it was from the University, confirming that they wanted to use the classroom facilities for two mornings a week in term time, and asking if they could discuss holding a dinner for pupils in the ballroom at some point.

Derek knew Amanda would be pleased with that, but when he got to the hospital he was dismayed to learn that she had been sedated again.

The reason, the senior nurse explained, was that in the night some feeling had obviously returned to her lower body, and she had shouted out in pain. Until this point the nerve damage had prevented her from having any real discomfort, but now that it was receding, Amanda was beginning to feel her injuries.

'I know it sounds cruel, but this is actually good news,' the nurse had said. 'Once the sedation wears off, we can start to manage her pain as she encounters it, and it demonstrates that the traumatised nerves are starting to react again.'

Whilst Derek saw the logic of that, he mourned in spirit at the thought that the woman he loved was in pain, and that there was more to come. He hoped she was strong enough to cope and that the nurses and doctors were able to quickly administer relief when it hit.

-oo0Ooo-

Chapter 35

'Yes,' said Pete, 'I see what you mean. I will get on to the fire protection people about the sprinkler system and see if I can speed it up.'

'What about the structural alterations to the cloakrooms and so on?' asked Derek.

'I was going to take some labour from the new houses to knock down a couple of walls where we need to make disabled access toilets, and then do the plastering …'

'No, I would rather you asked Dave to pop over and do that for you. I don't want anything to slow down the new build houses we have reservations on.'

'The new windows should arrive next week and the electricians start on Monday in the big classroom, so that bit is covered. But we need bathroom fitters. The old loos are functional, now that the new water tank is in, and the site operatives use them, but the plan to put in these huge disabled ones and alter the walls around to take them is going to disrupt all that.'

'And the idea is to bash through and pinch a bit of space from those two rooms either side of the central corridor to do that, isn't it?'

'Yes. We need about a metre and a half on each side and a new block-work wall putting up.'

'That sounds like a job Dave could do for you. I'll give him a call.'

'Then we need the plumbers. The original idea was to get temporary site toilets delivered near the end of the programme while that was going on, but we could bring that forward if you are prepared to live with the additional hire cost.'

'We can't have all these telly types using portable toilets. We will have to move the work to the changing rooms and toilets forward so it is done before they start.'

'Right-ho, I'll sort it out and let you have a revised programme.'

'Well done, Pete. Thanks for stepping up with all this.'

'No problem, Derek. I'm enjoying it. But there are two things I need to ask you.'

'Go on?'

'Well, firstly if the big extrusion machine is out of the workshop now, I had an idea to make some window boxes to hang on the front of the college to grow fresh herbs in, and break up that rather grim wall. I'll do it on my own time, of course, and I'll use wood from those old uncomfortable looking benches in the classroom behind the office, if you approve.'

'That is a lovely idea, Pete. When the new windows go in it will look better, but that will really improve the look of that side of the building. Don't feel you have to do it on your own time …'

'Oh, but I want to. It is my sort of "welcome home" surprise for Amanda …'

'That is a very kind thought Pete. But didn't you say there were two things?'

'Ah, well. Yes.' Pete started to clear his throat. 'I … I. Well, the thing is …'

'Yes?'

'Erm … Derek … Would you mind if Sarah and Emma moved in with me in the caretaker's house?'

'Well, that is wonderful news! Of course I wouldn't mind, and Amanda will be delighted! Congratulations.'

'You don't mind? Fantastic. Thank you very much indeed Derek.'

Derek was chuckling as he shook Pete's hand.

'Oh, and Sarah says you can rent out her flat to new people, of course, but she will continue to pay you the same rent, if that is OK.'

'No need Pete. If I can let her flat, I'm no worse off, and I promised you the caretaker's cottage rent free for two years, so it makes no difference to me if Sarah and Emma move in. Perhaps you can use the rent money to save up a deposit for a place of your own!'

-ooOoo-

The architect confirmed by email that the Planning and Building Regulations permissions had arrived for the replacement link between the catering school and the hotel.

Derek was on the phone to Pete, explaining that the final drawings were waiting for him in the office.

'Personally, I don't like it,' he said. 'It is like big blue glass pointy conservatory in the middle with bits of flat roof behind a parapet at either end.'

'I know, Sarah and I saw the sketches in the office. Sarah thought it would make quite an imposing entrance from the carpark, although I am surprised the Planners went for that, tacked on to a Listed Building.'

'Well, apparently even the Conservation Officer

liked it, so who are we to argue with that! It is what the architect called "a statement", apparently. The blue glass bit is going to be made by a company the architect knows and will be installed, by them, when you get the walls up.'

'I don't mean to complain, Derek, but I'm struggling for labour as it is with the new faster programme …'

'Oh, that's all right, I'm sending Dave and a couple of his brickies over to sort it out. It uses the same foundation pad, so it shouldn't take too long to do.'

'Thank you. That is a great relief.'

'Yes, but there was one thing. I was going to ask you if you could build a sort of reception desk to fit in there, and also if you would oversee the fitting of two sets of automatic opening internal doors at either end of the corridor. The architect will organise getting them made.'

'Automatic opening doors?'

'Yes, it is so hot food trollies and waiting staff can move easily between the classrooms and the ballroom.'

'I see. Right. I will pick those plans up later. Will there be a set for Dave as well?'

'Ah, good point. There will be as soon as I've got some copied for him!'

SARAH'S KITCHEN

-ooOoo-

Chapter 36

Emma had been overjoyed when Sarah asked her how she would feel about moving into what they now referred to as the 'caretaker's cottage' on the Barclay Woods estate.

She came up with a long list of advantages of such a move and finished by announcing,
'And I shall be able to walk round to see Auntie Amanda and help her with stuff after school.'

'You realise,' said Sarah, when she was alone with Pete, 'that my decision to move in with you did rest on what Emma had to say.'

'Yes, but I think what may have swung it was when I offered to decorate her bedroom however she wanted.'

'I don't care if she wants it decorated in pink polkadots, so long as we can be together, Pete,' said Sarah, nestling in his arms. 'Provided, that is, that there is no wallpaper or anything else featuring hares!'

'No hares? Oh dear, that's torn it,' smiled Pete. 'I was hoping to use up some of the stuff left over from the cafe ...'

'Just you dare!' said Sarah, giving him a playful push in the chest.

-oooOoo-

'So that's it,' said Carlos, 'I checked with Chesney first and he went to speak to Andrew Smallpond about it. They reckon the five percent I talked them up is about as far as the Network will go, and said if we wanted to do it, you should accept this latest offer.'

'Well done Carlos, please tell Chesney we accept,' said Derek. 'Although between ourselves, I would have been quite happy to accept their first offer, but your bit of negotiation does more or less cover the cost of speeding up the building works, so I'm very grateful.'

'Andrew Smallpond wants to come over next week with what he calls his "team" to make a start on the walled garden, if you agree.'

'That's fine by me. Don't forget to tell Pete. That is right outside his front door after all.'

'And Sarah's front door shortly, I hear.'

'Yes, I think it is great news, and so does Amanda.'

'I couldn't agree more, they make a lovely couple, and Emma is going to be happier with a garden to play in.'

'Carlos, I hope you can forgive me, but when the accident happened Amanda and I were preparing these, and I've only just finished them off.'

Derek handed Carlos a little pile of envelopes, each individually addressed to a member of staff at one of the 'Amanda's' restaurants or those who worked at Mario's.

'Would you mind handing them round. I hope I haven't missed anyone off, and please tell them I am really sorry that they didn't get this in time for Christmas.'

'What's this?' asked Carlos.

'There is one there for you to, of course. It is a Christmas bonus.'

-ooo0oo-

Amanda looked pale and tired, and although the bruises on her face were beginning to recede, she was not looking as well as the last time they had seen her.

Emma dashed up, stopped dead half a pace from the bed, and asked if she could hold her hand.

'I would like that,' croaked Amanda.

'How are you feeling?' asked Sarah as the child sat down and gently took her hand.

'Oh, not too bad,' said Amanda, with a wan smile. 'Let me show you something, Emma,' and with that she moved her fingers and gripped her hand.

'That's fantastic Auntie Amanda! Well done.'

'I've only been able to do that since this morning, after the physiotherapist worked on me,' smiled Amanda. 'It is not much, but at least it is a bit of progress.'

'That is terrific,' said Pete, 'and I couldn't help noticing that some of the tubes and things have gone.'

'That is a bit of an experiment, actually, to see if I have some control …'

'Ah, sorry. I didn't mean to embarrass you …'

'Don't worry, they remove your dignity before they hand you the hospital gown in here. I'm not in the least embarrassed.'

Amanda winked at Pete.

'Emma. If you run the tip of your finger round the palm of my hand I might be able to feel it. Would you like to give it a try?'

-oo0Ooo-

Chapter 37

The move to the adjacent private hospital, a few days later, went without a hitch.

Although Amanda was still connected up to some of the machines that were initially deployed in the Intensive Care Unit, she had regained enough control of her body to give her medics confidence that she was ready.

She could now move both her feet, as far as the cast on one of her ankles would allow, and was rapidly re-gaining control of her hands and arms. To her delight and relief, the daily physiotherapy she received was obviously working.

'Well, I can't say it is comfortable, honey, and it is certainly hard work, but there is no denying the progress,' she told Derek in answer to his concerned enquiries. 'I shall be dancing by the time the ballroom opens, just you wait and see.'

'Ah, well I wanted to talk to you about that, if you are

up to it. I've bought some swatches for the ballroom wallpaper proposals which Pete has mounted on a bit of board so I can hold them over your head to look at.'

'Pete is very thoughtful, isn't he,' Amanda smiled. 'We are very lucky to have such a great bunch of people behind us.'

'I've handed out all the bonus letters we were working on by the way, so they should know how much we appreciate them by now.'

'Oh, I confess I had forgotten that we had not finished those before …'

'Yes, well. It is all done now,' said Derek, who did not like to be reminded of the actual accident.

-oo0Ooo-

They decided that Sarah and Emma would not move in until the end of the month, which would give them time to get Emma's bedroom prepared.

Sarah insisted that she would help with the decorating, 'At least as high as I can reach,' she added.

'Well that is the skirting boards dealt with,' teased Pete.

Emma had also decided that the little nursery bedroom would become her playroom, with the imposing dolls house taking centre stage, and with a shrug Pete had agreed.

'I was going to make that into a gym with a treadmill and a cross-trainer,' said Pete. 'But I guess I can still go for a run around the estate instead.'

'Oh dear,' said Sarah. 'I will tell Emma that she can't ...'

'Yes she can, Sarah. She can have anything in the world she wants so long as I can have you.'

'All right, it's a deal,' smirked Sarah. 'I wonder if she would like a pony, or perhaps two ...'

'Within reason, I was going to add!' laughed Pete. 'Besides, ponies might eat Andrew Smallpond's vegetables and fruit in the walled garden, and that would never do!'

-ooo0oo-

This time, now that the nurses had sat her up slightly, and changed her neck brace for a more appropriate item, Derek was able to hold Amanda's iPad where she could see it.

'So these are the documents forming part of the public consultation on the Waitrose site,' he explained.

There was just a narrow road and the original graffiti covered factory wall separating the flats and the six shops, which they already owned, from the former agricultural machinery site. The plans, and particularly the newly proposed central "village green and swing park" would mean Albany Development's shops and offices would form the fourth side of a broad square. With the Waitrose store on one side, and on the other a new development of shops with flats above, it promised to improve the area no end.

Amanda commented that, as it included some more shops, she was glad that the Mad Hatters Tea Shop was already set up and running, as that would put off similar competing outlets from taking any of the shops.

Derek said he supposed they would have to tender to purchase the land to build the shops and flats like everyone else, but if they did and they won, and got to buy the site and build it out, it would at least enable them to control who leased the shops, to avoid direct competition with their cafe.

'Why don't you talk to the Frobishers, or Henry perhaps, and see if we can buy the site for the shops and flats without having to compete for it in an open tender. Then we could jointly develop it with them, using the company we formed with the Frobishers when we bought our interest in the hotel and college? After all, they own the land, don't they?' asked Amanda.

'A joint venture, you mean? Spot on,' said Derek. 'I shall do that as soon as I get home.'

Amanda agreed that the future looked bright for them if the public consultation was successful.

'It will make it very similar to the regeneration scheme I went to see on the other side of the river that the Council were keen to emulate. That looks pretty good, and so could this,' she said. 'I think you should write in offering our support. Goodness knows if they will take any notice, but we are neighbours of the scheme, holding several properties and a business there, so you never know.'

'I'll get the architect to word something up using the sort of befuddling language Town Hall Planners use, so they might take it more seriously,' said Derek.

-oo0Ooo-

Derek had agreed to meet Justin and Trudy at the big soulless pub on the corner, by the entrance to the hospital, before they went in to see Amanda.

'All the templates are done for the invitations and the brochure about membership is ready to go to the printers. All you need to do is agree the mailing list and I can press the button,' said Justin.

'And I've been a busy little bee too, Derek. I ain't stopped, have I Justin?'

'No love. I must admit I had no idea you knew so many people.'

'Well, some of them's stage door Johnnies, posh

blokes what hang about theatres trying to chat up the dancers, or the chorus girls or boys, according to taste. Some of them might be good for investing in membership ...'

'There is even a Lord amongst Trudy's list,' Justin pointed out.

'And three Rt. Hons, two Sirs, seven MPs and an Archdeacon.'

'Blimey,' said Derek.

'But shelving that for a moment, it's the list of acts what I'm most interested to hear what you think of,' Trudy handed Derek a type written list running to two pages, 'Here, cop and eyeful of this lot.'

'Do you actually know all these people?' Derek asked.

''Corse, or the ones on the second page, like, I know their Agents.'

'There are some big names on here,' said Derek, scanning the list.

'When you have been a hoofer as long as I have, round the West End, like, you do pick up a few names.'

'Yes,' said Justin, stretching out the word, and scowling. 'But going back to the list of potential members, we have had to have a discussion about how many of these you dated, were engaged to, or had to get injunctions against, back in the day.'

'He's exaggerating, Derek. Don't take no notice. I was only sort of unofficially engaged to one of them and the injunction was a mis-understanding caused by his wife turning up.'

Chapter 38

It was decided to put Andrew Smallpond in the best suite in due deference to his status, both as a TV personality and a Director of the Network company commissioning the cookery and gardening series.

Consequently it was a surprise when Jane encountered him at the reception desk in a dressing gown.

'There is somebody in my bath,' he informed her. 'And he is singing ribald songs at the top of his voice.'

'Oh Lordy! Uncle Frederick!' said Jeremy, who was standing nearby. 'Penelope was supposed to be keeping an eye on him in our apartment …'

While Jane made apologies, took the famous gardener to another room for his bath and tried to explain away the situation and her elderly relative's 'forgetfulness', Jeremy streaked up the stairs, eschewing the slow lift, and confronted his uncle as he splashed about happily in the bathtub.

-ooOoo-

In the main classroom, the electricians had arrived and were installing the complicated trunking and conduits, occasionally in accordance with the architect's drawings, while calling to each other and sharing jokes.

Above their heads, on the scaffolding, men in clean blue overalls worked to install the shiny machinery that would become the heat recovery, extraction and air conditioning system. They worked silently and efficiently and Pete felt watching them was like watching a carefully choreographed dance.

Their actions were in sharp contrast to the window fitters who, expected to work around the electricians, were annoying them and causing some friction as they ripped out the old wooden windows and pumped evil smelling caulk into cavities.

But, by the end of the third day, the building was watertight and even becoming gradually warmer, as the heating engineers commissioned their installation.

Having all these contractors working on the project at the same time, in the compressed sequence of works, was bound to be difficult. But by starting at seven each morning to be ready to organise the trades, and finishing on his own at around ten at night by pushing a broom around to keep the working area clear, Pete managed to soothe frayed tempers and keep the disparate teams of workers from each other's throats.

Fortunately the new build site was much less intense. The team working there were mostly the original tradesmen Derek had gathered about him years ago, and could be trusted to run the job pretty much on their own. A visit from Lauren, the Building Inspector, passed without incident and only the late arrival of a delivery of bricks upset the steady progress being made. The only cloud on this particular horizon was with the window manufacturers who kept pushing back the date they would be able to deliver their products. Pete and Dave were used to problems of this nature and Dave pointed out that as far back as he could remember it was always the windows that disrupted the programme.

Pete took occasional trips to the ballroom where he observed, with some respect, the artistry of the restorers working on the ornate ceiling. When they finished for the day, he took a moment to cut and remove sections of the carpet and deposit them in the almost full skips outside the tall glazed doors. He was ready for the next specialist company, engaged to restore the dance floor, when they arrived.

He had no time to start on the decoration of Emma's bedroom, and remembering only to send Sarah his love by text before he slept, he fell into bed exhausted each night.

-ooOoo-

Running two building sites was also stretching Dave, and as a 'hands-on' tradesman, he found working outside to build the link between the two buildings in the constant drizzle a distraction.

He enjoyed relieving his frustrations by knocking down the walls in the two cloakrooms and then building them up again in rough blocks in their new positions inside the buildings. But, having allowed himself that luxury, he returned to his own site and left his 'borrowed' team of bricklayers to get on with building what would become the entrance to the college, and the link to the hotel.

He would return to oversee the fixing of the odd blue glass structure in the middle of the link, and to make sure the plasterers knew what was expected of them when the structure was finished. But beyond that, with a substantial site of his own to run, however much he wanted to help Pete out, he had little time to spend on the project.

-ooOoo-

Now that the swelling had reduced, the x-rays showed a fracture in Amanda's neck.

There was an improvement in her ability to feel touch, and the tingling sensation had mostly been replaced by a dull ache across most of her battered body.

The clever hospital technicians had constructed a substantial cast using very precise measurements that fitted from the hard collar, she wore to hold her neck still as the bones slowly knitted up, to her hips, and the whole contraption was strapped tightly into place.

The therapists arrived with some mechanical engineers who, as she watched in some trepidation, built a trapeze like structure with wheels, winches and pulleys in front of her.

When it was done they wheeled the contraption over the bed and attached steel cables to hooks set into the moulded plastic and metal cast she wore.

Then as gently as they could, they winched Amanda into an odd leaning standing position with her feet slightly off the ground. This enabled the therapists to work on the muscles in her legs, her hips, and her feet. The plan was to gradually lower her to enable her to take her weight on her legs. It was agony, and it was going to be repeated each day until further notice.

On the first day she cried out in pain. On the second day she just cried, but by the end of the third day she managed to move her knees and the ankle unencumbered by the cast, and using the gravity defying frame she managed to move her hips and clench her buttocks. That made her laugh out loud.

Then it was time to take her for an MRI scan and the results contained a discovery which none of the staff expected and came as a complete surprise to everyone involved.

Amanda was pregnant.

-ooOoo-

Chapter 39

'And as I opened the envelope, I thought O.M.G!' said Sarah. 'When Amanda said something about a Christmas bonus, I certainly wasn't expecting a rise in salary as well!'

'I got one too,' said Pete. 'With no rent to pay when you move in, we are going to be able to save up some money. That is going to be something of a novelty.'

'It certainly will be for me,' said Sarah, pulling a face. 'I have spent so long scraping along, wondering if I can find the money for even the most basic things, like a new pair of school shoes for Emma, that this is going to be amazing.'

'New shoes?' said Emma, joining them in the kitchen. 'Are we going shopping for some new shoes for me?'

Pete and Sarah exchanged glances.

'Yes,' they both said together.

'Why not!' added Sarah.

-ooOOoo-

Amanda was actually sitting up in bed when Derek arrived.

'Of course I still need that thick strap attached to the hoist to stop myself falling over sideways, but I have to say it makes a very pleasant change to be upright. I feel much more human and part of it like this.'

Earlier the hospital's hairdresser had been round and washed her hair, and when they got chatting she admitted that she had previously been a make-up artist, so Amanda had talked her into applying a little eye liner and some mascara.

'You look fabulous, darling!' exclaimed Derek. 'How was this even possible?'

'Fast talking and playing on the sympathy factor,' giggled Amanda. 'Now, sit down, Derek. I've got something to tell you.'

-ooOOoo-

Sunday mornings were normally quiet on building sites, so Pete allowed himself a couple of hours to take Sarah and Emma to buy some new shoes in the big shopping centre on the main London Road.

Shopping complete, he bought them a pizza for lunch, and as they sat digesting it, while Emma investigated the ice-cream machine, he confided in Sarah that he had never been shoe shopping with a child before.

'What I can't get over is how many shops we had to go into. I didn't even know there were that many shoe shops. And then to come right back to the beginning and buy the very first pair she tried on ... well, honestly.'

'You have a lot to learn about female shopping habits, young man,' said Sarah. 'You should see me shopping for a new blouse.'

'Mummy is naughty,' said Emma from behind the vast dripping cone she was carrying to the table. 'Because she is little and they fit, she sometimes buys children's clothes so she doesn't have to pay the Government their tax.'

'Guilty, as charged, your honour,' Sarah smiled. 'Being on the shrivelled side of petite, I can indeed get into children's sizes, and there is no VAT on them. Helped me save quite a bit, that has.'

'Now that she has had this massive pay rise, I'm rather hoping Mummy will mend her ways and stay on the right side of the law in future, Pete,' Emma nodded sagely. 'I can't tell you the number of sleepless nights I have spent, worrying that the Police will come knocking on the door at any moment! Miss Carter-Bone says we must always strive to set a good example, you know, and I don't think her buying clothes meant for children did that, do you?'

-ooOoo-

On Monday morning, at last, the sprinkler system was being installed. Pete had had to have several quite angry conversations with the company involved to get them to commit to a date, and he was relieved that it was finally happening. He was expecting the plumbers to finish shortly and he did not want the painters and tilers to be held up by anything, especially as he had borrowed three teams from Dave, so that four teams would be working simultaneously on the hotel project overall.

Pete had to co-ordinate the floor sanding in the ballroom with the redecoration, of course. The industrial sanding machines the specialists unloaded from their van would create some dust inevitably and that would further delay painting.

It was fortunate that the dance floor in the ballroom could be restored. Laying a completely new sprung floor would have been prohibitively expensive. The experts they had engaged to inspect it found that it was certainly in need of work to bring the surface back to its former glory, but that it had been replaced within the last twenty-five or thirty years, so amazingly still met the current standards.

Shortly before they found out about that, Derek had learned the cost of the special reflective metallic wallpaper. Has it not been for the good news about the floor, the projections for the cost of the ballroom project would have been spiralling out of control.

-ooOOoo-

'And I don't think you are on the "shrivelled side of petite" as you said, Sarah. I think you are like a perfect little fairy, and I adore everything about you.'

'Yes, well,' said Sarah, embarrassed. 'Do you want brown or tomato sauce on your bacon roll.'

Before she could get a reply, Derek burst through the cafe door.

'Amanda is pregnant!' he beamed at the bemused looking customers.

'My goodness!' said Pete.

'Well, that's a surprise!' said Sarah.

-ooOOoo-

Chapter 40

The decorators and tilers had started now, in what was originally a separate bakery.

This room had deep windows looking out over the gardens and the carpark beyond, and shared the high open roof of the main building. It was destined to become Sarah's patisserie, where she would prepare her teas for each of the restaurants. The plan was to train up a specialist assistant to help her in this room in the fullness of time, and then to offer students who expressed an interest, the opportunity to learn how patisserie was created.

Most of the original kitchen units had been removed now, and it awaited the arrival of the stainless steel equipment currently used in the development kitchen at the cafe, along with some new ovens and various accessories, such as a floor mounted dough mixer, chillers, and gadgets to make the production of the delicate cakes and fancies easier, and keep them fresh.

This part of the operation would depend on precision timing when the room was ready. The plan was for Sarah to use part of the main kitchen if it was ready, or even her own kitchen in her flat if not, for a day or two while the existing equipment was transferred. The aim was to maintain the flow of production for the teas, and it was going to take some management.

From Pete's point of view the sooner he could get the new bakery section up and running, so that Sarah could stop using her own kitchen and move into the cottage with him, the better. But that private agenda was not going to be easy to achieve. Apart from anything else they had not even started decorating Emma's new bedroom yet, and Emma, having been made promises, would expect it to be done before she moved in.

-oooOoo-

Derek called a meeting in the office and invited Sarah, Carlos, Mario, Pete and Dave to attend.

Since the news of Amanda's pregnancy broke, followed by confirmation that the baby was fine, and as far as they could tell had not suffered any ill effects from the car crash, Derek had been like a man possessed.

He had something to plan for, and he was determined to be fully prepared.

'Right,' he said now, as everyone took their seats in the meeting room, 'we need to make sure we are ready.'

Rising now, he turned over the cover of a flip chart to reveal a blank new page and took the lid off a felt-tip pen.

'I'm going to need some help from you guys to make this right and I hope I can rely on you to step up,' he began.

There was a catch in his voice as he continued.

'I had a meeting yesterday with Amanda's consultant and we now know …' Derek removed his handkerchief from his pocket and blew his nose. 'We now know that it is possible, in the worst case scenario, that Amanda might need to use a wheelchair.'

Sarah should have stifled the little gasp that escaped her, but Derek heard it and addressed his next remarks to her.

'That is, as I said, the worst case scenario, the very worst case scenario. We all hope she will be able to walk again, of course, and her progress to get back the use of her lower limbs is looking very encouraging, so it might not come to that.' Derek blew his nose once again.

'Look,' he said now, nodding to Dave, 'apart from ties

of blood, I'd like to think that you guys are all our friends, rather than just our employees and I want to level with you.'

Derek went on to explain that Albany Developments and all its diversifications had become a busy and successful business, but that it was at a crucial point in its growth which could see it really blossom or begin to decline.

With a baby to look after, and especially if she had to cope with mobility problems, the amount of time Amanda would be able to give to the business was bound to reduce, he said.

'She won't want to give up any of it and would hate to hear me suggesting anything of the sort, so this is all absolutely between us. But I would like you to help me to plan for that eventuality.'

He turned towards the flip-chart and wrote "Mobility" at the top of the page.

'First, can we have a think about what we need to do to the house, the office and the rest of the business premises to make sure they are fully, seamlessly and easily wheelchair accessible. Who wants to go first?'

-oo0Ooo-

'Well Jack,' said Derek. 'I think one of the best suggestions was to ask you, as an experienced wheelchair user what we might need to do, and what barriers you face.'

'Of course, I will be happy to help,' said Jack, turning his wheelchair slightly to face the large screen he had linked to his mobile phone and used to project Zoom or FaceTime conversations into his office.

'Perhaps we could start,' he said, 'with perceptions …'

-ooOoo-

Pete and Dave met at Derek's house and let themselves in.

'First up, we'll need to make a ramp to this front door,' said Dave.

'Yes, and bearing in mind what Derek said about making the adaptations seamless and as invisible as possible, it should be easy here because the path and the drive are done in block pavers. So we can just build the path up a bit at a gentle slope underneath and then put the pavers back.'

'I've downloaded the requirements for slopes and ramps and all that so I know the angle we need to achieve, and as you say it will be easy on this door. But how are we going to do it on the big patio doors leading to the deck, round the back?'

-ooOoo-

Emma stirred the paint very carefully this time, she didn't want to risk getting any more on her clothes after her mother had snapped at her.

Sarah and Emma had borrowed a key to the cottage, and straight after school took a taxi there, and started decorating.

'That taxi man was smelly,' announced Emma. 'I'm glad Pete will be taking us home in his truck.'

'He was a bit, wasn't he,' said Sarah. 'And expensive too. But we won't have to do that, or go on the bus again very soon, because Derek is going to buy a little people carrier thing for us to use.'

'I thought you said he was going to lease it?' said Emma, who liked to get these things right.

'Well, yes. Lease it then, if you like.'

'And is it going to say "Sarah's Kitchen" on the side?'

'Yes, unfortunately.'

'Well I think it is terrific and I hope you will come and pick me up from school in it sometimes, so I can show everyone there.'

'I might pick you up if it is raining,' chuckled Sarah. 'But right now we need to get this painting done, or we will never be ready to move in here.'

-oooOoo-

Chapter 41

What drew his eye to it, he could not say, but when Sarah came down to the kitchen to wash out her paint brushes, she saw Pete on his hands and knees in the dining room, examining the bottom of the french doors.

'This door is obviously a replacement,' he said. 'The threshold is almost level with the floor so a disabled person could get in and out easily this way.'

'I wondered what you were doing down there!' said Sarah.

But Pete, still on his hands and knees, was on his phone to Dave.

-ooo0oo-

'I've had the story from Jeremy Frobisher,' said Derek. 'When he was just a boy, the caretaker who lived in that house had a wife with only one leg. She used to have to go round the back to get in through those french doors, Jeremy told me. He didn't know anything about the doors, but Dave asked the bloke from the housing association up at his site and apparently french doors with level thresholds are widely available. It probably means we will have to change one of the big sliding patio doors on the lounge for something like that.'

'If it ever comes to it, Derek,' said Pete. 'We don't know yet, and with any luck we won't have to do anything.'

'Let's hope not. By the way, I think what you said about turning the snooker room into a bedroom and poking in a bathroom to include the cloakroom under the stairs is a dreadful idea,' said Derek. 'But I have to admit it could work if we really need a ground floor bedroom.'

'Sorry Derek,' said Pete. 'But it is either that or sell up and build a bungalow, if you can find a plot.'

'I hate bungalows,' said Derek. 'Too land hungry. You can get two or even three houses on the land a bungalow takes up. Did I ever tell you there was a huge bungalow, that some old dowager from the original Barclay Court family lived in, where our house is now. When she died and they knocked it down, they built ours and the one next door on the land, and you are not allowed to build more than two houses per acre up on our estate, so it must have sat on over an acre.'

'Very grand, up there, isn't it. I sometimes jog round

the estate looking at all the big houses in the evenings.'

'You mind you don't get stopped by the estate's security people, they are always on the look out for loiterers!'

-oo0Ooo-

'Derek? It's Justin.'

'Hello Justin.'

'How is Amanda?'

'Improving slowly, I think, Justin.'

'Great, give her our best. Now then, you know we did that flyer drop on Trudy's A1 prospects ...'

'I beg your pardon?'

'Sorry. We sent out leaflets and emails about the dining and dancing club to some of the people on Trudy's list of contacts ...'

'Oh yes. How did it go.'

'The response we got was amazing. You can usually only count on about a two to five percent click through rate on unsolicited but targeted mailings ...'

'Sorry?'

'Er, the response rate is usually poor ... but we got several really good expressions of interest and even requests to see the prospectus ... the details of how to join I mean, from just the first trawl, er, mail out.'

'I see. And this is good, is it?'

'Good? It's unheard of! We got over forty serious expressions of interest and loads of people asking for a brochure!'

'Oh! That *is* good! I'll tell Amanda.'

'Please do. And that's only the qualified A1's ... I mean the most likely people. We hit, I mean contact, the next group tomorrow.'

'Thank you, Justin ...'

'And you wait until we can start advertising. I think we will be up to Amanda's target two hundred members level in no time!'

-ooOOoo-

'Excuse me. Sorry to trouble you. I'm looking for someone called Sarah.'

The shiny suited individual standing by the cafe door smiled winningly.

'And you have found her,' said Sarah.

'Great. I'm Darren Teasdale,' he said producing a business card like a conjurer from the recesses of his costume. 'I'm from the Vauxhall dealership. I believe you are expecting me ...'

'Ah, yes,' said Sarah. She had been looking forward to

this.

'I heard,' said Jenny returning from the kitchen and waving aside an explanation. 'You get off and mind you don't bump this gentleman's nice new car.'

'Great,' said Darren. 'If you don't mind, before we head off, I need to get you to sign the insurance forms and so on …'

That done, Sarah reached for her coat.

'Great,' said Darren. 'I've bought our Vauxhall Combo demonstrator over for you to try. It does have a few more extras than the one you have been enquiring about, and it is the next model up in terms of trim, but it is the same engine and body so not many differences, really.'

'Right-ho,' said Sarah, who couldn't have cared less which model it was so long as the wheels went round.

'Great,' said Darren. 'Shall we get off then?'

'Great,' said Sarah.

Chapter 42

The sanding operation did not take long at all. It was very noisy, and Pete made a point of apologising to the Frobishers while the operatives were working, but at least it was soon done.

The special treatment they put on the wood removed any residue of dust, and then, wearing masks and goggles they started spreading the sealant over the top, and suggested that Pete should leave and return in about two hours when it was done to sign off their paperwork.

'If you can keep everyone out of here for twenty four hours until it has fully cured, that would be best,' announced the team leader. 'The smell will subside, and in about a week you won't notice it any more.'

For Pete the all pervading and very strong smell reminded him of fish, but Jeremy Frobisher had a much ruder description as he firmly locked the ballroom door and hung a 'no entry' sign on the handle.

-ooOOoo-

'And we have got another reservation on one of the Barclay Court new houses,' said Derek.

'Well, by the sounds of things you don't need me at all, Derek. It is all going brilliantly.'

'Oh Amanda,' said Derek. 'I need you more than I can say. I miss you so much. I … I'm sorry. I shouldn't have said that …'

'That was a lovely thing to say, and it is how I feel too. But you know what the Consultant said, we have to remain strong for each other and not wallow in sentiment.'

'I'm not sure she said that bit about wallowing in sentiment, Amanda.'

'Well, maybe not, but sometimes I could do with a good wallow … and a glass of wine!'

-ooOOoo-

Fortunately, Pete had already painted the ceiling, and when he got back to the cottage he found Sarah standing on the top of a short set of steps trying to apply a self-adhesive paper frieze to the area at the top of the walls in what would become Emma's room.

'Hello,' he said. 'I didn't expect to find you here.'

'Dave gave me a lift over and Jenny is giving Emma tea. I hope you don't mind, but you did give me a key, and I've got to get this awful stuff done.'

Even standing precariously on tiptoes on the top bar of the little set of steps, Sarah could only just reach and Pete wound his arms around her and lifted down to the floor.

'You are not supposed to stand right on the top like that, you could have fallen off. That was dangerous.'

'Well, pardon me, tough-guy!' said Sarah. 'I may look like a delicate fairy to you, but I'm as tough as old boots, you know. I would probably just bounce, if I fell off.'

'But I would rather not find a beautiful broken fairy lying on the floorboards when I return home tired from my labours, if you don't mind. I have quite enough to do without having to bury any dead fairies in the garden, thank you.'

'Oh yeah? And where would you like to find a fairy then, plonking this horrible sticky paper thing half way up the walls?'

'Leave it. I'll do it in a minute. I'll show you where I would like to find my favourite fairy ...'

And with that he picked Sarah up as if she was weightless, and carried her into the biggest bedroom.'

'Oh you big strong brute! Help, help!' whispered Sarah.

-ooo0oo-

'So, now the bosses have been over for a look and Derek has sent the documents back signed, Andrew would like to send his gardening contractors in to start the work,' said Chesney. 'If possible they will stay four days, so that is three nights in the hotel. Andrew was quite concerned to ask you to ensure that old Mr Frederick Frobisher was either back in his care home or firmly under control in the family's apartments. He was quite amused to find him in his bath, but maybe once is enough.'

Carlos laughed as he promised to ask for assurances from the Frobishers about their Uncle Frederick.

'How many of them will there be, Chesney?' he asked.

'There are nine coming, as far as I understand. Andrew is not coming himself, it's just his contractors; and before I forget, they will have a low-loader full of mini-diggers, and that sort of thing, that they want to park up safely, if you can arrange that.'

'I will just check that they have the space in the hotel, but I'm sure it won't be a problem,' said Carlos. 'The hotel can provide bed and breakfast, but do you think they would like dinner at one of our restaurants, and how about we make up some picnic lunches for them, to keep them going?'

'I'll ask Andrew about that and let you know. Now then, on the Friday, I would like to come down briefly and see how they have been getting on, and I wondered if I can come with a cameraman, and watch you cook a meal for me. Call it a screen test if you like. I would also like to have a meeting with Amanda if possible about the filming dates, please ...'

'That is very exciting Chesney, and thank you very much,' said Carlos. 'But there is something I need to tell you about Amanda.'

-oo0Ooo-

Chapter 43

Amanda was bored.

Normally such an industrious person, now with only a view of the carpark, diverting though that might be at times, and the hospital TV to distract her, she was becoming frustrated.

The television had been thoughtfully adjusted on its bracket so that she could comfortably see it from her bed, and now that she could operate the remote control, positioned by her hand, the hospital orderlies felt they had done enough. However, no amount of button pressing could convince the TV to show any more than three channels, one of which seemed to only show French soap-operas through a snow-screen.

The antics of those coming or going in the carpark was mildly more amusing, on occasions at least. So far, she had witnessed one minor collision, an exchange of paint between two vast luxurious four wheel drives, and a row between two drivers who wanted the same parking space. But that was it for entertainment.

Now that she had more control of her arm and her fingers she had hoped to convince the nurses to let her use her mobile phone. But when it was retrieved from her handbag, it was discovered that the batteries were flat, and until Derek remembered to bring her charger from home she was unable to use it.

Amanda's frustration had reached a peak when Derek visited yesterday and had to admit that he had forgotten to bring the charger, and sharp words had been exchanged.

At least she had her exercises to do. The physiotherapist had told her to run through a sequence of moves and squeezes once every couple of hours, but Amanda, being Amanda, had been doing them at least hourly. She was absolutely determined to get back a full range of motion and keep up her strength.

She detested the wheelchair, now parked in the corner of the room, which was used to take her backwards and forwards for scans and so on, and was determined that it would not feature in her future plans.

Now though, as sleep refused to come, she sighed deeply and tried once more to lose herself in a re-run of the dreadful soap-opera, "Southenders". At least it was in English, of a sort.

-ooOoo-

'So, the thing is, Derek,' said Henry, 'The Frobishers are quite happy to enter into a joint venture whereby they put in the land for the shops and flats above, so long as you will sort out the fine details of the planning permission and build them, and then take responsibility for selling the flats and letting the shops.'

'That is just what I hoped they would say,' said Derek. 'Easy for them and a profit share when it is all sold in return for waiting a bit for the land money.'

'Quite,' said Henry. 'They were also nice enough to say that the partnership arrangements you already have at the hotel are exceeding their expectations and they are convinced they found the right company to work with, so that is good.'

'Well, that is very gratifying to hear,' said Derek. 'It has worked well so far, and since we did the deal with the TV company they can look forward to a rapid increase in occupancy of the hotel part of it, so everyone's a winner.'

'Indeed so,' said Henry. 'Now, assuming you are happy that we have covered all that, could I ask you one small favour, please. My wife and I celebrate our wedding anniversary next week and I have been trying to book a table at Mario's without success. It always seems to be so booked up …'

'For you, Henry, not a problem. There will be no charge, of course. When would you like to go?'

-ooOOoo-

'And so,' said Jack, 'If Desmond Tweedy and I could come over and you could meet us there one day next week, we could finalise the lighting and sound arrangements and then get the big chandeliers delivered, if you have somewhere to store them.'

'I will have a word with Pete,' said Justin. 'I'm sure we can sort something out.'

'Oh, by the way, has Trudy told you Desmond can bring his support act over for the opening night as well, if Derek and Amanda are interested. Desmond describes them as a "foot-tapping sophisticated jazz and swing combo with a wide repertoire," and I think he is hoping to find them a job. You see they won't be included in his new act when it goes on tour, and having worked with them for a long time, he is wondered if he could ease them in to something like the "Carlos at Barclay Court" club as the resident band.'

'Well that might be handy,' said Justin. 'Have they got a demo-tape or whatever they call them these days?'

'They can do better than that, I suspect. They have had several records out in their own right in the past. They also found a good market recording the sort of thing you hear in hotel lobbies and lifts, I understand.'

-ooOoo-

On his own initiative, Pete bought and installed a selection of powerfully perfumed air fresheners, in an attempt to reduce the fishy smell in the hotel reception and adjacent rooms.

In the ballroom itself, when he briefly looked in, the smell was overpowering and the chemicals used to seal the dance floor made his eyes water. So in order to contain it he covered the joints in the entrance doorways with wide decorators masking tape and also ran some along the floor at the bottom of the doors.

Pete was anxious not to upset the Frobishers and their guests, of course, but he was also concerned that, as things were, the decorators could not start work in there, and there was a lot to do.

When the team who expected to be working in the ballroom arrived, if it was still not possible to start work there, Pete suspected he would have to re-deploy them to assist with the more mundane painting and decorating required in the catering school.

-ooOoo-

The painting and decorating in Emma's new bedroom was finished at last, however.

Pete and Sarah had chosen and ordered a new carpet to complete the room which would match the curtains and furnishings they would be taking with them from the flat, and everything was nearly ready for them to move in.

But first, because Sarah would still have to bake in her flat while the development kitchen equipment was moved, the decoration work on her new kitchen and bakery had to be finished at the college at pace.

The tilers and painters working in there must have wondered why they saw quite so much of Pete, and although he assured them he knew they were doing their best, why he kept asking them how it was going.

-oooOoo-

Chapter 44

'It was lovely, Pete. It is very tall but not as big as I had feared, fortunately, but it does have two seats in the back, or three at a pinch, and still plenty of room to deliver the cakes.'

Pete had taken a moment to make a call to see how Sarah got on with her test drive.

'What was it like to drive, Sarah.'

'Well, it was better than I expected. I thought it might be more like a rattly van than a car, but it was actually very quiet. I had to slide the seat right the way forward, of course, but my worries about how hard it would be to push the clutch were unfounded, it was easy.'

'That's great. I'm pleased for you. If you tell Derek to go ahead it will certainly be more comfortable for us to use when we go out as a family than my old truck.'

'Family? Are we a family, Pete?'

'We are going to be, if you will let me join in.'

'Oh yes please, Pete.'

-ooOoo-

'There is another bit of good news,' said Derek, adjusting the wire leading to the phone charger, 'there has been some feedback from the Waitrose Planning consultation.'

'Oh yes? I was wondering about that,' said Amanda.

'All pretty positive, and the architect put something in our letter of support asking if we could put tables and chairs on the pavement outside the cafe when the side road gets turned into a footpath.'

'That was a good idea.'

'It was, and they said that, in principle, yes we could, although we will have to apply properly if the Waitrose thing goes through.'

'There is only a couple of weeks left on the planning consultation thing, isn't there?'

'Yes, and then, if there are no big problems, they will take it to the Planning Committee for a decision.'

'And that will mean the Frobishers get their money?'

'Assuming permission is granted, yes,' Derek lifted Amanda's phone and checked that it was charging. 'Jeremy was telling me that there is a bank involved who will need paying off, but other than that they are ready to sign a joint venture with us on the flats and shops as soon as the deal goes through.'

'You said you had been talking to Henry about the specifics, didn't you?'

'Yes, he told me that they have had the usual blizzard of unsolicited approaches about selling the site, but the more interesting thing is the number of shops who have shown an interest in the new build proposal. Henry said the best of those is "Bridal Daze" that he described as a 'destination' shop which could attract specific types of shoppers to the area.'

'Brides, I assume.'

'Well them, obviously, but there are what he called 'companion' businesses that sit well alongside that. For example, if you are going to get married, the chances are you are going to want a honeymoon, so a travel agent next door makes sense, and what about a hairdresser to do their hair? Henry says they have had approaches from three travel agents and loads of hairdressers.'

'That companion business is a very good idea,' said Amanda. 'What other sort of businesses have approached them?'

'I wrote it down,' said Derek fishing in his pocket. 'Yes, here we are ... there are approaches from all sorts of things, but Henry thought these might be the most appropriate if we can nail down Bridal

Daze. There was a posh dress and hat shop, a shoe shop, a couple of florists, and an electrical retailer.'

'Why on earth do you want an electrical retailer near a Bridal shop?'

'To buy the happy couple a washing machine, of course!'

Amanda laughed at that.

'Old Watty, the Estate Agent has also approached them, Henry said. He is interested now, but he didn't want to know about one of our shops before the regeneration scheme got going.'

'Offer him one at an inflated rent,' said Amanda. 'That will teach him not to be so short-sighted!'

-oo0Ooo-

The Frobishers formed a little welcoming committee in the porch of the hotel for the group of nine landscape gardeners, as they pulled their bags out of their cars and trucks.

Pete introduced himself and rode in the cab of the big van towing the trailer as they moved it round to the back of the walled garden and reversed it in through the tall gates.

'Why don't you just un-hitch the trailer here and we can shut the gates and leave it while you get settled in and relax,' he suggested. 'I've got hold of a pretty substantial padlock and fitted the gates with a bolt to lock it up from the inside, so it will be quite safe.'

Pete met the team, which included three women, in the hotel Reception an hour later. He walked them round the walled garden and gave them a glimpse of the interior of the catering school.

'Who lives in that funny little cottage?' asked a large lady in a tweed jacket and wellington boots.

'I do,' said Pete. 'So if you can't find me on one of the construction sites, just knock on the door if you need anything.'

'Power,' said a tall man who looked like a Viking. 'Where do we get power?'

'I have had the electricians install an external double power point over there, by the doors leading to the college,' said Pete, pointing. 'And there are two taps over by the gates. One is tap water and the other comes off a big old rainwater tank on the other side of the wall.'

'Excellent. Most convenient,' said a little man emerging from behind the Viking. He was carrying a clipboard, and appeared to be in charge. 'It seems you are very well prepared for us to start work. Did Andrew ask you to arrange to provide these things?'

'Well, no, actually. I just sort of thought out what you might be needing.'

'What I need,' said the large lady in the tweed jacket,

'is a very large scotch, with or without soda. Do you also provide a bar, young man?'

Pete led them back to the hotel reception, established that they would require breakfast at half past seven in the morning, and prepared to leave them to it.

'Can you smell fish?' said the little man with the clipboard, sniffing. 'There is a quite overpowering smell of fish in here.'

'Ah,' said Pete, 'I can explain that ...'

-oooOoo-

Chapter 45

'Auntie Sandy and Uncle Matthew are coming over to see us on Saturday, Emma,' announced Sarah.

'Wahoo! How long are they staying?'

'It is only for the day this time. They are on their way to a function, in London, in the evening.'

'What's a function, mummy?'

'It is ... it is what Auntie Sandy and Uncle Matthew are coming over for, in London.'

'You don't know, do you mummy,' said Emma as they arrived at the school gates. 'I shall ask Miss Carter-Bone, and inform you of the definition when I get home.'

-oo0Ooo-

Now that the window fitters had finished, Pete was working on the outside of the building when the landscape gardeners turned up to start work.

'What is that you have got there?' said the little man, still clutching his clipboard.

'These are just some window boxes I made to grow herbs for the kitchens, I was about to install them.'

'You made those, young man?' said the large lady now dressed in bulging blue dungarees. 'They are very pretty. I like all that delicate filigree work you have put around the top and the colour matches the shutters on your little house.'

'They are just made out of scrap really, I carved the decoration out of a bit of an old school bench I found inside here and the boxes are made out of oak panels originally forming the backs of the seats ...' Pete was blushing as all the gardeners had now gathered round to admire his work. 'I ... I was wondering if you might give me a few tips on what to plant and whether herbs need special soil, or anything.'

'Herbs for kitchens?' boomed the Viking. 'My speciality. Let me plant them up for you? I'd like that.'

'Well, I don't mean to impose ...' stuttered Pete.

'Better let Damian here have his way,' said the large lady. 'We had enough tears and tantrums in the car on the way down.'

'Yes,' said small clipboard, 'You mount them on the wall and leave it to Damian. There is some lead in the van to line the planters with, Damian,' he called to his back as he stomped off.

'I know, I put it there,' said Damian and continued on his way to the van.

-oo0Ooo-

Derek handed round face masks as he approached the ballroom doors with Justin, and Sparky, the owner of the firm of electricians Derek regularly used.

Sparky wasn't his real name of course but he didn't like being called Julian; and now that name was reserved only for use by his mum.

Sparky felt being called Sparky was also a useful advert and avoided those awkward questions people asked about what you 'do' when introduced at parties. He went to quite a lot of parties. His mother was a professional party planner and Sparky was often called in to arrange and install the lighting for her events.

'They said the smell would have gone off by now, but I think it is as strong as ever, I'm afraid. Please don't step on the wooden dance floor, by the way. It has just been treated, and that is what you can smell.'

They managed to stay in the ballroom for a little under three minutes, before retreating back to the hotel reception. It was just enough time for Sparky to take some photographs with his mobile phone, unscrew a fuse panel, and press a little implement with lights on it into the wires he had exposed.

As Derek closed the door and did his best to re-attach Pete's masking tape, Sparky tore off his mask and made his feelings known.

'Gawd-and-actual-Bennett! What sort of fish have you been cooking in there? Whales?'

'Whales are mammals, actually,' said Penelope who was passing by. 'Coffee is being served in the dining room if you would like some.'

-oo0Ooo-

Amanda was delighted, and even though it hurt like hell, she couldn't wait to do it again.

Mounted in what she referred to disdainfully as her trapeze, with the help of two very determined physiotherapists, she had lowered her weight onto her good leg and taken one step forward landing on her other foot, still encased in its plaster cast.

As soon as it was accomplished, the physiotherapists yanked her back into the air so she did not topple the frame forward, or put weight for too long on her broken ankle, but all three let out a little cheer. It was, quite literally, a step forward.

-oo0Ooo-

Chapter 46

'So, just to make sure I have got this right, Sarah, you want the Blast-Chiller over there and the new floor standing pastry sheeter over there?'

'Yes please, Pete, then it works with the flow, you see.'

'No, but I am only here to serve. Your wish is my command.'

'Get on, you daft lump!' laughed Sarah.

'Easy for you to say, but the special sealed flooring for this room arrives tomorrow and, ready or not, they are going to want to know where to put things very shortly after that.'

'Why have you had this bakery done so far ahead of the other kitchens, Pete?'

'How do you mean?'

'Well all the plumbing and power points are in and the tiling is all done so there are only limited things left to do in here, but all the other rooms are not nearly so advanced.'

'I think it is rather sweet,' said Emma standing in the doorway in her oversized HiViz vest. 'He has done it so we can move into the cottage and I can have my new bedroom quicker.'

'Quite correct, Emma. Well spotted,' said Pete.

'I hope you are not going to get wrong with Derek when he sees what you have done here.'

'Don't worry my little flour fairy, Derek is fully aware of the plan. Look at it this way, the sooner we get you in here and working, the sooner he gets you out of the flat so he can rent it out for more money than he is getting from you!'

'He is not that mercenary … you made that up, Pete.'

'Oh, alright I admit it, but he does know what I'm doing and he is as keen to make sure the flow of patisserie and teas is uninterrupted when this is ready as I am. There are elements, relating to the positioning of cameras and so on which are not decided in the main kitchen so it made sense to get this one done first while we are waiting.'

'Really?'

'Yes and I need this team of tilers and painters out of here and working on the much bigger main kitchens as soon as possible. The TV crews are coming to agree all the things we need to provide for them next week and until we have that sorted we can't take the main kitchen much further, and I've only got limited labour to juggle with so I can't have them standing about waiting.'

-ooOOoo-

'So I thought,' said small clipboard, 'If you let us plant a row of semi-mature conifers in front of it, it will separate it up from the garden area, give the chap living there a bit of privacy, and avoid any accidental appearances by other people while we are filming.'

'Well, yes, I see the point of that,' said Derek, 'but I thought you gardeners didn't like conifers.'

'Quite correct. Can't stand them, but this is telly. We will whip them out and burn them when we finish filming if you like. I only suggested them because it will provide an instant natural looking solution and appear less contrived than a bit of new fencing.'

'And this is OK with Pete and Sarah is it?'

'Pete I have spoken to, but I don't think I know Sarah …'

'Sarah is going to be living here, in the cottage, soon with Emma, her eight year old daughter.'

'There are going to be children on the set? Oh my! That could make it difficult. Perhaps we had better go with close boarded fencing ... or maybe a brick wall ...'

'What is the problem with children?'

'Well, there is no problem with children *per se*, except that they are infernally inquisitive, and no matter how hard we try, if they are around they are quite likely to peep at us.'

'I see,' said Derek, who didn't.

'You see the problem with this sort of thing is that we only have the celebs here for a very short space of time and if we have to keep re-doing bits to remove a peeper, the schedule quickly goes to pot. That is why a walled garden is so ideal for this sort of thing. No peepers. But if there is going to be a child actually living on the set ...'

-ooOOoo-

'Thank you very much for coming to see me,' said Amanda as Justin and Trudy placed their basket of fruit on the seat of the wheelchair, for want of anywhere else to put it. 'And thank you for the fruit. I had only just finished the last lot you bought!'

'Well they don't seem to like you bringing flowers no more,' said Trudy. 'We thought about trying to smuggle in a bottle of wine, but decided fruit was safer!'

'Have you had time to take a look at that clip of

Desmond Tweedy's support band I sent you?' said Justin.

'I've never had so much time in my life since I came in here,' said Amanda, 'so getting that clip was a welcome distraction. I have played it several times.

'What do you think?'

'They are good,' said Amanda, 'but I don't think we should offer them a residency until we have seen them perform properly.'

'That is fair enough, I don't think they expected anything else, but it would be handy to have them ready as a possibility, don't you think?'

'Certainly. We are going to need a core group of musicians who we can rely on. I can't see us being able to book big name acts all the time. That will be the exception rather than the rule.'

'There's quite a few good troupes of jazz musicians floating about as would give their eye teeth for a regular spot at this club, y'know. I'd audition a few if I was you, Amanda.'

'I'm sure you are right Trudy.'

'I know I'm right. Some of them backing bands what play in the shows are really just a collection of session musicians, but they are all desperate for regular work, like. So what you have got to offer is what they want. You should have your pick.'

'I wondered if it would be a good idea to put on a couple of dance troupes every now and then. I don't want to try to recreate the Royal Variety Performance, but maybe something for the diners to look at when eating would go down well.'

'A cabaret act, you mean?'

'Well, not comedians or anything like that. I was just thinking of something musical with a bit of pep to it to amuse the diners occasionally.'

'Sometimes dance troupes from the shows will come out and do a number for clubs and that. It's good practice for them as well as an advert for the show. Maybe I could find you something like that.'

'Derek would say I'm trying to run before I can walk again, if you will excuse the very obvious reference to my current situation, so perhaps I ought not to get too involved in that sort of thing, yet. But it is certainly worth bearing in mind.'

-ooo0oo-

Chapter 47

The visit from the Wine Merchant was unexpected but Derek, who had never met him, shook his hand and offered him a seat in Albany Developments offices, when he called in.

He had quietly run his business, in the only consistently occupied shop in the block, since the shops and flats were built and had wanted to hand the business on to his son when the time came.

Now, he explained, with the Waitrose consultation concluding shortly, he had seen the writing on the wall.

'As an independent we can't possibly compete with the supermarkets selling the same products, and it is all too easy to settle for what they are offering,' he explained. 'So, given that my son left the business and went into IT some time ago, it is with a heavy heart that I have decided to give up and retire.'

He went on to explain that his son was now buying

his own home and that he would be able to vacate both the flats they occupied, and the shop, in three months time.

The business premises, which was originally two largish shops knocked together shortly after they were built, was quite spacious and Derek wondered what he would do with it.

After wishing the wine merchant well and showing him out of the office, he picked up the phone and called Henry, the accountant.

'What other businesses were on that list that expressed interest in the new shops,' he asked. 'And were any more of them these "destination retailers" you spoke about?'

'Well, not really, but there was a gym, part of a big group actually. It's a different sort of destination, I suppose. That sort of thing might attract sports shops or clothing outlets, possibly. Why do you ask?'

-oo0Ooo-

The short letter from the solicitor was attached to a copy of a longer letter which was signed by Professor J G Wimbish on behalf of Dr Gerard Foyle, the Vice Chancellor of the University. It set out the detailed financial arrangements for their use of the main classrooms at the Barclay Court Hotel catering school.

It contained no surprises and accurately set out

their agreement, and all Derek and Amanda were asked to do was sign a copy and return it, at which point the agreement would be dated and would become a contract.

It had taken this long to arrive because of the Christmas and New Year shut down at the University, the solicitors note explained. Now, however, there was some urgency to tidy up the legal side because the University needed to start offering their new courses and adapting existing ones ready for the new academic year. They also wanted to organise a visit to inspect the works.

'But at least we have got it all in a legal form now, Amanda,' said Derek, as he helped her position the document to sign it.

'That is the first official thing I have had to sign since …'

'And you did it with no trouble at all,' said Derek.

'You don't like me saying "accident", do you honey. I've noticed you always interrupt when I'm about to say it.'

Derek looked embarrassed.

'You got me there,' he said. 'It may seem rather wimpy, but after it happened every time I heard that word I couldn't stop myself crying …'

'Oh Derek …'

'I have got over it now, more or less, but it was embarrassing and … and un-manly.'

'I think it was lovely, and shows yet again that the roughty-toughty facade you present to the world conceals a heart of pure gold.'

'Pure mush, more like,' said Derek, gently kissing his wife's hand.

-oo0Ooo-

The progress the landscape gardeners had made in the few days they had been working on the walled garden was astonishing, and it now looked as though the beds and borders with their immaculate rows of vegetables, fruit and herbs had been productively growing and producing for years.

A compromise had been reached over how to screen the cottage, and avoid any 'peepers' looking through the glazed doors of the college building into the area where the celebrities would be filming, and Emma declared it to be 'Naff.'

In the end a temporary green wire fence had been erected about three meters in front of the house and stretching along past the college doors. This was then draped with dense artificial leaves on a bamboo frame to give the impression of an established hedge.

'It will have to do,' said small clipboard, and left it at

that.

Much more attractive however was the delicate creation with kitchen herbs Damian the Viking had made in the window boxes which now supported a range of fully grown as well as immature plants.

'So long as you water it and don't over crop it,' Damian advised, 'it will last for years and still be providing for your kitchens long after we have gone.'

-ooOoo-

Chapter 48

'Three steps today, and very nearly four,' said Amanda delightedly as Sarah and Emma stood at her bedside. 'And tomorrow the cast comes off my ankle.'

'Terrific, Auntie Amanda,' smiled Emma.

'Tomorrow Chesney Marriott is coming down to give Carlos his screen test and see how Pete is getting on at the college,' said Sarah. 'Everyone is very excited.'

'And they are going to agree the camera positions in the main kitchen, Derek told me,' Amanda observed.

'Yes, that will please Pete. He has been waiting for that, to be able to finish the tiling and decoration in there. They had to get matt tiles to go on the walls so they don't reflect in the TV lighting and they only arrived this morning, apparently.'

'Yes, and I see the plan is to move the equipment from the cafe to the new bakery on Monday. It is very good of you to offer to use your own kitchen while the move is going on, Sarah.'

'Pete has promised Mummy that it will only take a couple of days,' said Emma, 'and then we can move into the house, and she can work from the new place.'

'You must be excited about that, Emma.'

'Oh, I am. Pete has borrowed one of Dave's vans … one with a proper roof, unlike Pete's rattly truck, to move all my stuff.' Emma was dancing on the spot. 'And then he will go back for Mummy's stuff while I get settled in and unpack.'

'Emma has got it all organised,' said Sarah. 'And luckily there is one of those "non-pupil" days on Friday, so we should be able to do it then.'

'Friday!' exclaimed Emma. 'I told everyone Tuesday or Wednesday at worst. Miss Carter-Bone, our form teacher is not expecting me in!'

-ooOoo-

'Initially "Gym-Fit", the company I contacted, thought the off-licence shop unit would be too small, but they were very interested in the location,' said Henry. 'But then I remembered you saying there were two flats over the top of the wine merchants shops. Would it be possible to join them up, Derek? They like the idea of having rooms for things like Pilates on upper floors. They would want to provide massage and physiotherapy in separate rooms, if they could, and they need a small amount of office space as well.'

-oo0Ooo-

At long last, the smell of fish in the ballroom had reduced enough for the decorators to start work, so long as they kept the windows open.

Using the scaffold tower, which seemed to have become a permanent fixture in the vast room, they installed the very expensive metallic wallpaper with great care between the gilded decorative plaster columns that stretched from the broad skirting to the elaborate coving at ceiling level. This reflective fabric closely copied the style and design of the tired old stuff they removed, and created a feeling of opulent luxury, no doubt as the original designers intended.

Another group of technicians were working in the room alongside them, occasionally borrowing the tower to mount concealed loudspeakers and lighting projectors here and there. Their main focus, however, was on the broad raised stage, where broken and possibly dangerous spotlights had been removed and replaced with state of the art equipment.

Up on the balcony further work was underway to install a complicated looking mixer panel and computer screens which, when commissioned, and concealed behind a discrete dividing panel arrangement, would become the control centre for all the lighting and sound management and would be the domain of a highly qualified theatre technician appointed and trained by Jack Bolton personally to 'drive' the show.

Carefully wrapped up awaiting installation, further along the balcony sat the new black-out curtains which would cover the floor to ceiling windows, and which had been made by a theatrical scenery producer known to Trudy. Next to them, under heavy canvas covers, lay the enormous chandeliers, concealing clever electronics, projectors and spot-lighting. They were due to be winched into place when the decorators finished, after the carpets were laid and before the new tables and chairs arrived.

Pete videoed the scene on his mobile phone and sent his slightly wobbly efforts as an amateur cameraman to Amanda's phone.

-ooo0oo-

'I'll just have a coffee, please Sarah,' said Derek.

I popped in because I have just had the vehicle leasing firm on the phone. They can deliver your new car on Wednesday, if you are prepared to accept a blue one.'

'Well, you are buying it, so ...'

'We ordered a white one, but apparently there has been a run on those, and airport taxi firms particularly seem to be snapping them up. They have found a pale blue one at a dealership somewhere though, so if you were happy with that they can get it here next week.'

'It doesn't matter to me what colour it is,' said Sarah. 'I'm just really grateful that you are prepared to let me use it, Derek. Thank you very much.'

'Yes, well. That's fine, I'll get it ordered then, shall I,' smiled Derek. 'Would you mind dropping your driving licence into the office at some point so we can make a copy for the file, please Sarah.'

'Of course. Emma is really excited about this, and is on at me about taking her to school in it when we get it. Would it be all right if I did that? Just once I mean.'

'Of course it would, Sarah. It is for your use, not just for the business. If you want to take Emma to school in it everyday that is fine by me.'

'Oh no, only when it rains!' said Sarah. 'The exercise is good for her on nice days.'

-oo0Ooo-

Chapter 49

'Well, I confess I was jolly nervous, but Chesney seemed to think it went all right,' said Carlos. 'And fortunately I didn't mess up the cooking, so I think they liked their lunch.'

'Well done,' said Mario. 'Soon you be the big telly star and forget all about the poor Mario, ay?'

'Highly unlikely, that is! Chesney is only talking about me appearing as the resident chef at the hotel in the first episode to introduce the place.'

'But from the little acorns grow the big apple trees, eh?'

-oo0Ooo-

Derek was becoming impatient.

It was cold in the tiny untidy customer reception area of the sign company and it seemed to him to be taking ages to attach the sticky plastic signs saying

'Sarah's Kitchen, & School of Culinary Arts' to the sides and rear doors of the new people carrier/van thing.

He regretted volunteering to take the vehicle to be 'liveried' as soon as it had been delivered, principally because of the time it was taking. But also, now that he had seen it, he felt very conspicuous driving a vehicle in quite such a childish shade of pastel blue.

The idea had been that it would be complete and ready to use when Sarah first saw it, but he had not realised how long these things take, and although he used the time to make some calls, he didn't think his mobile phone battery could last much longer.

He was glad about one thing, though. He was pleased to see the tall vehicle had two individual back doors.

He made himself smile with a vision of the diminutive Sarah dangling in mid air, hanging onto the handle of a top hinged tailgate and shouting for help. That illusion faded, however, as the words of Emma came back to him, telling her audience that we are supposed to *celebrate our differences* and it was *inappropriate* to laugh at them.

In his mind, he would never be able to forget hearing her say, "Miss Carter-Bone says we are all identical inside, and God made us all equal," when she was first told that Amanda might need to use a wheelchair and be classified as 'disabled'.

-ooOoo-

Now that the requirements of the camera crew were clear, Pete could really crack on.

The decorating team chosen to work in the ballroom, principally because they were the tidiest and most careful, were now hard at work, with all the windows open, and going well alongside Jack Bolton's engineers. Progress there was good, despite the lingering smell of fish and their discovery that the expensive metallic fabric 'wallpaper' stretched, which made hanging it a challenge.

The team who worked on Sarah's bakery had moved on to the open plan area of the classroom kitchens, and at Dave's suggestion Ivor's team now got to work on the main kitchen, where the filming would be done.

'Honestly they are a bit messy, but so long as you clean up after them each night, they really are quick,' Dave explained. 'Ivor is the craftsman. He does the tiling while the others slap paint about and mix up grout for him. We use his team when we need a house finishing off quick for a hand-over.'

The fourth team were Derek's old mates who he trusted to fit kitchens, tile, and decorate the brand new houses he built. They would be starting next week in the lecture room with its raised staging and separate cooking area used for demonstrations. The new 'theatre style' seating and tables and chairs for this area was due to arrive shortly, so they would not have much time.

Dave had reluctantly agreed to 'lend' them to Pete on the understanding that he did not upset them or get under their feet.

Pete surveyed his busy little ants nest, now humming with activity and the smell of fresh paint. Now he could turn his attention to transferring the catering equipment from the cafe to the new bakery and getting Sarah producing her teas in her flat for the absolute minimum amount of time possible.

And then, at last, she would move in with him, and that he was sure, made him the happiest man alive.

-ooOOoo-

'Well, you told me to ask him, so I did. And guess what … he said I could have your flat for the same rent as I'm paying now!'

'Well that is lovely, Jenny. I'm glad for you.'

'And my full time hours start at the end of the month so I am going to be much better off. It won't affect you, now you are moving out, Sarah, but I have set up a rota of mums to collect and deliver each other's kids to school, so them that don't have jobs helps them that do, and then the employed ones baby-sit to pay back when we are not at work, to give them a breather.'

'That sounds a good idea, Jenny. By the way, I meant

to say, there might be jobs up at the college when it gets going. It might be cleaning or something else, but if I tell you about them, can you pass them on to the mums?'

'Sure. Regular little self help group we are, aren't we!'

-oo0Ooo-

'Oh no, Mummy!' said Emma when Sarah pulled up at the school gates. 'Quick, get out of here before anyone sees!'

'What's the matter, Emma?'

'It's baby blue! It's horrible. Please don't tell me you chose this colour. It looks like a baby's rattle on wheels!'

'I take it you don't like our new car then, Emma.'

'It would be all right for a playgroup, I suppose, but I thought it would be white, or even a smart red ... but this! I shall be teased unmercifully at school! Take me home, quick!'

-oo0Ooo-

Chapter 50

Morning sickness affects everyone differently.

For Amanda it started suddenly in the middle of the afternoon, which was unfortunate, particularly as she was wearing her high neck collar and was about to be winched into her 'trapeze'.

At least she had some people around her when it happened. The staff expressed some concern that she could choke if it happened when she was on her own and unable to get rid of it.

That led to medication being prescribed to control it which worked almost instantly until, as they made to winch her up again the next day, the same thing happened.

'It must be when my stomach gets stretched and moved about,' she told Derek, 'But at least I do feel pregnant now!'

'Of course we don't know how many weeks pregnant you are, but I've been looking it up, and what I found out indicates that it subsides in about week 12 in many cases.'

'Well, they have put me on some drugs and changed my diet. Now it seems all I get to eat is bananas and stewed apple, or toast and a bit of chicken with rice. Carlos would be horrified.'

'Not very appetising, I'm sure.' said Derek.

'You know, honey, the food in here has actually been jolly good until now, so I suppose I mustn't complain, but I wish I was at home and being made a fuss of.'

'Once they have got some strength back into your ankle, they said they would review the possibility of letting you come home, you know that. And the plaster on your arm is coming off next week they said, didn't they?'

'They said it might, yes. Derek, if I still can't walk when they send me home, how are we going to cope?'

'Can't walk? You told me you did nine steps yesterday. At this rate you will be doing the London Marathon by Christmas!'

'Oh, ha, ha.'

'No really love, we will manage. And of course I can't wait to get you home … Even I can cook you a banana and open a can of stewed apple, so you certainly won't starve!'

-ooOoo-

'The link structure is done, so you can tell the architect we are ready for the ghastly blue glass thing now,' said Dave. 'I've got a plasterer on standby, who will also screed the floor when the lid goes on.'

'Thanks very much Dave, that is great,' said Pete. 'Is there any chance the plasterer could be doing those new loos while we are waiting. Then I can get them decorated and the sanitary-ware installed. The TV people will want them finished.'

'All right, yes, I'll send him over. But you can't have any more of my decorators and I've got completions coming up so I will need them back here very soon.'

'Don't worry Dave, we are swimming in paint at the moment, so you will soon have them back.'

'How are you getting on with that peculiar wallpaper in the ballroom?'

'That is all up, thank goodness. The guys found it stretched so getting it up on such a huge fall was quite a task.'

'It's fabric rather than paper, isn't it?'

'Yes, the guys say they have never worked with anything like it.'

'Let's just hope it stays up then so I can have my best team of decorators back.'

-oo0Ooo-

'So, I hope you will forgive me for collaring you about this,' said Andrew Smallpond, 'but it occurred to me that it could interest you.'

The telephone call from the TV gardener had slightly surprised Derek, but as Andrew continued, he became increasingly interested in what he had to say.

'When my wife was involved, it was called "The Ultimate Graduate Domestic Training Institute", but that was a bit of a mouthful so now it is just called "Pinnacle Training", but the idea is the same. They train up Butlers, Footmen, and domestic or hotel waiting staff and they have built up quite a reputation here and abroad over the years.'

'I see,' said Derek. 'And you think we could help them in some way?'

'Yes. The hotel they use as a training base has been sold … I think they said it is going to be turned into flats … so they are losing their venue to train people. My wife is still a shareholder, and Non-executive Chair, although she is not involved in the day-to-day business so much. She was down at your walled garden last week, you may have met her. She may have introduced herself as Dame Amelia Runacres-

Smythe, her professional name.'

'I don't think I ...'

'No? She was one of the team of gardeners I sent over to prepare the walled garden ... No matter. The idea was that, if you are not fully booked up, they might well be interested in using your classrooms. I'm thinking particularly of the one which had tables and chairs and seating facing a stage, on the plans you showed me. Could she get their Director, Hugo Meadows, to give you a call?'

-oo0Ooo-

Pete, Sparky the electrician, and the decorators were the first to see it.

With the enormous chandeliers and curtains now in place, the lighting and effects were ready to be tested.

Jack Bolton had traveled down with Justin and Trudy, and after half an hour or so, announced that he was ready.

Jack's wheelchair had a mounting for his laptop and his fingers flew over the keys as he sat at the edge of the dance floor, facing the stage.

With a whirr and a swish, the enormous curtains all closed and some background lighting came on, along with some illumination on the stage.

Then as Jack sat back to watch, there was a flash and

a pop, and the wall behind the stage seemed to erupt into hundreds of tiny stars, before an image resolved itself and, to the gasps of the onlookers a scene appeared. Apparently viewed through a set of tall french windows, which appeared to open out onto a terrace and a large swimming pool, surrounded by dazzling blooming rose arbours, behind little groups of chairs and tables, the view filled the entire area of wall behind the stage.

'Hmm. Bit bright,' muttered Jack, and with a few keyboard strokes, the roses took on a more subtle, old fashioned, hue.

'Wow!' said Sparky. 'That is so realistic. It feels like you can reach out and touch it, or dive into that pool!'

'Thank you,' said Jack. 'Now let's try something else.'

Once again his fingers danced over the keyboard, and the image on the wall dissolved to be replaced, almost immediately, by what appeared to be an extension of the very room they were in, again viewed through tall doors, but this time with tables and chairs occupied by elegant diners in the full evening dress of a bygone, more elegant, era.

As they watched, white jacketed waiters appeared to move between the tables and the diners seemed to be engaged in silent conversations.

'Of course you have to imagine it with the band playing and people dining in here,' Jack said. 'But it is pretty realistic, I hope you will agree.'

'It's brilliant,' said Justin, 'and the ballroom looks just like a mirror image of this one!'

'That is because it is a mirror image of this one, just with the diners and so on superimposed on the image,' smiled Jack. 'Watch.'

And with a few more clicks, the curtains in the real ballroom began to open, and a few moments later so did those in the image!'

'I've filmed the ballroom in real time so what you are seeing is a playback of the curtains opening by running the film of them closing backwards, so they appear to be opening, see? The superimposed people stay the same, the waiters are still moving forwards as you see. It is one film running behind another, if you like.'

'Genius!' said Sparky. 'If my mum could get hold of something like that for her party-planning business, she would be over the moon!'

'Well she can, if she can afford it,' said Jack and produced a business card which he handed over.

-oooOoo-

Chapter 51

'So when I spoke to him, Amanda, it was clear this 'Pinnacle Training' are pretty desperate to find somewhere else to train their butlers and waiting staff people, and they will pay us an initial figure to cover what he calls "set up costs" and then so much per student depending on the training time they require. He is coming down tomorrow for a look at the facilities.'

'Well that is great, Derek. There was a danger that room could be underutilised, as the University only really need to use the training kitchens.'

'Yes, and I was relieved when he said that they would bring all their own equipment, like silver service, glasses, table cloths and what-have-you. I thought that might be what he meant by "set up costs" but all he really wants is to ensure is that we have a white board and so on, and can keep the place clean.'

'That reminds me. Cleaners. We need to sort that out, don't we.'

'As it happens, I popped into the cafe this morning and Jenny was telling me about this group of mums who she is in touch with who ...'

'Sarah told me that the last time they tried to set up a cleaning round on our estate, when the original company folded, it all came to nothing because of their inability to get insurance.'

'Yes, Jenny was part of that little group. However, the problem was that they had no track record, so couldn't get the insurance companies interested. The only other way for them to do it was if they became direct employees of the estate management company, and that was a non-starter. But the Barclay Court Hotel has its own registered cleaning company according to Henry. They set it up like that years ago because of something to do with tax. Henry said if the Frobishers are interested, he could use that company to get insurance for our cleaners as well as their own, and if we pay the insurance premiums, plus say five percent to them for the use of the name, he will recommend that they do it.'

'And we get to control it? Excellent!' said Amanda.

-ooOoo-

Pete's wobbly mobile phone video of Jack Bolton's trial run in the ballroom accompanied his text with a message to say that, apart from a bit of a polish up, everything was ready, and should he ask the company providing the tables and chairs to deliver them now.

Amanda excitedly showed Chesney Marriott the video, when he unexpected turned up to visit her.

'Normally I avoid hospitals like the plague, Amanda, and I apologise for not having to come to see you sooner. I don't know why, but these places creep me out.'

'Quite understandable,' said Amanda, 'I'm not any too keen on them myself.'

'The reason I came in person is that I want to sort out the filming schedule with you, now the garden is ready and the kitchen is nearly done, and I also had a new idea to run past you.'

'I see. What have you in mind?'

'Right, well, this is between us because Andrew and the Network people don't know about this yet, and if I suggest it they might muscle in and veto it.'

'Go on,'

'To be honest, the show, as scripted, lacks a bit of a punch at the end and just sort of fizzles out. But if we had some sort of a glitzy dinner where the celebs are filmed serving up their efforts to friends and family, it would end on a high note. And perhaps if other celebs and chefs who would be on later editions come to this dinner it will introduce them, and whet the viewers appetite for the next one in the series, if you see what I mean.'

'That's very clever. I like that idea.'

'You do? Marvellous! Well, what I was thinking was that Carlos and I could host these events, with me helping the celebs to get their dishes out and Carlos running the professional kitchen. There are a couple of problems with that, however.'

'Oh, what are they?'

'Well firstly, Carlos is a dear boy and very keen, but he works for you, not us, and then there is the venue.'

'If Carlos wants to do it and can work it in around his other duties I don't mind. But what is the problem with the venue?'

'We would have to hire your ballroom obviously, and you know how mean the Three Blind Mice are ...'

'If we can sort out scheduling around our other plans, I see no problem, and if you are going to fill the place with celebrities and well known chefs on a regular basis, on the telly, that could really help us, so long as we could have our members along to make up the numbers for these dinners.'

'Yes, making up the numbers is a good idea and most celebs love a chance to show off in front of an invited audience ... my worry is the cost. I can't guarantee I can get it past the Three Blind Mice. How much do you charge to hire out your ballroom, Amanda?'

'Will you want a dance band?'

'Er, yes, I suppose so,'

'Well, subject to Derek's agreement, of course, if you will pay for the band and the food; and Carlos, of course; so long as we can sell tickets to our members and let them meet the celebrities, I should think that would about do it. How does that sound?'

-oooOoo-

'Well that is amazing,' said Justin. 'One round of that on the telly and we will have potential members beating a path to our door. We might even have to start a waiting list.'

'I thought you would like it,' said Derek. 'All Amanda's idea, of course, and it depends on Chesney getting it past the Network people. But if he can do that, I think it will give us the sort of, what is it you people call it ... exposure ... we could only dream of.'

'And if we handle it right, folk who see the show will be queueing up to pay good money for cookery classes in the school to say they have done a course with you.'

'It does all look pretty exciting, doesn't it.'

'I wonder if we can get Sarah to do patisserie lessons and demonstrations ...'

'There, I have to say you might be running before you can walk, Justin. Sarah is not the most self confident of people and I would hate to frighten her away by pushing her into something she might not want to do.'

'Fair enough. It was just a thought. So, Derek, are you happy for me to launch our advertising campaign for the dining club now?'

'Just hang on a few days, Justin. If Chesney pulls this off we will be able to hint at the telly connection, perhaps, and that must help.'

-ooOOoo-

The arrival of the first of the stainless steel kitchen units and appliances resembled organised chaos, and there were one or two sharp words exchanged between painters and delivery men. But it sorted itself out in the end and Sarah was invited to inspect her new domain.

'Don't forget the stuff from the cafe isn't here yet, of course, but when you are set up at home tomorrow it won't take them long to get that over here,' said Pete.

'And then we can move into the cottage. Wahoo!' said Emma.

'On Friday,' said Sarah.

'Yes, Mummy, on Friday. At least there will be less danger of my friends from school seeing us in the baby-blue bus then, I suppose.'

'I like the colour,' said Pete. 'I can't see what your objection is …'

Chapter 52

'Yes, they have agreed,' said Trudy. 'So long as you will feed and water them they will do it for nothing as a sort of extended audition, on the date you suggested.'

'Great, well done Trudy! What are they called by the way?'

'They have performed under several names over the years, but just lately, the current line up calls itself "Showstoppers". Was there anything in particular you wanted them to play, or any style of music you want?'

'Do you think we could safely leave that to their judgement, Trudy? They must have done this sort of thing before.'

'I think so. I think you are wise doing it this way, Amanda. A whole evening of them playing will really give you confidence if you are going to consider them becoming the resident band at the dining club. It's not like they are just auditioning for a one off gig, is it. It's a big opportunity and a big decision for you and Derek too.'

-ooo0oo-

'That is excellent news, Chesney, although …'

'Is there a "but" coming, Amanda?'

'Just a tiny one. You see I have one little condition, that will be just between you and I.'

'Oh?'

-ooo0oo-

'So I'd like you to give each of the staff one of these, Carlos,' said Derek, 'but don't go into too much detail about what it is all about.'

The invitations Carlos now held were for the Albany Developments and associated businesses belated Christmas dinner for staff and partners.

They set out that smart casual dress was expected to be worn and that a meal, followed by dancing to a live band would be provided in the newly refurbished ballroom. There would, the invitations stated, be a pay bar after 9:00 but free drinks would be served from 7:30, before dinner was served at 8:15.

Carriages would be at midnight.

-ooo0oo-

The complicated blue glass structure, which would sit in the middle of the single storey link and create the entrance and part of the roof, was being installed by the company that made it.

Pete watched them carefully as they lowered sections of grey aluminium into place from a 'cherry picker' and attached the large glass panels as they went.

He hadn't realised that the raised pointed section over the door would bear the words 'Sarah's Kitchen & School of Culinary Arts' in the same style as the signs on the side of the new van, and he wondered what she would have to say about it, when she saw it.

Now that it was in place Pete had to admit that it looked very imposing. It would make what architects call a 'statement entrance' to the building beyond.

'That looks very flash,' said Dave's plasterer, now standing beside him. 'Classy, I call that.'

-oooOoo-

Chapter 53

With the equipment now removed from the cafe and installed in the new bakery, Pete had to manage a series of other tasks and deliveries.

Ivor's decorating team had finished in the main kitchen, and with some relief, given the messy way they worked, Pete returned them to Dave's tender care.

There was a rush to oversee the installation of the special sealed rubberised non-slip flooring, which turned up at the edges to facilitate easy mopping. That had only just been done in time when the new ovens and stainless steel cabinets and benches started arriving.

The area was once again swarming with people, and as the painting team working in the lecture room finished and were packing up for the day, the theatre style seating arrived along with the tables and chairs for use in that room.

The last decorating team were making steady progress in the large teaching kitchen and the flooring company would be working round them to finish fitting their special floor into the space first thing in the morning.

Late in the afternoon all the rest of the catering equipment, new and refurbished benches and cabinets arrived and the plumbers began to connect up all the sinks, while the gas engineer commissioned the hobs and the electrician tested and issued safety certificates for all the electrical appliances and the vast extractors that covered the working areas.

As Pete was locking up, Carlos popped in with Steve for a look, and both declared themselves mightily impressed with progress, before Pete, exhausted, finally went home.

He was asleep in the chair before the microwave 'pinged' to announce that his dinner was ready.

-ooOoo-

The news that the 'Waitrose land' proposal had been approved, following the conclusion of the public consultation came as a great relief to the Frobishers, and Penelope, who had been gathering up holiday brochures, spread her three favourite options on the dinner table that night, for the consideration of her siblings.

There would be no holidays for a while for anyone working for Albany Developments or its subsidiaries, however, as the filming began in the walled garden and kitchens, the membership enquiries for the dining and dancing club started arriving, and the level of completions on the building sites ramped up as building work reached a peak after the seasonal break.

The restaurants were also all busy, particularly with the demand for afternoon teas, and the cafe saw more and more house-buyers, as the number of visitors to the show-house down the road increased.

A new deal was in place with 'Pinnacle Training' for the lecture theatre. Dame Amelia Runacres-Smythe, Andrew Smallpond's wife, who Pete recognised as the large lady who had worked in the garden dressed in bulging blue dungarees, signed the papers on their behalf.

For Amanda, detached by necessity from all the hustle and bustle, it was like watching a beautiful flower open and she redoubled her efforts to get back into the thick of it.

The physiotherapists had started to take her to a therapy room to use a new contraption, like a bridge, to help her walk. With the wooden beams in her armpits, taking her weight, and her feet firmly on the track between them, she forced herself to push one foot in front of the other until she could haul herself along its whole length, several times.

She worked on her balance, which frustrated her initially but showed signs of slight improvement, when she didn't rush. And now with the plaster removed from her arm, she started a punishing regime of exercises to strengthen her muscles. Her aim was to be able to walk with crutches, and she had a clear target to aim at.

The Consultant had agreed that if she could stand safely, just using crutches, but otherwise un-aided, even if she still had to use the wheelchair to get around, she could go home.

Unlikely though it seemed at first, Amanda was determined that she would be out of hospital and able to attend the belated staff Christmas dinner in the ballroom, and she gritted her teeth and drove herself ever harder with her exercises.

-oo0Ooo-

On Friday Sarah and Emma moved into the cottage at last.

Once Sarah worked out how to fold up the rear seats in the new vehicle, it was pressed into service to shuttle boxes of clothes, the precious Edward Bear and Emma's dolls house, all of which were considered too precious to go in a van with the furniture.

To amuse those helping, Emma put on the hard hat

Pete had given her and directed operations with an efficient hand. All she needed was a clipboard.

There were a lot of stairs to come down in the flat, and as the high level bed and desk from her bedroom arrived there initially 'flat packed', it caused some little difficulty in getting it out and some more getting it up the stairs in the cottage, and into it's new position.

But at last it was done, and as Pete did a final run to the dump in his truck, Sarah and Emma collapsed onto the sofa and declared themselves to be home at last.

'And I don't think anyone saw me in the baby-blue bus, either,' said Emma with a satisfied smile.

-ooo0oo-

At the weekend, and on odd evenings, in Barclay Court Gardens, Dave and Suzanne had been quietly working with Derek on measures to make life easier for a wheelchair user.

They had created a gentle rise from the drive to the front door and replaced the block pavers on the surface so that, unless you knew, you might not notice anything had changed.

They made a similar ramp from the edge of the raised deck down to the wide path and the lawns beyond and Derek made a series of gently rising wedges in the workshop, to slip against the raised lips of the wide patio doors, inside and out, to facilitate easy access with a wheelchair, or for that matter with a pram.

Snatching a little bit of time where he could, Pete made a frame using some of the oak from the old benches and Derek asked his most trusted plumber to use it to mount a bathroom sink with flexible pipes and an expanse of marble worktop, which could be lowered to 'wheelchair height' in the spacious new bathroom they had converted from the original downstairs cloakroom and part of the snooker room.

The snooker table had gone into storage, and an electrically adjustable bed and hoist had been installed instead. The wide sliding door installed in the partition dividing the new bathroom from this re-purposed bedroom was designed to leave space to comfortably turn a wheelchair, and odd corners of the house had been subtly altered for similar reasons.

While a decorator 'made good' and disguised the alterations, Derek agreed that it might not be immediately obvious to Amanda that much had changed.

All it needed now was for the Consultant to confirm that she could return home, at last.

-ooOoo-

'Erm, could you come ...' said Andrew Smallpond,

standing at the reception desk in the hotel. 'He's in the garden.'

The cameramen and three celebrities stood huddled against the far wall, awaiting events as Jeremy and Jane hastened after the famous gardener. And there, sitting in the middle of a fine row of lettuces, sat Uncle Frederick, without his trousers, happily eating radishes.

Small clipboard was hopping from foot to foot as Uncle Frederick's nephew and niece helped back him into the hotel. They were unable, for the moment, to locate his trousers and vowed to return later to find them.

'Look at all that damage!' squeaked small clipboard. 'We will have to film the whole sequence where Victor Bottle picks the lettuces all over again!'

'And those radishes were supposed to be for Chesney's Mediterranean cucumber and radish salad,' wailed Damian the Viking.

-ooOoo-

Chapter 54

It took two attempts, but at last the hospital consultants were prepared to accept that Amanda was sufficiently stable on crutches to go home.

Derek had organised for a private nursing agency to send a visiting carer to help Amanda twice a day, which she was not happy about, but had to accept as a pre-condition of her release from the hospital. She also had to attend intensive physiotherapy sessions twice a week back at the hospital, where her progress was being carefully monitored.

But now she was home. And the improvement in her state of mind was immediately obvious to anyone.

She feigned dislike, but was quietly impressed and very grateful for all the aids and adaptations Derek had arranged at the house, and she was soon navigating confidently around the ground floor of her home.

Jack Bolton surprised her, when he visited with

Justin and Trudy, by installing a black box under the big television in the lounge and positioning her laptop on a clever folding table which she could sit at in her wheelchair. The black box connected her laptop wirelessly to the television which now showed her emails, and whatever she had on her screen as well as controls for the heating, lighting and a camera on the front door. The gadget could also summon help via a dedicated emergency call service if she needed it, and when Derek got round to fitting the motors, he explained, it could also open and close the curtains.

Various junior chefs and trainees and occasionally Steve or Carlos delivered meals each day and Amanda started to improve rapidly, both physically and in terms of how she felt.

Her sister Suzanne came over every day and made sure she had everything she needed as well as keeping her company. Their sibling bond grew closer each day as a result.

Her smile was back, and Derek smiled too, for the first time in a long while.

-oo0Ooo-

They started working in the main kitchen at a little after three o'clock in the afternoon, with the door firmly shut.

Derek was at the hospital taking Amanda for her physiotherapy, so he did not see the Christmas decorations being put up, or the preparations going on to dress the new dining tables with cutlery and glasses and position the chairs, and he was unaware of the hive of activity going on in his absence.

Everwhere you looked, preparations for the delayed staff Christmas dinner and dance proceeded at pace.

-oooOoo-

'You know it really doesn't matter if you don't feel like going tonight, Amanda. I could just nip over and put in a brief appearance for a couple of minutes and then come home. I'm sure they don't need me there to have a good time'

'No Derek, I will be fine. So long as you don't expect me to dance I'm looking forward to it.'

'Well, all right, but look, if you get tired and want to go at any point, you just say and we will come home, OK?'

'OK, fine. If you insist. Wasn't it good of Carlos and Mario to offer to do the catering? I mean fair enough they are partners in the business rather than just employees, but it is supposed to be their Christmas do to. We could easily have got caterers in.'

'I don't think Carlos wants anyone touching his smart new kitchen, and with all the TV cameras and equipment in there he probably wants to keep an eye on that too.'

'I assume they are doing a traditional Christmas dinner with turkey ... I hope nobody is too fed up with turkey to want it!'

'I've no idea what they are doing, and to be honest, what with one thing and another, it has not occurred to me to ask. Do you want me to ring up and find out?'

'No, honey. Whatever it is, it will make a welcome change from bananas and stewed apple.'

'At least, if you do feel able to come along, we will be able to get a good look at this band Trudy came up with. Then we can make a decision as to whether or not we are going to offer them the residency at the ballroom.'

'Yes, it will be good to get that sorted out. It is not long now until the Grand Opening of the club after all.'

-oooOoo-

'Uncle Matthew and Auntie Sandy will be here very shortly, Emma. Now, you are going to be good this evening, aren't you. You know we are only going to be next door if anything ...'

'Mummy, stop panicking. I have our evening all planned out. Auntie Sandy is bringing over some of those new hares she has made and wants to put in the display cabinet in the hotel foyer for sale.

Edward and I will need to check them out carefully and discuss pricing arrangements with Auntie Sandy. Then I need to show them my new dolls house and we can play with that for a while before I read them some of 'The Adventures of Robin Hood.' I expect they will be tired by then so ...'

'It seems you have got it all worked out, Emma,' said Pete.

'Certainly, Pete. Don't worry, I am quite capable of entertaining our guests until you get home.'

-ooOoo-

Chapter 55

Dave helped Derek lift Amanda out of the car and into her wheelchair before, with Suzanne in attendance, they went into the hotel reception together.

What greeted them there made Amanda gasp.

"Welcome home Amanda!" read the huge banner draped across the tall ballroom doors and as Dave and Suzanne pushed them open, a huge cheer went up and the band started playing 'Welcome home'.

While lights danced around them as they entered, a mirror image of the ballroom, complete with diners appeared on the wall behind the the band, and a large St.Bernard dog appeared to run across the stage carrying another 'welcome home' banner.

'Oh, Derek!' said Amanda, but Derek was blowing his nose and wiping his eyes.

-ooOOoo-

'Thank you very much for this wonderful surprise,'

said Amanda. 'But now I've got a bit of a surprise for you. Your dinner tonight is going to be rather special.'

Spot on cue, Chesney Marriott emerged from the servery dressed in his chef's whites and brandishing a long ladle.

'It is going to be prepared for you by star TV chef Chesney Marriott, no less!' she added.

There was another cheer and much clapping.

-oo0Ooo-

The dinner was superb, of course, and Derek helped Mario and Carlos to serve it up.

As coffee was being served, Derek called for three cheers for the chef, and Chesney emerged once more, and took a bow.

Then at a signal from Derek, the band struck up and the dancing began.

'This is going really well,' said Dave. 'Almost everyone is up on their feet ... oh, sorry Amanda.'

Amanda laughed and then, looking over his shoulder asked what Suzanne was doing.

Her sister had been talking to the band leader, and now gestured to Dave to join her.

The band started to belt out an up-tempo swing medley as, to everyone's astonishment Dave and

Suzanne gave a polished demonstration of energetic Lindy-Hop dancing, which impressed everyone.

They spent the next few numbers showing everyone how it was done, and while Amanda sat with Chesney and Mario, even Derek got dragged onto the floor.

Things quietened down after that and Pete and Sarah returned to their table to catch their breath.

'I don't think I have ever danced so much in my life,' said Sarah, 'Phew!'

The band sensed the change of mood, and began to play slow dances, first to swing music and then to modern classics, where two of the band members sang.

Now recovered, Pete and Sarah began to dance again as a smooth version of Chris de Burgh's 'Lady in red' floated across the gently swaying dancers on the floor.

Pete cleared his throat.

'Sarah,' he said, and cleared his throat a second time, 'will you marry me?'

-oo0Ooo-

Chapter 56

'So there are seventy six of the eighty tickets sold, so far,' said Justin.

'Given the maximum capacity of one hundred and twenty and my calculation that we need twenty five to thirty spaces for us and our guests, we are pretty much there already,' said Amanda, 'That is amazing.'

'Thank you,' said Justin. 'Although it is mostly Trudy we need to thank. She has got some really top flight people coming to this before we even add in the celebrities from the telly programmes and all the chefs.'

'And with Desmond Tweedy's new show and well as our new resident band now all signed up it should be a very grand "Grand Opening" indeed.'

'Trudy said she had been talking to a couple of the guys from the "Showstoppers" band and obviously they are very pleased that you have given them the residency, but they were saying they really enjoyed your firm's do and thought there was a great bunch of people there.'

'Please thank Trudy once again for putting us on to them, they really were fabulous.'

'I will. Now, I thought we had better discuss the membership applications. We are up to one hundred and ten now and after the first dinner dance next month where we have invited interested parties to a one off ticketed event, I confidently predict that going well over two hundred. We have already sold a hundred and two tickets for that.'

'Wow!'

'Yes, and you will be amused to hear that amongst others, we have sold tickets to Dame Amelia Runacres-Smythe, or should I say Mr and Mrs Andrew Smallpond, and to Chesney Marriott and partner.'

-oooOoo-

Pete and Sarah were preparing to go shopping in the 'baby-blue bus,' and planned to pick Emma up from Amanda's house on the way back.

The idea to move the dolls house into Amanda's living room was entirely Emma's and meant that she had an excuse to go to see her 'Auntie Amanda' regularly.

There, between dolls house play sessions, she made

Amanda tea, read to her, and kept her company. For her part Amanda had been busy 'on-line shopping', and now the doll's house was pretty much fully furnished with every conceivable little piece of miniature furniture, she loved watching Emma's delight as each new piece was positioned.

'When we get home tonight,' said Pete now. 'There is something I want to show you.'

'What is that?'

'It is a little surprise for Emma, I hope you are going to approve.'

'What have you done?'

'Well, if you don't mind. I would rather it remained a secret until we get there.'

'Well, how are you going to know if I approve?'

'Oh, I hadn't thought of that. Well, if you don't like it you can always go back to living in the flat,' grinned Pete.

-ooOOoo-

'Here, you might need this torch,' said Pete, opening the French door to the garden.

'What am I looking for?' said Emma.

'Have look in the shed.'

'What are you up to, Pete,' said Sarah. 'Why all the

mystery?'

Emma was opening the shed door.

'There is a light switch on the left hand side ...'

'There are some bikes ... Mummy! Come and see. Quick!'

'The two adult bikes are my mum and dad's, but they don't use them any more,' said Pete. 'I'm afraid I didn't do much of a job of wrapping it up, Emma, but I hope you like it. Sorry it is several months late, but Happy Christmas anyway.'

'Is it for me? What, really? It's a bike! Mummy, Pete bought me a bike!'

'I thought we could all go for rides round the Barclay Woods estate ... you can ride a bike, can't you, Sarah?'

'Oh yes, I certainly can,' said Sarah. 'This is incredibly generous of you, Pete!'

'Yes, thank you! Oh, thank you, Pete!' squeaked Emma, who was dancing from foot to foot.

'Right, shall we get it out and have a proper look at it?' said Pete. 'Then you can unwrap it.'

Sarah was going through the pockets of her coat.

'Are you all right, Sarah,' asked Pete. 'Oh. Are you crying? Don't cry ... here use my hankie.'

'Mummy?' said Emma, concerned.

'These are happy tears, Emma. Isn't that a beautiful bike!'

-ooOoo-

==

Disclaimer:

Note: All rights reserved. No part of this book, ebook or manuscript or associated published or unpublished works may be copied, reproduced or transmitted by any means, electronic, mechanical, photocopying or otherwise, without the prior written permission of the author.

Copyright: Bob Able 2024

Photo Credit: Brooke Lark

The author asserts the moral right under the Copyright, Design and Patents Act 1988 to be identified as the author of this work.

This is a work of fiction, Any similarities between any persons, living or dead and the characters in this book is purely co-incidental.
The author accepts no claims in relation to this work.

-ooOoo-

==

*And now, an excerpt for **'Bobbie and the Spanish Chap'**, the first in the Bobby Bassington series of stories recently published by Bob Able:-*

Chapter 1

'I don't think we have met Rosy, have we?' asked Geoff.

'No, I don't think so. You would know if you had. Outdoorsy, all-for-it type. We were up at Girton together,' said Bobbie. 'She was a bit of a blood for rowing and all that sort of thing. Fearsomely bright, of course. One of those clever girls who got into University early. She was a year below me but graduated at the same time and was always heaps of fun.'

'I see,' said Geoff. 'You have been on holiday with her before, haven't you?'

'What? Oh, the foul, frightful, failed river trip you mean. When her awful oaf of a brother put me off boys of his particularly loathsome type for life.'

'Yes. When you came scuttling back here early, halfway through the planned trip, with all sorts of tales of woe.' Geoff smiled at the memory.

'I do not "scuttle", Uncle Geoffrey. I may have made a retreat at a few more m.p.h. than my usual elegant glide, but you could not accuse me of "scuttling"! And I was sorely pressed by events, so allowances must be made.' Bobbie pulled a face and continued. 'Let's not forget what I had to endure on that revolting old tub Brice-Waterman had the raw cheek to call a River Cruiser. Take, for example, the shower. I shudder at the recollection!'

'Oh, it can't have been that bad. A bit like camping, I would have thought.'

'Camping? You don't really expect a young girl of my delicacy and fragrant loveliness to want to subject herself to anything resembling camping, do you?'

'No, of course not, Bobbie. If you can't spend an hour in the shower followed by another one messing about in the bathroom every morning, you consider the day wasted,' chuckled Geoff.

'Don't tease, Uncle Geoffrey. A girl has to follow her beauty routine, you know. Otherwise the radiant vision you see before you now would just become another fading rose in a sea of so many. To stand out one has to work at it!'

Bobbie danced a few steps towards the front door where she heard Janet turning the key as she returned from work.

Their effusive greetings forced Geoff to shelve his enquiries into Bobbie's no doubt ambitious plans for a while, as the excited conversation flowed backwards and forwards between his two favourite females.
It was not until after supper that he got the chance to pick up the threads again and press Bobbie further on the plans for her trip abroad.

Janet was asking about Rosy Brice-Waterman and Geoff saw his chance to join in.

'So,' he said now, 'Your idea is to go to Spain with Rosy and visit your boyfriend there?'

'Orlando,' said Bobbie, looking at him censoriously, 'is not my boyfriend in the fullest sense of the word. Well, not yet at least.'

'Oh. But I thought you said …' began Janet.

'I may have mentioned that we have had a few casual dates …' said Bobbie.

'Including a trip to The Proms, the ballet and Goodwood,' interjected Janet.

'Yes, all of that. But he has not yet qualified for the title of "boyfriend". We are still enjoying each others' company as friends.'

Geoff chuckled, which earned him a gentle slap on the arm from a reddening Bobbie.

'I thought he was nice when he picked you up here,' said Janet.

'In his drop-head Porsche …' added Geoff.

'All right. Yes, I admit I like him.' Bobbie squirmed.

'Who wouldn't?' said Janet. 'He works for his father's international law firm, where it seems he has his own department, dresses like a designer's model and is as handsome as they come!'

'And you said he was well off and had a sexy Mediterranean accent, too,' added Geoff.

'Oh stop it!' blushed Bobbie. 'I grant you he is quite a catch and I'm not immune to his charms. But he still has some good old-fashioned wooing to do before I am prepared to refer to him as a boyfriend.'

'And this trip you plan with Rosy Brice-Waterman might change that?'

'It might. I regard it as another stepping stone along the way,' said Bobbie. 'We shall be visiting him on his home turf, as it were, and seeing him in his native land.'

'Are you going to meet his mother and father?' asked Janet.

'You make it sound like a formal sort of thing.' Bobbie looked surprised. 'The contingency of meeting any parents is not on our somewhat loose agenda. The plan is to soak up some Spanish sun whilst being taken here and there and, no doubt, spoilt by Orlando. There may even be a chance to meet some of his friends and Rosy might select one as a companion during our stay, perhaps.'

'Making up a foursome in sunny Spain. How romantic!' said Janet dreamily.

'Well, be that as it may,' said Geoff. 'We don't really know very much about this Orlando chap, and going to spend a week in a foreign country with him is not like going on a boat on the Thames just down the road, you know. You can't just scuttle back home from Spain if it doesn't work out, Bobbie.'

'Ten days, actually, and we have covered the issue of "scuttling" before, Uncle Geoff.' Bobbie scowled. 'If, like mother, you are proposing to invoke the Spanish Inquisition on the matter, let me say that Rosy and I are staying in a rather nice tourist hotel which we booked through a proper British Travel Agent, and we will be sharing a room. So you can put any of those sort of ideas right out of your head!'

'You will be sharing a room with Rosy?' asked Geoff.

'That is what I said, Uncle Geoffrey. Although, in these enlightened times, it is not really any business of yours, I can state that Orlando and I are at the stage of holding hands occasionally, and nothing more.'

'Holding hands. How romantic!' said Janet.

'I'm sorry Bobbie. I didn't mean to pry. I merely want to be sure you are going to be safe.'

'That's rather sweet, Geoff. But I'm sure Bobbie knows what she is doing,' smiled Janet.

'It is sweet of you to care, yes, Uncle Geoff, and since my father died you have always stepped up to fill the parental role, for which I am, of course very grateful. But be of good cheer. This little jaunt will be fun and, if nothing else, will allow me to top up my healthy tan and experience some of the culture of Spain.' Bobbie wrinkled her nose. 'If you like, disregarding the expense and increased pressure on my already stretched ex-student's finances, I will call you every couple of days and let you know how I am getting on.'

'I'm sure there will be no need for that ...' said Janet.

'You will call your mother though, won't you?' said Geoff, who would have been happier to have a regular call from Bobbie and slip her a few pounds to cover the expense.

He suspected he would have to make a 'donation' to Bobbie's always-precarious finances anyway nearer the time of her trip, and was expecting her request for funds imminently.

-oo0Ooo-

Thursday morning dawned bright and clear and Bobbie, re-arranging her suitcases in the hall once more, was excited.

'Come on, Uncle Geoff! Rosy will be at the station at any moment and we don't have time to waste!'

Geoff, pausing only to kiss Janet as she left for work, was ready with the keys of his Jaguar in his hand.

'Come on then, young Bobbie. Let's go and get her,' he said.

-oooOoo-

Rosy Brice-Waterman was one of those solid girls who would do well in the light heavyweight class.

She was substantially built and had a laugh like a hyena in a drain, which she deployed at regular intervals.

'Isn't it a scream!' she stated as she swung the heaviest of her cases into the boot of the car with ease. 'I've never been to Spain before, so it will be quite an adventure!'

'You've bought rather a lot of luggage, Rosy,' said Bobbie, 'We will probably have to pay "excess baggage" charges for this lot.'

'Just let them try!' bellowed Rosy, 'It is quite clear on our booking confirmation what we can take. The travel agent chappy told us the maximum weight and that is precisely what I have packed!'

'Ah,' said Bobbie, squeezing into the back seat beside a vast holdall. 'I think I see what has happened here, Rosy. The figure you refer to is the total amount for both of us, and by the look of things, you have snaffled the lot.'

'Oh, I say! Surely not! Blimey, that puts the fox among the pheasants rather.' Rosy turned in her seat to look at Bobbie. 'I'm frightfully sorry, old girl, I may have rather overdone it!'

'Don't worry,' said Geoff. 'If we hurry there is still time to nip home and unpack some of this and start again.'

'Splendid!' shouted Rosy. 'Thank you. I'm not the sort who can holiday with just a bikini and flip-flops, I'm afraid, but I'm sure we can find a solution!'

-oooOoo-

What they found themselves engaged in, however, when they reached the house was a full-blown row.

In the spare bedroom, with the bathroom scales to hand to weigh the cases, and mountains of clothes on the two single beds, the floor, and spilling out onto the landing, the girls argued over every garment and as their voices were raised, Geoff left them to it.

'Don't forget we need to leave in an hour, and I'd be grateful if anything you want to leave here was stacked neatly out of the way,' called Geoff over his shoulder as he retreated down the stairs, just as Rosy enquired in a loud voice why Bobbie needed to take quite so many dresses.

The journey to the airport was conducted in a strained silence as the girls sat surrounded by their hastily repacked luggage.

The only comment Bobbie made as they unloaded their cases onto a couple of trollies at the terminal was to the effect that she, Rosy, had to pay any excess baggage charges, which drew a growl but no further comment from the more substantial of the pair.

Having made sure they both had their tickets and passports, Geoff wished them well and made his escape.

-ooOoo-

What awaited him back at 2 Easton Drive was something resembling an explosion in a clothing factory.

There were dresses, trousers, tee-shirts, blouses, and even a pair of wellington boots scattered about all over the bedroom.

Geoff was particularly horrified to find a matching tweed

jacket and skirt hanging from the lampshade on a coat hanger!

Geoff knew that Janet, whose house this was after all, liked to be tidy and this eruption of clothes cast carelessly around the room would be bound to irritate her, so he started folding up the clothes and positioning them tidily on one of the two beds, Rosy's on the left and Bobbie's on the right.

The process went well initially, as the differences in size made it obvious which belonged to whom, but Geoff felt acutely embarrassed when he came to some of the smaller garments, and he hid four very substantial bras under a tweed jacket on Rosy's bed, and after a moment's indecision two pairs of very brief black lace knickers under a little jacket on Bobbie's.

The process took some time but, topping Rosy's pile off with a copy of Horse and Hound Magazine and Bobbie's with a pair of strappy, cork-heeled sandals that he remembered seeing her wearing, at last it was done. Geoff retired downstairs to catch his breath with a mug of strong coffee.

-ooOoo-

'I think it is a lovely idea to go to Spain for a few days to get to know Orlando,' Janet was saying as they finished their supper. 'I've always wanted to go to that part of the Spanish mainland.'

'Have you?' said Geoff who had long held the opinion that the Costa Blanca was exclusively and entirely Benidorm.

'Yes. Did you know that the highest concentration of Michelin-starred restaurants in the world is there among the lovely little towns where you can buy the catch straight off the fishing boats?' Janet warmed to her theme. 'There are over twenty kilometres of pure sandy beach in one area, dotted with little *chiringuitos*, that means beach bars, by the way, right on the sand for romantic dinners watching the sunset.'

'Amongst the "kiss-me-quick" hats, and Union Jack swimming trunks, a short walk from the British pubs selling all-day breakfasts and fish and chips, I suppose.'

'What? Don't be silly, Geoff. You are muddling that up with somewhere else. The place I'm talking about has a little open-air restaurant on the rocks by the sea where they catch and hang up octopus in the sun to dry, and luxurious, expensive villas overlooking the endless, blue, Mediterranean sea.'

'You've been reading a travel brochure!' exclaimed Geoff.

'Yes. The one Bobbie left behind. The area she is visiting sounds idyllic.'

'Not Benidorm, then.'

'No. Certainly not Benidorm. I think that is on the same stretch of coast line, but it is miles away and nothing to do with the places in Bobbie's brochure.'

'I thought it was all Club 18-30, boozy stag-dos, and that sort of thing.'

'No. I don't think so. Here, take a look for yourself.'

The well-thumbed travel brochure Janet handed him did sing the praises of an area renowned for fine dining, quality wines, and culture as well as stunning beaches and spectacular mountain scenery. Geoff had to admit it looked delightful.

'Don't you think it would be romantic if we took a break from house hunting and went somewhere like that for a week or so, Geoff?'

Geoff, who thought that being anywhere with Janet was the most impossibly romantic thing that had ever happened to him, looked at her smiling face now.
That dazzling smile always did it for him.

'Anything I do with you is romantic,' whispered Geoff, swallowing hard. 'I don't need exotic scenery and beautiful locations to take my breath away, Janet. You do that everyday.'

'Have you been drinking?' said Janet, breaking the spell.

'No. Apart from this small beer,' Geoff held up his glass, 'But if you want to go on holiday somewhere like that, I shall be delighted to take you.'

'Really?'

'Certainly.'

Janet moved her chair closer to his.

'And did you mean all that stuff about my taking your breath away?'

'I did,' said Geoff, suddenly feeling very hot, 'I may have mentioned that I love you, Janet, and I simply cannot believe that you even gave me a second glance, let alone invited me to share your life. You are the very best thing that has ever happened to me, and if you can put up with me a little longer, until finances allow, I will take you to watch the sunset in all the exotic locations you like!'

'Oh come here, you soppy old sod!' said Janet, and they left the washing up for the morning.

-ooo0oo-

All Bob Able's books are available as ebooks and paperbacks on the Amazon bookstore.
www.amazon.com/author/bobable

About the author:

Bob Able is a bestselling writer of popular memoirs, fiction and thrillers. He describes himself as a 'part time ex-pat 'splitting his time between his homes in coastal Spain and 'darkest Norfolk 'in the UK.

His memoir **'Spain Tomorrow'** was rated as the **third most popular travel book** by Amazon in September 2020 and continues to top the charts. With the sequel **'More Spain Tomorrow'**, and then **'Third Helpings of Spain Tomorrow'**, these charming lighthearted insights into his life continue to amuse readers.

If you like Bob Able's distinctive writing style and would like to read more of his work, here is a little more information…..

Bob Able writes with a lighthearted touch and does not use graphic descriptions of sex or violence in his books, that is not his style. He prefers to leave that sort of thing to the reader's imagination.

He has also produced a **new series** of **lighthearted thrillers** which will amuse as well as captivate readers. They are ideal 'beach reads' to take on holiday. The Bobby Bassington Stories include:
'Bobbie And The Spanish Chap',
'Bobbie And The Crime-Fighting Auntie',
'Bobbie And The Wine Trouble'
And' **Auntie Caroline's Last Case'**

Bobbie makes her first appearance in 'Double Life Insurance', and all these books can be read on their own, although if you read them as a series, 'Auntie Caroline's Last Case 'draws all the strings together and completes the tales of the lives of all the characters we meet along the way.

Early reviewers had suggested that these stories would make an engaging TV series and of course Bob would be pleased to hear from television companies and promoters to explore that option!

His fictional novels include **'Double Life Insurance'** a fast moving but lighthearted thriller, where Bobbie Bassington first makes an appearance, fresh out of university, **'No Point Running'** which is set in the world of horse racing in the 1970's, **'The Menace Of Blood'**, which is about inheritance, not gore, and the sequel **'No Legacy of Blood'**. They are engaging thrillers, with a touch of romance and still with that gentle, signature Bob Able humour.

His semi-fictional memoir **'Silke The Cat, My Story'**, written with his friend and wine merchant, Graham Austin and Silke the Cat herself, is completely different. Silke is a real cat, she lives today in the Costa Blanca, and her adventures, which she recounts in this amusing book, really happened (also available as an audio book).

Contact:

bobable693@gmail.com

This is a 'live email address' and is monitored by Bob himself, so do not expect automated replies ... Bob hates that sort of impersonal thing.

You can find details of how to buy all Bob's books and also follow him at:

www.amazon.com/author/bobable

Or just enter **'Bob Able books'** on the Amazon site or Google and the full list should appear.

Thank you for reading.

Printed in Great Britain
by Amazon